THE BALLOT

It didn't matter a d
those decisions we
duty, driving the he
correct Lobby. The
peaceful co-existe
liberty and Party di

Every now and the
faces before him had fought back. He actually enjoyed his arguments with a rebel or two. So far the force of his arguments, the force of the obedience clause, the waving of a bad voting record under noses, the mere threat of writing to the rebel's constituency management committee had been enough.

No, an awkward squad was not so dangerous to the Labour Party as rows and rows of uncritical, acquiescent, non-dissenting back-benchers. They were the kind of people who would watch the party die of inertia before they did anything about it. It had happened before, not only on the back benches . . .

ROWLAND SUMMERSCALES

The Ballot

MAGNUM BOOKS
Methuen Paperbacks Ltd

A Magnum Book

THE BALLOT
ISBN 0 417 05280 4

First published in Great Britain 1979
by Robert Hale Ltd
Magnum edition published 1980

The Ballot is a work of fiction. The names of real politicians occur occasionally, but all characters are fictitious, and any resemblances to real people are purely coincidental

Magnum Books are published
by Methuen Paperbacks Ltd
11 New Fetter Lane, London EC4P 4EE

Reproduced, printed and bound in Great Britain
by Cox & Wyman Ltd, Reading

This book is dedicated to my brave wife, Peggy; our daughter, Jill; and in loving memory of her sister, Janet.

"Conscience has no more to do with gallantry than politics." – Sheridan

1

Lying in his bed in his bachelor flat in Artillery Mansions, Edwin Battle was not a prepossessing sight. He slept on his back, bare to the bottoms of his pyjama set, and the chest thus exposed was flabby, with breasts almost as heavy as a woman's. A few golden hairs grew there.

His thick lips were partly open and, as he slept, they bugled little musical snores as he breathed in and out. He had a high, domed forehead, but the dominating feature of his face was a bulbous nose, pitted and red, a strawberry type replica of the W. C. Fields organ. It was such a convincing replica that, when Edwin Battle could be persuaded after a heavy overdose of Haig, he would give a convincing parody of the great man's hilarious golf act.

Edwin Battle, therefore, was not a handsome man. In addition, he was proud rather than ashamed of his non-athleticism. He never ran to catch a bus, he had never worn a boxing glove; he had never, even at school, risked limb, in ruck or maul; he had never wielded a driver, niblick or putter, except in his impression of W. C. Fields. But he slept peacefully with a clear conscience, bugling out his musical contentment. His piggy eyes were closed up in little sacks of fat. Later, when he opened them, they would unroll into folds of dissipation.

He slept well for two reasons: one, the bottle of whisky on the bedside-table was nearly empty; and two, he had been busy for the last few days since Prime Minister Hargreaves, to the surprise of Westminster, had gone to the Palace and asked for a dissolution. The general election campaign proper would begin in a few days.

Edwin Battle tried always to be prepared for any emergency. Ready on the bedside-table were the pad and ball-point pen, the luminous-faced alarm-clock, the bottle of laxative, and the remains of the whisky. But, primarily, there was the telephone, the instrument which dominated his life. He had been heard to say often that he spent half of every day on the blower. Unheard by Edwin Battle, Big Ben struck a solitary stroke. It was one o'clock and to the sleeping world all might have seemed well.

But then the telephone shrilled. Edwin Battle's eyes remained closed but his response was instantaneous and Pavlovian. His right arm reached out unerringly for the instrument, lifted it, and placed it to his ear as he turned over in the bed on his elbow. Slowly his eyelids ungummed themselves, showing the dissipation as he pulled the cord, and switched on the light.

The voice had not waited for an acknowledgment. It was feminine, and it was intoning a message in a monotone, like an answering device. But to Edwin Battle it was part of the camouflage. He listened in silence until the message ended and the instrument clicked.

Then he showed his elation and excitement. He slid out of the sheets and, heavily and flabbily, descended to the bedroom floor. It was Stella, Stella Martin, his golden goose. Stella Martin calling at one o'clock in the morning, without identifying herself, meant only one thing. News in Whitehall. Big news. A capital N.

The most efficient switchboard in Europe, the Downing Street complex, was working at top pressure. Called in to deal with the emergency, Miss Thwaites, the supervisor, patrolled the area behind her staff, noting with pleasure, but without surprise, the coolness and quiet speed with which the girls worked.

One by one the Ministers in the Cabinet were being summoned to No 10. At each successful connection, the girls read to the recipient the one-paragraph message passed to Miss Thwaites by Arnold Prestcote, the deputy-Prime Minister and deputy-leader of the Labour Party. No further information was given. Miss Thwaites was highly satisfied. She did not know about Stella Martin.

Stella was waiting her chance, surreptitiously watching Miss Thwaites, envying her grave assurance and authority, the trim figure beneath the dark skirt and spotlessly white blouse. Above the waist, Miss Thwaites was constructed like a television model, advertising a bra., breasts uptilted, nipples attracting Stella's jealous eyes.

Suddenly alert, Stella heard the message being passed: "The deputy-Prime Minister wishes to see you in the Cabinet room, Miss Thwaites." This was her chance. Miss Thwaites came up behind her and gave her the clipboard with the names. Some, those who had received the emergency call, were already ticked off.

"Keep the list, Stella," instructed Miss Thwaites, and strode off, leaving Stella in charge. It was, she thought, her rightful place, if seniority, and not personal charm, had been the test. The fact that she was not supervisor was one of the motives for the act she now perpetrated, carefully dialling Edwin Battle's number, making sure her neighbour couldn't check. She had done it before, and never without a flicker of fear; she felt the fear now as she visualised Edwin Battle stretching a bare arm across the bed.

The dialling tone stopped, the line clicked. Before Edwin Battle had time to commit himself, she read the typed copy in front of her:

"This is No 10, sir. I am afraid I cannot tell you the reason, but you are summoned to an emergency meeting in the Cabinet Room as soon as possible. Do you wish for an official car from the pool or will you use your own transport? Thank you, sir. I am sorry I cannot be more informative."

She cut the line. Her mouth was dry. Once the act was done she had to refuel her envy of Miss Thwaites, her grievance against the promotion system, her hatred of the God who had made her physically unattractive, big-hipped, waistless, topheavy with bust. Whatever the mystery of her sex life, she wanted to be like Miss Thwaites.

Resentfully, her fingers stroked her top lip as if they could feel the shadow still left after the removal of the disfiguring moustache which had appeared at puberty and had required removal by painful electrolysis. She was still conscious of the hairs on her legs: the more she shaved, the thicker and stronger they grew.

Mechanically, she resumed her routine, next dialling the Foreign Secretary's official home in Carlton Gardens. He was testy at being awakened at one o'clock, and was positively rude when Stella had to tell him a second time she couldn't explain why he was being summoned. She ticked his name off the list. So far, only six had been successfully contacted.

She rose from her seat and began, like Miss Thwaites, to patrol behind the girls, exercising her temporary authority with undisguised pleasure. She had got over the flicker of fear: when she thought of Edwin Battle now, she felt moist between her thighs as her prolific sexual juice flowed.

She remembered their first meeting, two oddities coming together at a party given to the Downing Street staff by the Lobby – the drinks, the first clumsy fumblings of sex, the subsequent secret meetings, the treachery in which he had involved her. She wasn't ashamed. She always furtively avoided facing the knowledge, but she knew that she was being used.

The supervisor returned and Stella handed over the clipboard. The brief moments of authority had been deeply satisfying as she secretly rejoiced at the service she had rendered to Edwin Battle. She looked at Miss Thwaites. Perhaps, after all, she need not envy the other: she had Edwin, despite her shapelessness, plainness and lack of physical or intellectual attraction.

The official cars had begun to arrive in Downing Street outside. By now, she thought, Edwin Battle would have dressed and would be on his way. Once again she felt fear, but it was quickly superseded by defiance. She was not sorry for what she had done. She had done it before and had not been found out. If the opportunity arose, she would do it again.

Long before the first official car had drawn up at the entrance to No 10, Joe Hepworth, sitting in his pyjamas at his desk in No 12, the office of the Government Chief Whip, had already by-passed the Downing Street switchboard.

On his outside line he had spoken to the Lord Chancellor and to Nick Hayling, the secretary of the Parliamentary Labour Party. First things first, he reflected. He didn't know what Prestcote had done, but Joe Hepworth hadn't hesitated. In the power struggle which was about to begin, he had moved unerringly to form the alliances which mattered most: with the most powerful authority on the country's constitution; and with the acknowledged expert on, and custodian of, the standing orders of the Parliamentary Labour Party.

For a flabby man, overweight from a sedentary life, with a liver already cirrhosed from Haig, with the motor part of his mind irretrievably damaged by the same cause, Edwin Battle moved with commendable speed. All his adult life, spent in Fleet Street or Westminster, he had been accustomed to being despatched on missions, deprived of the time to pack even a toothbrush or razor.

In the circumstances, it was a miracle of co-ordination which allowed him to pull on his trousers with one hand and zip the fly while, with the other hand, he dialled the *Daily News.* He put down the telephone momentarily to use both hands to pull on his shirt, in time to pick up the receiver when the office answered.

"Give me the Art Room," he said, and with the adrenalin now freely flowing, he added exultantly: "Make it snappy. This is hot."

He sat on the bed putting on his shoes, telephone receiver professionally gripped between neck and shoulder, earpiece at the ear. He fretted at the delay. When Art answered it was a voice obviously awakened from sleep.

"Battle here. Lobby. This is an emergency. I want a man with a camera at 10 Downing Street at the double."

"What's the flap, old man?"

"How the fucking hell do I know? I've just had a tip from an exclusive source. It could be a Middle East war, a Warsaw Pact conventional attack on N.A.T.O., or Russia may have made a pre-emptive nuclear strike."

"Then they've kept it very quiet."

"Cut out the comic cuts, old man. All I know is that the Cabinet has been called to an emergency meeting at one o'clock in the morning. Just get a man there pronto."

Ferociously, not waiting for another exchange of incivilities, Battle slammed the receiver back in its cradle. Beneath the flab of the abused and slowly deteriorating tissue and internal organs, there was the hardness of steel. He had survived thirty years in Fleet Street and in that time many had coveted his job. He was still there, a legend at Westminster, the secret confidant of Cabinet Ministers, the man informants 'phoned surreptitiously when they wanted to fly political kites, or damage a colleague.

He was not a generous or grateful man. He did not pretend that he was a fair or impartial chronicler of political events or character. He was almost totally untroubled by conscience. He was, he boasted, a professional hatchet-man. Even in the era of the massive influence of the tube, which he hated pathologically, he was still a phenomenon – a newspaperman to be flattered or feared.

That was why, as he finished dressing with a speed which belied his past indulgences, his sudden glow of tenderness and gratitude was totally out of character. Edwin Battle, he told himself, you're a cunt; for Stella, discovery would mean dismissal, disgrace, loss of pension rights and, very likely, Holloway. But, for him, discovery would be different. Fleet Street would create a martyr of him, accord him accolades for striking a blow for freedom from the constricting bonds of section two of the Official Secrets Act, the odious Catch 22 behind which Ministers and mandarins of the Civil Service sheltered in their cowardice. And if Edwin Battle was sent to prison for conspiracy it would be in triumph, with the banners of freedom fluttering, blessed with the eulogies of the prose of the leading articles of the *Times, Telegraph* and *Guardian*.

Conscience endured a few moments in the snake-pit of his mind. Then he picked up his jacket, slung it over his shoulder and left the flat. He ran down the corridor towards the lift-shaft. For once it was working; within a few minutes he was on the street, flagging down a taxi which was fortunately cruising by.

No one knew the value of stealth more than Edwin Battle. Secrecy was part of the Lobby code, the art of the game. Unobserved, he had a chance of solving the mystery of the emergency but, once his presence was known or suspected, lips would be sealed, tongues would dry up.

For these reasons, he paid off the taxi at the Whitehall junction with Downing Street and went forward on foot to reconnoitre, clinging to the shadows and making for the dark haven of the archway entrance to the Foreign Office quadrangle, opposite the doorway of No 10, where the policeman stood.

His trained eye surveyed the prospects. One car was drawn up outside No 10, pointing towards Whitehall. Deduction: some visitor was due to leave. But official cars were still arriving. The waiting car did not bear the insignia CD, which ruled out the visit of an ambassador, and international complications.

While he stood there, official cars delivered the florid, heavily-jowled Lord Chancellor; the trim, neat Pam Bruce; the thick Tom Westwood, built like an oak; and finally, young Eric Bassett, the *enfant terrible* leader of the Workers Control group, which was as destructive to the Labour Party as the death-watch beetle in Westminster Hall.

At the sight of the deceptively innocent-looking Bassett, Edwin Battle almost broke cover, momentarily thinking of the prospect of the direct approach. He could stay under cover for hours while the time for the last edition came and went, and still learn nothing. He had already ruled out the other possibility – telephoning the No 10 Press Secretary, and asking point-blank what the hell was going on? From that source, Edwin Battle never got anything but dislike, distrust and evasion, if not downright misleading answers.

As Bassett made for the door of No 10, Battle actually started to follow him, ready to seize an arm and force a direct confrontation. But, as he changed position, he had a clear view of the red-carpeted lobby and of the tall, slim, dark-suited man approaching the exit from the direction of the staircase. In his right hand, the man held a black bag, the mark of his profession.

Recognition rang in Battle's brain with the impact of a bell. Sir William Lawson, the Harley Street doctor, whose one National Health Service patient was the Prime Minister.

So that was it; Hargreaves was sick. In a way, it came as an anti-climax. It could, thought Battle in disgust, be something relatively trivial. Then the evidence struck him with renewed force. An emergency meeting for something trivial?

All the time he thought, he had acted. He was out in Downing Street, approaching round the front of the car, ambushing Sir William as he was about to open the door to the driving-seat. Where the hell was the photographer he had ordered? He was going to miss the picture.

Battle laid a restraining hand on Sir William's arm: the object was two-fold, to shock the news out of him, and to delay departure until the arrival of the cameraman. He heard a taxi turning the corner into Downing Street.

"Sir William, would you excuse me a moment. . . . ?"

"Yes?" The testy eyes, the suspicion, the delay, would have deterred a pessimist. The cunning Battle chose his question carefully, priming the charge.

"How is he, Sir William?"

"Who are you?" The eyes measured the unprepossessing figure, the signs of hasty dressing, the evidence to the professional eye of years of booze. The question was hostile. But the photographer was stepping out of the taxi and Battle indicated his target by signalling over Sir William's shoulder with a thumb. Once again, in a time of crisis, Edwin Battle's instinct for self-preservation worked.

"I'm the P.M.'s new Special Branch bodyguard, Sir William." He lied without a quaver in his voice, although he knew the penalty for impersonation of a police officer. Fleet Street forgave such frailties: after all, it was only a little lie. Germany had lost the war but that didn't of itself invalidate Dr Goebbel's hypothesis that the bigger the lie, the surer the belief. "How is he?" he asked again, sincerely hoping that it was serious.

Sir William said curtly: "He's dead. Very dead. A coronary."

The photographer's flash went off, briefly illuminating the street like sheet lightning. It lasted long enough for Battle to see the outrage on Sir William's face. His hand tried to grasp Battle's arm. But Battle was too elusive.

"I want to see proof of your identity," commanded Sir William, in a voice filled with scandalised rage. But Battle was already running down Downing Street, staggering because of the alcoholic damage to the motor in his brain. He was full of joy and triumph, yet already out of breath before he reached Whitehall. But he knew he had not far to go: the location of all the telephone-kiosks in the Westminster area were plotted in his mind like little flags on a map. He headed for the nearest: at the entrance to the Home Office opposite the Cenotaph.

As the breath left in his body seemed to strangle him, his mind went cooler and cooler in inverse proportion to his physical distress. The sentences and paragraphs formed up behind his tongue, ready and memorised for dictation.

The light in the telephone-kiosk beckoned his struggling body as a harbour beacon welcomes a returning craft in a storm. He almost fell through the door, stood there panting helplessly before he had the strength to feel in his trouser-pocket for the necessary coin. The hand which inserted it in the slot when the *Daily News* answered, trembled. But the voice was resonant with exultation:

"News Desk. Quickly."

The News Desk answered promptly. The telephone was an instrument of divine providence. The Post Office was merely the installer.

Edwin Battle said calmly, with the authority of the sole possessor of cataclysmic news: "I am going to put over an exclusive story. Hargreaves, the Prime Minister, is dead. He has had a heart attack. Get ready to pull out all the stops. Art has a picture of Sir William Lawson, the Prime Minister's doctor, leaving Downing Street. Dig out the old boy's obit from the morgue. I will deal with the political angle. Now put me through to news telephones and I'll dictate."

Edwin Battle was not a vain man; he was too conscious of all his physical and character defects. But he had always wanted to win the Granada prize for the Political Correspondent of the year. And because, instinctively, he guessed that Prestcote would want the news kept under wraps until the morning, he knew that this year he would achieve his ambition.

Joe Hepworth, the Government Chief Whip, toyed with the beige Ministerial folder before him on the coffin-shaped table of the Cabinet Room, listening to the unenlightened buzz of conversation among the twelve Cabinet Ministers who had managed to respond to the summons. The coffin shape, introduced by Macmillan, was very appropriate in view of the corpse upstairs, he thought, without feeling. His steely mind recalled that Campbell-Bannerman had been the last Prime Minister, before Hargreaves, to die in No 10 Downing Street.

In this Corinthian pillared room, lurked the ghosts of history; memories of moments of glory and honour, but of squalid intrigue and conspiracy, too. Here, Asquith and his Cabinet had waited for the guns to start up along the Western front as the lights of Europe went out; in this room the crafty, under-estimated Baldwin, had plotted the destruction of the Triple Alliance and the collapse of the General Strike; here, the War Cabinet had assimilated the shock and shame of the falls of Singapore and Tobruk; through this room, according to Lady Eden, the waters of the Suez Canal had flowed in 1956, and had washed away Sir Anthony.

For what would Hargreaves be remembered? His sexual promiscuity? And what of Joe Hepworth? He had been Hargreaves' butcher. He felt no guilt of association because his motivation had always been honourable – to make Pam Bruce the next Labour Prime Minister. The puzzlement at the table, above and below him, confirmed what he had already guessed from his assessment of Prestcote's character.

No one fitted better than Prestcote, Beatrice Webb's category of a "gentle Jesus" Socialist. He hadn't had the foresight to line up his alliance in advance. He was simply going to break the news and rely on persuasion. His eyes met those of the Lord Chancellor and acknowledged their secret: they were the only two in the room who knew that Hargreaves was dead.

The door opened and Arnold Prestcote walked in. His stride was confident and there was no doubt he had an outward presence, with a fine head: something, Joe Hepworth thought, like the early Ramsay MacDonald. He was older, of course; but he had grown old in a distinguished sort of way. All that was wrong with him was that he hadn't the brain and he hadn't the guts. Joe Hepworth had known him since the 'thirties, and had been heard to say in Annie's bar that, on a clear day, you could see right through Arnold Prestcote.

He watched Prestcote walking quickly, and with an air of authority, towards Hargreaves' chair. He did not sit down at once but put his hand on its back, and smoothed it. It was the revealing act of a man staking a claim. Just as Joe Hepworth had figured, Prestcote was going for the *fait accompli*.

He waited a moment, savouring the puzzled silence. Then he spoke, the resonant voice of the accomplished public speaker. Only Hepworth detected the nerves.

"Pam, and gentlemen, I am afraid I have some very bad news for you." Prestcote paused for dramatic effect. Overdone, thought Joe Hepworth critically; he was going to do a Mark Antony, 'I come to bury, not to praise,' oration.

"The Prime Minister died about an hour ago. His doctor is certain it was a coronary." In the time it took for the members of the Cabinet to examine the import of his words, to face the consequences, Prestcote had slipped into Hargreaves's chair.

It doesn't fit, Joe Hepworth thought cynically; you couldn't fill it. But the movement was clearly a declaration of intent. 'The King is dead, long live the King.' Over my dead body.

Along the table, Joe Hepworth and the Lord Chancellor

conspired silently. The remainder were still shocked into silence. Because of that, Arnold Prestcote retained the initiative he had seized.

"Of course, I have already informed the Palace," he said, in the tone suggesting it was the most natural thing in the world that he should take over. "I shall be talking to the Queen's constitutional advisers later in the morning. I thought we had better meet immediately to make the necessary decisions before I inform the leader of the Opposition. It seemed to me the first decision to take is whether to postpone the general election time-table."

Joe Hepworth watched him closely: beneath the calm exterior was a very nervous politician. He had to go on speaking as if the sound of his own voice strengthened him.

"We shall all miss him, especially you, Joe."

"We worked well together," said Joe Hepworth, noncommittally. He could still see Hargreaves sitting in the Prime Minister's chair at the Cabinet table, dominating his Cabinet even in silence, pausing reflectively every now and then to restart his pipe with a lighter which worked like a miniature flame-thrower. He wondered what Hargreaves would have thought if he could see Prestcote, the politician he had gelded, sitting in his chair, usurping his authority.

He decided to play for a little time because Nick Hayling, secretary of the Parliamentary Labour Party and so essential to the success of his plot, hadn't arrived yet, although Hepworth had sent an official car for him. So he said, prolonging discussion:

"How's Janet taking it?"

"I've just left her. She's standing up to it very well. But it was a great shock."

Prestcote was gaining in confidence every minute; it would soon be imperative to stop his little gallop before he imposed his presence on the innocent. He knew only too well how Janet Hargreaves would be taking the death of her husband, the Prime Minister: however black the widow's weeds she wore, there would be an overwhelming relief that she would no longer be humiliated by the spreading whispers of his sexual exploits.

"Mercifully," said Prestcote, "according to Janet, he didn't suffer. He didn't even cry out. Death was quick and painless."

And clinically clean, thought Hepworth. The sod didn't deserve to go easily like that; he ached with the sense of the Labour Government's failures, a knowledge of the creaking machinery and overstuffed bureaucracy of the National Health Service, and those compelled to a slow, obscene death in overcrowded and insanitary conditions; Nye would turn in his grave if he could see the squalor which had become of his bequest to the nation: death was not only at St Thomas's, Westminster, Barts and Guys, eased by consultants and the best of medical science.

Prestcote said: "Does anyone disagree with the proposition that the general election campaign should continue exactly as planned? A postponement would create chaos. More important we daren't wait for unfavourable economic indices. We can observe the proprieties by a political truce on the day of the funeral. I'm sure the Opposition parties would agree. So, if everyone accepts, I'll arrange that with the Opposition later today."

No voice was raised in dissent. Prestcote looked smug; he obviously thought everything was going fine. Once again Joe Hepworth's eyes encountered the Lord Chancellor's: bereft of his full-bottomed wig and knee-breeches, and the quaint dignity of squatting his arse on the Woolsack, the Lord Chancellor had the appearance of a gentleman Sussex farmer, a port-and-pheasant face, with florid dewlaps overhanging his white collar. Thanks to Miss Thwaites' tip, Joe Hepworth had been able to agree a plan with him based on mutual knowledge: Prestcote as Prime Minister would be an unmitigated disaster. What made the Lord Chancellor such an invaluable ally was that he was never so obsessed by legalism that it could deflect him from the right political decision.

"Well," said Prestcote, maintaining his determined, businesslike manner. "Since the House isn't in session and there can be no tributes there, I have asked the secretariat to draft a statement lauding the Prime Minister's achievements in his

Ministerial capacity. That will go out under my signature from No 10 immediately his death is officially announced. "Tom – " He addressed Tom Westwood – "as chairman of the Executive's Organisation Committee, would you have Transport House put out a eulogy of the Prime Minister's work for the Movement as a whole?"

"Of course."

Give him a little more rope, Joe Hepworth argued within himself, and passed the message silently to the Lord Chancellor. Then pull the noose tight and string him up. Westwood, he saw, was making his own calculations and knew Prestcote's game. As far as Westwood was concerned there would be no *fait accompli*. But Hepworth wanted to see Hayling sitting down at the table before he made his move. Most of the faces on either side of him were still dazed by shock.

Only a politician long past his prime would have failed to line up his backers before calling this meeting. But Hepworth was not surprised by Prestcote's error. Prestcote's nerve had really been broken years before on the wheel of the Treasury. His efforts to expand the economy had resulted in a frightening run on the pound, loss of international confidence, and terrible trade figures. The only alternative to another devaluation, so soon after Callaghan's was to appeal to the I.M.F. for a gigantic stand-by credit. The terms were degrading, the strings so tight, that they put Britain's economy at the mercy of unsympathetic international auditors.

And, thought Joe Hepworth, callously, although the Cabinet had backed Prestcote's expansionist policies, the belief that the buck stopped at the Prime Minister's desk was all crap. When it came to the choice of the downfall of Hargreaves and his Labour Government, or the humiliation of Prestcote, there was never any question what the answer would be.

On Prestcote's resignation, Hargreaves offered to make him Lord President, Leader of the House, and deputy-Prime Minister. That was when Prestcote made his biggest mistake. He should have gone to the back benches and restored his battered self-confidence, renewed his friendships, rebuilt his reputation. Instead he had taken empty honours: everyone at

Westminster knew he was frozen out of the decision-making, that he was just a figure-head, an object of pity. His only duty was to maintain the rights of back bench M.Ps. And everyone knew Hargreaves had never given a bugger for those. Oh yes, he and the Lord Chancellor had a lot of ammunition with which to stop any take-over bid.

Joe Hepworth knew precisely what he would have done in Prestcote's situation: he would have rung up every member of the Cabinet, making his case, offering inducements, appealing for loyalty, explaining that after Hargreaves, the Party needed a caretaker while the general election was fought. And, if the Party won it, he could then appeal to the Parliamentary Party for a vote of confidence, only as a caretaker, of course. And a happy Party would show its gratitude to the victor and Labour would be stuck with Prestcote for a long, long, time. By now, Joe Hepworth would have had it all fixed. As he had now. But in a reverse direction. For Pam Bruce. Prestcote was about to find out it was never a case of Buggins' turn in the Labour Party. Intrigue and manoeuvre were certain.

There was a knock on the door. Twelve pairs of eyes turned to see Nick Hayling standing on the threshold, mute and tense. Hepworth motioned him to the vacant chair next to him. On Prestcote's face, he identified surprise and suspicion. Hepworth nodded at the Lord Chancellor and the attack was launched without delay.

The Lord Chancellor said in his deceptively guileless voice: "Arnold, you have referred to contacts you have had with the Palace. Could you explain what these amounted to?"

"Mainly courtesy. And to inform them I would be conveying the decisions of this meeting as soon as it ends."

"I hope there is no suggestion that the Palace may have any constitutional rights in this situation? Perhaps I had better explain quite clearly what the position is: the Monarch has only three constitutional rights: to be consulted, to advise, and to warn."

"But, as deputy-Prime Minister –"

"Perhaps I ought to remind you, Arnold, that this is a title unrecognised by constitutional authority. True, it has been used by various Governments from time to time. But it is an empty title, serving the same sort of purpose as a flag of convenience."

The Lord Chancellor had the mastery of the advocate, skilled in the vocal inflection of contempt. He dismissed Prestcote's title with a wave of the hand, signifying that Hargreaves' bestowal of it denoted the termination of Prestcote's political value – the pay-off, the sop to preserve his dignity after his disaster at the Treasury.

"But we must take decisions now. Someone has to lead the Party into the general election. Someone will have to take over the leadership, fulfil his speaking engagements, preside at the campaign committee meetings, conduct the Press conferences, take over the eve-of-poll television broadcast. And all the time the Queen's Government must be carried on.

"This isn't a question of who is next in the pecking order," ended the Lord Chancellor, brusquely.

By now, Prestcote's smile seemed to have been gummed on to his face. Joe Hepworth, feeling that his plan was already successfully launched, wondered whether there really was a life after death: if so, he had no doubt that Hargreaves would be buttering Peter to open up the pearly gates, but one cynical eye would be pointed downwards, watching Prestcote's performance.

"Sudden though the Prime Minister's death was, it left me time to consider the situation and study precedents," said the Lord Chancellor. "The situation, as I see it, is that the Palace has only one role to play in this: the Labour Party should elect its leader immediately, and the Queen would then have no alternative but to send for him –"

"Or her," interposed Joe Hepworth, nodding down the table at Pam Bruce.

"Or her," agreed the Lord Chancellor. "The Queen would then make the elected leader Prime Minister to take charge of the country's affairs during the general election campaign. It could be very temporary, of course. But there is no other way."

"There is nothing to prevent the Queen asking my advice,"

said Prestcote. But his face had reddened, his voice was a bluster. He was already afraid of defeat. He never had been a no-holds-barred fighter.

"And, of course, the advice of others." The Lord Chancellor had adopted his court-room technique, firmly grasping the lapels of his jacket in both hands. Somehow, in the limited time left for him to look up the precedents he had found the opportunity to shave, and his dewlaps were pink and smooth. Just like a baby's bottom, Joe Hepworth thought; a camouflage for his devasting skill as an interrogator, a skill which had left hundreds of writhing wrecks in witness-boxes at every assize court in the land. If she sent for anyone for advice, it would have to be him. He would eliminate Prestcote. Prestcote knew it.

Hepworth thought it was time to make his intervention. He said: "Since this meeting obviously has no power to take decisions on the leadership," he said smoothly, "I think it right to ask Mr Hayling to put the position from the Party political point of view." He challenged Prestcote directly. "That is why I asked him to attend. In his capacity as custodian of the Parliamentary Party standing orders." Prestcote did not dispute the change of ground. He seemed stunned by the loss of his initiative. "Mr Hayling, have you had time to examine the precedents?"

Prestcote's glazed eyes were now recognising him as his worst enemy: he retaliated with his deadly, cherubic smile.

"As usual in the Labour Party," said Nick Hayling, turning over his books of minutes, "There is no exact parallel. Over the years, I've been able to study the records, salvaged from the blitz, going back to 1906. The closest parallel I could find was the case of Harold Wilson."

"But," protested Prestcote, with renewed hope, "there is no resemblance. Wilson timed his retirement to leave ample time for an exhaustive ballot. The nation wasn't left like a rudderless ship."

The Lord Chancellor said, ominously: "I hope, Arnold, you are not advocating going into a general election without an elected leader? It would rob us of our biggest advantage of having been in office at the time of dissolution. We must be led into battle by a person with all the authority of the office of Prime Minister. Otherwise there would be no strategic advantage over the Leader of the Opposition."

"I'm suggesting there is no practicable alternative."

The issue was out now, as naked and as visible as a document on the coffin-shaped table. "I don't see how we can go through the exhaustive ballot procedure before the Prime Minister is decently buried, especially as it would coincide with the general election campaign. We cannot postpone that."

"That will not be necessary," said Hepworth. "Let me ask Mr Hayling his professional advice on how quickly the ballot would be completed. After all he is the Party's *Erskine May*." He had played his ace, the Lord Chancellor; now came Hayling, the Joker.

"Yes, let's hear the programme." It was Westwood's first intervention, the indication that he too was seeing himself as the next Labour Prime Minister.

Bassett said: "I agree we must have an elected leader before the election."

The battle lines were being drawn, just as Hepworth had anticipated. Pam Bruce (he would see to that). Tom Westwood. Young Bassett. Prestcote? He wondered whether Prestcote would have the guts to fight. He wondered too, whether he and Janet would marry after a decent lapse of time. He knew all about their unconsummated love. Through his intelligence system, the best at Westminster, he knew of practically every peccadillo, every whim, every character weakness, and every sexual deviation among his troops.

"Well, Mr Hayling, you are the expert. How long would it take?"

"Forty-eight hours would be enough. First, we should ask the broadcasting authorities to include in all their news bulletins a message to members of the old Parliamentary Labour Party to return to London for a meeting tonight to make arrangements for the emergency ballot. There should be adequate time for them to get back to Westminster."

"And just how would you allocate the time-table?" demanded Prestcote.

"I would propose that nominations close at 10 am the following day. Balloting hours would be governed by the number of candidates. There would be no time for refinements but extra staff could be called in from Transport House to duplicate the balloting forms. It could be done."

Westwood asked, softly: "Couldn't the whole matter be settled more expeditiously by a simple show of hands at the Party meeting?"

"Theoretically – " Hayling looked quickly at Hepworth for guidance. "Theoretically, I don't see anything against it. But –"

"But I do," said Joe Hepworth, grimly. He saw through Westwood's game at once: he didn't want to allow him time to organise Pam Bruce's campaign. He feared Joe Hepworth's system, the way he would use the old Whips. "It's got to be by secret ballot."

"There's no alternative," said the Lord Chancellor. "We couldn't face hostile Tory crowds asking our candidates who was the real leader of the Party, the worst possible posture for a Government fighting to preserve power. We must be able to confront the electorate with a Party united behind an elected leader."

"After two days of internal intrigue and conflict?" asked Prestcote, looking at Joe Hepworth with hatred.

"I hope you don't intend to make it that kind of a ballot," said the Lord Chancellor, cuttingly.

Joe Hepworth watched Prestcote's face. If he hadn't been a hardened, ruthless politician, he would have felt pity. Attlee had clung to office waiting for Gaitskell to emerge just to dish Herbert Morrison. Now Hargreaves had done an Attlee on Prestcote. Joe Hepworth knew, because he had faithfully carried out Hargreaves' orders and played his dirty tricks. But the only love he felt was for Pam Bruce, whom he now saw, elbows resting on the beige covering of the table.

"If I could make a suggestion," said Westwood, "this meeting should now resolve itself into the Party's liaison committee. Those not on the committee could retire and the rest could draw up a time-table to recommend to the full Party. Agreed?"

There was a chorus of approval. Prestcote had been downgraded in his role of deputy-Prime Minister but, in the absence of the Parliamentary Party chairman, Golding, he was next in line to preside over the liaison committee.

Westwood said: "May I make way for the Lord President?"

"This," said Prestcote, through gritted teeth, "is not a task I would perform. I wish my dissent to these proceedings to be formally noted."

"There'll be no minutes," said Joe Hepworth. "This is a meeting which was never held." Save it for your memoirs, he thought. He was utterly content: as soon as Miss Thwaites had given him the tip of Hargreaves' death, his mind had concentrated on one thing: there must be a ballot, time to organise, even though the time would be limited.

"I propose to withdraw," said Prestcote, and, summoning up from the reserves in his body, he left the room, a humiliated man. The silence continued a long time, like a commemoration, an embarrassed acknowledgment of a defeated politician.

"In view of the changed position, I move Mr Westwood to the chair," said Hepworth. His reasoning was simple: in the event of odium within the Party for the treatment of Prestcote – and Joe Hepworth knew Prestcote still had many friends – it would rub off on Westwood, the emergency chairman.

"Second," said the Lord Chancellor. He was one of the lucky ones, Joe Hepworth thought: whatever happened politically, *he* was assured of a fat pension. He had reached the pinnacle of his profession. He was fireproof.

A chorus of agreement confirmed Westwood, and the voices began: all the dirty work had been done, all that remained was to instruct Hayling to draw up time-tables for submission to the Party meeting.

Joe Hepworth felt a glow at the complete success of his plot: so far, so good. He had eliminated Prestcote. All that remained were Tom Westwood and the British electorate. Bassett would get his turn, but definitely not this time round. With Bassett, it was a case of Eric, or little by little.

The bedroom of the flat in No 10 was filled with the lavender-water smell of death. Janet Hargreaves, the widow, stood at the foot of the bed, looking without expression at the familiar face, already set in its waxen mask.

She felt no grief, but no bitterness, just a sense of deliverance from the shackles which had bound her so long to the corroding influence of his political life. It did not help to know that many, many women would have made great sacrifices to have spent so long at No 10 in the shadow of the most powerful man in Britain.

In a few hours, she thought, after the news had broken, his enemies would be busy; particularly the leader writers, perhaps touched by shame and guilt at the memory of their calumnies and defamations of the past years, even before he had gone to No 10. Above all, she hoped for contrition and expiation from the Street's lackeys who had pursued him from hotel to hotel, hoping to catch him in one of those infidelities to whch rumour had attached him. Oh, she had known of them. She could have told them, but for loyalty. She knew, but she had no longer cared. Love had left them many years ago.

She acquitted herself: she had not failed him, either in the daytime or, in bed, at night. There had been no stress or strains in their early sex life. Nor could any other woman have gratified him because of his constant search for variety, his lack of faithfulness to principle. Whoever he had married, he would have remained a compulsive philanderer.

Now, looking impassively at the face of the dead, she felt no need to force forgiveness. She just did not care; her sacrifice had been buried in the past, her own musical career. She had the one other bitter regret which had tainted their marriage: her barrenness. It had been before the miracles of the fertility drugs, or artificial insemination.

Suddenly, she did feel grief, the grief of her sacrifice. From the past she recalled the moment of the début, sitting at the Steinway in the Aelian Hall, fright-frozen fingers poised above the keyboard. Then she had unfrozen and the début had been a triumph. It had been the culmination of years of dedication, of climbing the mountains of aspiration, hours of practice in the morning, hours of teaching to provide the money in the afternoons.

But she had been only a child prodigy the first night she had seen Thomas Hargreaves. It was in 1931 after the decimation of the Labour Party at the polls when she had heard him speak, when the magic of his voice had woven its spell. Caxton Hall was half-empty, a judgment on the Party, and on the inexperience and lack of pulling power of the young speaker. But with what success he had mimicked the rich Scottish burr of Ramsay MacDonald, what scorn at the treachery, what threats of retribution and revenge!

That night there had been no foresight that it would be for Thomas Hargreaves, then prospective Labour candidate for an unassailable Tory seat, she would give up her chosen career; no indication that she would stand with him on the steps of No 10 the night he saw the Queen and received her commission to form a Labour Government.

Before that she had played in Vienna, the beautiful Vienna before its rape, the Anchluss. She had been blessed by the Pope, she had known the great musicians. Now, contemplating the dead face, lamenting the lost prestige, she knew it had not been worth it; he had never acknowledged her sacrifice, the dedication with which she had accompanied him through the trickery and chicanery of his political life.

She looked round the bedroom. She had her own priceless treasures safely under lock and key – the musical scores dedicated to her by international composers – possessions she loved while mourning the others ruined in the blitz. But this room carried its own coldness, a coldness from the warehouses of the Department of the Environment, the furnishings and even the bed on which his corpse lay, the dressing-table which caught her eye.

On it stood the evidence of her sacrifice, the wedding photograph on the steps of the Kensington Register office. She mourned the day, the beautiful Dunkirk weather, Britain's crisis, the miracle of the little boats while cricket matches went on all over the country. She stood in the middle, arms linked with Thomas Hargreaves, now M.P. for a safe Labour seat, a politician the newspapers had tipped as a man to watch.

A few days later he was to achieve notoriety with the speech in which he recognised, as an M.P., he was in a reserved occupation but, in any event, he would have been a conscientious objector. Some had called it courage; the Tories had always taunted him afterwards. To them it had been cowardice. She had lived with him a lifetime but she had never known which it was. All she knew was that he was incapable of being faithful to a principle or wife; he would sacrifice any truth for any expedient.

She herself had always felt the shame as she stood at his side in Whitehall while the Queen laid the annual wreath at the Cenotaph. His chest was bare; there were no medals for falsity, guile, political intrigue and cunning, lack of loyalty. That had been the man and it was all now snuffed out like a candle. There was no prevarication or political accommodation capable of keeping death at bay.

Now she knew she had been wrong to take a route she thought was love, to sacrifice her own life to sustain and strengthen his twists and perjuries, to help him as he met his antagonists like a wrestler covered in oil.

Was she being fair to the man on the bed? Should one think evil of the dead? Were there no vices, jealousies, and dirty tricks in the professional world of music? Was it not the whole of life she was despising, not just the world of politics? No, she thought; he had used her just as he had used everyone round him. Because she was closer, he had used her most.

And most of all he had used her name and skill, her reputation, her friendships with the great. He had used them on the way up from a junior job in Attlee's 1945 Administration. How soon he had demonstrated his competence and slyness. How quickly Hargreaves had been promoted to the Cabinet. How ruthlessly he began his climb up the greasy pole to the moment of victory, waving for the cameras and sight-seers from the doorway of No 10.

He had never forgotten the débâcle of 1931. His aim had always been to unite the party at any cost. He knew that Labour was a coalition: like all coalitions his Governments had been administrations of the lowest common factor. She faced the truth, staring at the man on the bed: the judgment of history would be that he was a Prime Minister it would be charitable to forget.

The silence in the death room had become oppressive. She felt her own guilt. She had collaborated in his career by running No 10. She had queened over Chequers week-ends during which, at the Steinway, she had entranced heads of state from whom her husband hoped to wheedle favours.

She had used her talent and her professional skill to charm Kings and Queens, Nixon, Brandt, Trudeau and black Presidents of the developing Commonwealth: Kenyatta, Kaunda, Nyerere, Seretse Khama and Banda.

Now he had died, leaving with her the burden of guilt for the squalid secret political bargains often struck at Chequers under her influence. The dirt had rubbed off on her conscience; she was corrupted by her contact with power. She had seen the dead waxen face flushed with brandy and aglisten with triumph after her performances of Brahms, Mendelssohn and Beethoven.

The modern-day heads of African states were not so eager to visit Chequers as their predecessors. Some of those who had, found themselves deposed by new despots as soon as their Boeing was out of the country. They had begun their political lives as terrorists in colonial British cells; they had finished them in exile at Claridges or Brown's.

She turned her back on the dead and went into the living-room. She opened the lid of the Steinway and, standing at the keyboard, composed a few chords of a requiem for a Prime Minister. It was not a mark of respect. Not homage. Not honour. A formality one accorded the unmourned dead.

Prestcote stood with Janet Hargreaves at the foot of her husband's bed. His arm was round her shoulders protectively, the only indication that there was anything between them, unconsummated love. Looking at the face on the bed, Prestcote thought: the harm he did lives after him.

"In anything that really mattered he was such a meagre little man," said the widow.

"Do you think he knew – about us?"

"He knew all right. But he also knew you were too honourable to cheat. It was his last great laugh – hanging on to power just to rob you. It was even worse than I thought. Lawson, his doctor, told me after he died, that he had been going to his Harley Street surgery for secret treatment for nine months."

"He had been ill – and no one knew?"

"He knew he had arterioscelorosis with angina pectoris. He knew all the time he was in danger of a heart attack. Well, Providence did intervene."

"I wonder who will reap the benefit? Westwood? Pam Bruce? Bassett, I'm afraid, we'll have to be patient." He saw the sudden alarm touch her eyes.

"Arnold, what do you mean? You – " The alarm had deepened. "Arnold," she said, suspiciously, "the meeting didn't last very long."

"It's still on," he said, dully.

"Then what happened?"

"I made my case for Cabinet backing to fight the election as deputy-Prime Minister and was thrown overboard." He said, bitterly: "I summarily dismissed myself when the meeting resolved itself into a liaison committee to draw up a time-table for an emergency leadership ballot. Whoever wins will be made P.M. *pro tem.*"

"You are going to accept that kind of treatment?"

He was surprised at her vehemence. She had always given him to understand she hated her No 10 life and intrigue at Chequers. As always, he found himself torn between desire to wield power, and doubt of his physical and emotional calibre to do all the unpopular things necessary to rule a Cabinet and country. He knew in his heart and soul, from a lifetime's experience of self, that he was not a strong man, but his mind and its ambition refused to accept the judgment as final. That's what his enemies said: he was indecisive, a ditherer.

"You know what Trueman said: 'If you can't stand the heat get out of the kitchen.'" He feared the heat but was still dragged towards it.

"You mean you're not going to fight?" She stared down at the face on the pillows. She couldn't accept that he could win even in death. "You can't stand for treatment like that. It's an insult. After what you have done for the Party and country as a loyal deputy. They are an ungrateful lot of bastards."

"Janet," he said, wearily, "there never was any gratitude in politics. There's no easy way. The only way is to compete in the ballot."

"Then you'll compete."

"And, like Morrison, be publicly humiliated?"

"Then what do you propose to do?"

"Oh, fade out slowly. I have my farm."

"So you'll grow turnips for the rest of your life?"

"You have your music." He assumed they would be together. "We could settle down to a quiet old age."

"I gave up my music once for him. But it was out of a sense of marital duty. I would give it up willingly a second time for love. For you. But only if you fight back and show him – " she jerked her head contemptuously at the bed – "that you were always the better man."

"I never knew it mattered to you. I'd always thought – "

"It was him I loathed not the life; the squalid way he did things. I'd like another chance to see things done decently, and honourably."

He realised with humility that she had a strength he would never possess. He felt it stimulate him. Perhaps, together – Then the reality intervened. He shook his head.

"We've got to face the truth, Janet. I would be beaten." Ridicule, shame, humiliation, pity – those would be his experiences if he fought Westwood and Pam Bruce. "You must see that. I'm a has-been, a relic."

"There must be some way to beat them." She looked at the bed again and he knew she was thinking: Hargreaves would have found a way, a devious but successful way.

"The Labour Party leadership was never a line of succession, Janet. It's a democratic election." Her anger, her courage, her attempts to stiffen his backbone – all were hopeless.

"You must think of a way. Appeal to the Party over the

heads of those men down there."

"It just isn't practical, Janet. My mind is full of layers of cotton wool." His bitterness suddenly concentrated on Joe Hepworth. It was Joe Hepworth who had kept him out, he thought, viciously. Joe Hepworth had lined up the Lord Chancellor and Hayling.

"Are you absolutely sure you wouldn't win the ballot? There must be some loyalty for service."

"I'm absolutely sure." Hargreaves had made sure by years of denigration, silent but subliminal.

"You have your friends."

"That's what Chamberlain thought. He made the mistake of boasting about them. At least, I shall not make that mistake. The only way I could have taken over was the way I tried – to fight and win the election as a caretaker. I would then have won a formal vote of confidence."

He felt a new surge of anger against Joe Hepworth who had plotted his downfall tonight. He suddenly saw that by standing down, he might ensure Westwood's election on the first ballot. Defeat for his beloved Pam Bruce would wound Hepworth more than anything. It would mean turning the Party Left. But what the hell! He had cared too much for the Party: the first thing Westwood would do would be to sack Joe Hepworth because he was Pam Bruce's man. But he couldn't be elated: he felt old and tired.

"Janet," he said, "I'm sucked dry."

"I forgave his infidelities," she said, "I can't forgive what he's done to you." Mixed with compassion was a bitter disappointment in him: he felt he had let her down, she was ashamed of his lack of strength in a crisis. She said: "I don't feel like burying myself in the countryside like a beaten animal."

"Not even with me?"

"Not even with you, Arnold. I'd rather see you fight and lose."

"And end my political career like Morrison's? It embittered the rest of his life."

"You owe it to me to try. That man dirtied me. He used me. I was his prize asset to show off. I was just part of his apparatus, like his detective and his baggage man."

"He used us all." It was still impossible to believe the silent body lying so near was bereft of power, that he had in some ghostly way predetermined the outcome of the fiasco of the meeting downstairs, probably now breaking up after the disposal of Prestcote's political future. "I wonder how history will judge him?"

"I'm more interested in what tomorrow's papers will say about him. And about you." She was fighting still, clinging to a hope he had already abandoned. Despite his depression he felt the glow of a little spark in response.

"You don't want to be another R.A.B., do you? Too much of a gentlemen to take power when the chance is presented to you. Look what happened to him. A thin volume of memoirs."

"The art of the possible. At least R.A.B. was a civilised man."

"A civilised man. But if he'd had the nerve he could have led the country. Like you" – she accused him openly – "he was outsmarted by more ruthless but not better politicians. That's what the papers will say when they learn you're not entering the ballot."

"If only there was some other way than the ballot." All the bitter memories flooded back, the memories of Hargreaves' insults, the relegation to the background, the sly hints of his similarity to Ramsay MacDonald, the seeds of suspicion so assiduously but discreetly sown by Hepworth on his master's behalf. He was the number two, but Hargreaves had always seen to it that he never sat on the right hand of power. "The odd thing was," he said, "that although he made enemies wherever he went, the public went for his charm. He was miles ahead in last week's popularity stakes in the public opinion polls." He remembered his own derisory percentage. But he had done no worse than the others.

"Yet the whole country knows of his whoring about. It's a talking point in the public bars. No one seems to care about the wronged woman at No 10. Do you think I like that, Arnold? That's one reason why I want to win with you. It would be my compensation." How, she asked herself, could she rob the dead of triumph? "You'll feel differently in a few hours' time. The meeting has depressed you. I'm sure you would have a chance in the ballot."

He shook his head. Nothing was certain in politics. But he *knew*. A lifetime's experience, the touch of the finger-tips.

"Let's not deceive ourselves, Janet," he said. "This is the end of the political road for me. I'm sick of the whole charade."

"I never thought you were a quitter. Let's get out of here." She acted as if she thought Hargreaves was eavesdropping and would have enjoyed her shame. He was crossing the carpet towards the living-room when the little spark fanned into something brighter. Hope emerged.

"Just a minute," he said. He stayed her with his hand. Perhaps there was a way of winning without a ballot? Perhaps he could outsmart Joe Hepworth? His mind raced free again, drenched in adrenalin. He saw her looking at him with hope.

"I've got an idea," he said. "Don't ask me what it is. But there is a chance. I'll have to play my cards right. Up to now I've let Joe Hepworth get away with it because he's organised. I'll have to fight him with his own weapons."

Secrecy. Planning. Preparation. He had learned something tonight. He would prepare a nice surprise for Joe Hepworth. He kissed Janet on the lips. She clung to him, surprised at the change in him.

"Keep your fingers crossed," he said, and left her standing in the middle of the sitting-room. He went down the staircase swiftly and into the Cabinet Room. He picked up the Prime Minister's telephone. The switchboard answered.

"I know what time it is," he said. "But get me Mr Adam Bolt. He'll be in his constituency." He took the pad off the table and began to write down a list of names. Any politician would have recognised the names of senior back-benchers, all men of influence. He went on writing until he had accumulated nearly twenty names. At the moment of completion of his list, Adam Bolt answered the telephone.

Arnold Prestcote set his plan in motion.

The meeting was over and the tired Ministers were leaving the Cabinet Room in little groups. Joe Hepworth took Pam Bruce by the arm and indicated that she should remain behind with him.

"Would you like to make a bet?" he asked.

"It depends on the subject, and the odds."

"The bet is that Prestcote won't stand in the leadership ballot."

"I can hardly believe that. He's been the number two so long, he must think he's the natural successor."

"He hasn't got a chance and knows it." She was shrewd, he thought; she had the mind of a political animal, all right. But there was still a lot Joe Hepworth could teach her. He made it a vow, watching her face wrinkle thoughtfully, that he would make her great. The basis was already there: she was tough, steeled by hardihood, grown from good collier stock. Pam Bruce was the modern Ellen Wilkinson, he thought, mourning his legendary heroine. He said: "It isn't only the fear of humiliating defeat which will deter him."

"Then what else?"

"Now that he knows his *fait accompli* has failed, he will want to hit at me. By seeing you are defeated in the first ballot."

"Me?"

"Of course." Hepworth, he thought, you're a callous, political thug. His first task was to ensure that she would stand. "He knows I idolise you, that I would go through fire and water to further your political life." Hepworth had no difficulty convincing himself he was acting out of patriotism: that was the first essential. Once you were a patriot, you could take any decision, go either way. He had convinced himself she was in the national interest.

She threw her head back and laughed uninhibitedly, her mouth wide. Despite the adolescent years of starvation in the Scottish coalfield, she still had all her own teeth. Like the others, her parents had deprived themselves for the sake of the bairns.

"What makes you think I would even stand? But if – a big if

– if I did, who would it be beating me in the first ballot?"

"You know as well as I do, Pam. Westwood, of course" He knew the name had been in her mind already. At its sound her face went hard with the dedicated enmity. He knew the rough outline but had always respected her reticence on the Bruce-Westwood family feud.

"Are you sure Westwood will stand?"

"You're dodging, Pam. We both know Westwood will stand. He'll have a good chance with his Transport House base." He was using Westwood as the spur. Now was the time to have it out.

She said: "Why aren't we talking about you, Joe? You have played the part of the silent Whip too long. You would be a natural. You ran the whole show, not Hargreaves."

"Me?" He laughed harshly. "After ten years as Chief Whip? How can I ask for votes after putting the boot in, treading on toes, making enemies, tearing strips off on the carpet in the punishment room, all the telegrams recalling M.Ps from the foreign beaches and bars, to vote in divisions? Joe Hepworth has more enemies at Westminster than any other one man, and the one who feels it most is Prestcote."

"Try again, Joe. You have more friends than enemies at Westminster." She stabbed her own breast. "And right here is your best friend. Why don't you think of all the patronage you've dispensed, all the *quid pro quo's* owed to you? You are being too modest. You could win."

"I'm just a political thug, Pam, and you know it. With the right nature to be the Prime Minister's hangman. I prefer, like the hangman, to work behind the scenes." He switched his tactic deliberately. "I don't mind confessing to you that I'd be worried about the future if Westwood won."

"Why, Joe?" She gave him no encouragement.

"He's a Transport House man. He could prove to be a prisoner of the National Executive. He could be vulnerable to pressure."

"From the Left-wing dominated executive?"

"Exactly. It would be a predominantly Left vote which

made him Prime Minister and the Left would expect its reward."

"Surely, things haven't changed? Hargreaves had a constant fight with the Left extremists. He mastered them. And you think this poor miserable body of a woman, vulnerable as hell in a man's world, would be capable of uniting the Labour Party under my leadership?"

"Vulnerable? We both know you're as tough as an old boot."

"And as good-looking."

"You know that's all balls."

"That's what I lack for the job – balls. My guess is that it will be fifty years before the Labour Party is conservative enough to elect a woman leader."

"Pam, listen. You're a natural on television. And it's television that wins elections today – not the new Beaverbrooks and Rothermeres. They don't matter a damn with their dying anti-labour sheets. Nor do the public opinion polls."

"Beneath everything, Joe," she said, "what it amounts to is dangling before me like a carrot, a battle to the political death with Westwood. He's the carrot. Where's the stick?"

"I'm the stick. The promise that I would be your campaign manager. Think what that means. The full support of the Whip's machine. No other candidate would have such support. It could be decisive in a short campaign. It's all there, a ready-made intelligence system, strings to all regional M.Ps at our finger tips. I could give you an accurate estimate of your support even before you were nominated. I tell you Pam, I could put you in No 10. But Pam –" He paused.

"Yes, Joe?"

"Your feud with Westwood. I've never asked you for the full story but it could be important if you're fighting each other for the leadership."

"I'll tell you everything, Joe." Was it for him, he wondered, or was it balm to herself to talk at last? "You probably know we came from the same Scottish coal town. More of a village, really. There was only one pit and the Coal Board closed it years ago. The last time I saw it the tips had all been landscaped. The Westwoods and the Bruces were colliers for generations. My father and brothers and Westwood's father and brothers were the last in line to go down. We lived next door to each other in the terrace of miners' cottages."

He waited patiently for the spasm of pain to pass. It was for her own good, the evil memory must be exorcised. When she began again, her voice shook.

"One day there was an explosion down the mine. Fire-damp. You know what that means. It brought down a roof and twenty-five men were entombed."

She straightened her shoulders, conscious of the boast that though she was a woman she was hard and tough. But he knew what she was seeing – the bleak pithead, the spinning wheels and the taut cables, taking the cages up and down – down with the rescue squads wearing the breathing apparatus on their chests, lamps in hand; up with the injured and the dead; beshawled wives and sisters, waiting and watching tearlessly for a life-or-death verdict on those they loved; and a safe distance away the Press, hiding their cameras, conscience-stricken vultures only doing their job, exposing pain, searching for bad news, sensation and sorrow. . . .

"My father and three brothers were all dead when they brought them up. The inquiry found Westwood's father, a deputy, had been guilty of negligence. There was a lot of talk about manslaughter but there was no prosecution. It went on for years after that, the Westwoods and the Bruces living next door to each other, refusing to move, but never exchanging a word."

"The other Westwoods? Were they down the pit?"

"Aye. Westwood lost two brothers."

"It must have been a hard cross for the father to bear."

"It killed him. The Bruces never shed a tear."

"It hasn't done your life any good, Pam, bottling it up like that. In the name of charity – "

"Don't speak to me of charity." But she laughed suddenly, a bitter but resigned sound. "In the end it isn't charity which is going to end the feud. It could be love. Or it could just be sex."

"That's a puzzle to me, Pam."

"The new generation. Liz is sleeping with Westwood's son, Richard."

"How is Liz?" This was one secret which had never leaked at Westminster or elsewhere: Joe Hepworth was the father of Pam Bruce's daughter, Elizabeth.

"She's fine. I'm lunching with her tomorrow."

"Give her my love. I hope to see her soon. How did they meet?"

"At some Chelsea party. I can't do anything about it. But for God's sake don't try what you're thinking."

"What am I thinking?"

"How convenient it would be if you could arrange a technicolour reconciliation between me and Westwood on the eve of the ballot."

"Well, all Westminster knows about the feud. We don't want to lose any votes over it. And I'm glad about the kids. It's wrong to hand hatred down from generation to generation."

"You think that? Then tell me, Joe Hepworth, how much of Socialism is really hatred?"

"Hatred of past exploitation, certainly. But we are all comrades inside the party. Oh, I know we periodically tear ourselves to bits, but that's part of the ritual – "

"You are trying to sell me brotherhood, Joe. If I had wanted that, irrespective of politics, I would have joined the Salvation Army."

In the silence he knew what she was thinking about the leadership – Was the Labour Party fit to be governed? Sometimes it was a coalition they both despised – cryptos and Marxists, Trotskyists, and now the Maoists on one side, snob intellectuals on the other, society's top layer which had found Socialism fashionable since Gaitskell's Hampstead days. . . ..

"You're actually proposing to make me Prime Minister, Joe. Tell me, do you seriously think I am strong enough to achieve the real purpose – true comradeship within the Party and the unions? How could I do that when there is nothing in my heart but ice for Westwood?"

"It might help you," he said. "You'd have to work more closely with him."

"Still thinking of the great reconciliation, Joe?"

"You've got time to make the decision, Pam."

"There's plenty of time to say No. I don't know whether its long enough to say Yes."

"Don't be obsessed by the lack of comradeship in the Party, Pam. Think of the Tories you'll be fighting. They have even less brotherly love. The only difference is that they do their blood-letting in private. They are all the more sinister because of that."

"I know you can't make any promises, Joe – but could I win?" She was suddenly appalled at the consequences of victory in a leadership ballot. It would mean public meetings at all the big towns and cities, split-second dashes from place to place in fast cars, flights by chartered aircraft and helicopters, making basically the same speech, timing the calculated insults at the Opposition leader with the precision of the actress. "You know me better than most, Joe. You know I've never had any greed or lust for power."

"I know that."

"Have I the strength of an ox, enough self-control and vitality? Have I the judgment, the courage? Could I be a butcher and slaughter colleagues?"

"You've got everything it will demand, Pam. Above all, integrity and self-honesty. You could never fool yourself. You've got the personal charm too."

She said ironically: "But then, Joe, you're one of my fans." She knew, he thought, that he loved her but also there could never be another man in her life after her husband's death in the International Brigade. He'd died young for Stalin. No more than an idealistic boy. Like so many others. "We both know what the physical strain is at No 10 these days –"

"Times have certainly changed since Baldwin used to disappear to Aix-Les-Bains. One crisis follows another."

"And usually during the recesses."

She realised that her mind had taken an incline in the last few minutes, was moving towards the excitement of the challenge. She forced another part of her mind to resist, to erect obstacles, reminding herself that half the time at No 10 she would be fighting her own Party, not the hated Tories. She would have to manacle the Left without stirring up ineradicable hatreds; she would have to resist the madder instructions of the annual Party conference, without alienating the activists who knocked on doors, the Party's salesmen. Above all, she would have to reconcile the Westwoods and the Bruces. All that, and then the taming of the Civil Service mandarins who had broken previous Labour governments.

"Joe," she said, "you're trying to thrust greatness on me, I've never sought it."

"But you're not afraid of the responsibility?"

She hesitated. "No," she said, at last. "But I'd like to see what the newspapers say – and of course, the views on television." She saw his face.

"Don't worry," she said. "I'm not afraid of criticism." Unlike Wilson she hadn't a love–hate relationship with the Street: she never flinched from their bullets. What did worry her was the thought of Workers' Control extremists marching up Whitehall, chanting: "Bruce out, Bruce out, Bruce out." She did not think she would be corrupted by power, but did one know in advance? Joe would watch over her, she thought. But Joe was ruthless. Could she be sure Joe wouldn't try to manipulate her, priding himself that it was Joe Hepworth who had put her there? She felt shame immediately, knowing that Joe was the finest friend she had ever had. The father of her child, the provider of the sperm but not her lover.

They walked out of the Cabinet Room arm in arm. In the red carpeted corridor they parted, he to return to his camp-bed in No 12, she to the parked official car drawn up at the door. There was no parting word. He simply kissed her lightly on the cheek. They both knew she had already taken her decision.

2

Edwin Battle awakened slowly, but without pain. He was so addicted to whisky, his system so accustomed to its quota, that he never suffered a hang-over. Something was different. He sniffed, and the cooking smell reached him – bacon and eggs were frying in the miniature kitchen. Oh Christ, he thought, Stella is here. She had come to claim her reward. He should never have given her a key.

Edwin Battle groaned. He had always been indifferent about sex, even when young and long before the growth of the steady, relentless intake of whisky had diminished even that urge to practically nothing. This morning, the thought of sex with the bulky, unattractive Stella, was repellent. He turned to the bedside-table for solace: the bottle was empty.

Gratitude, he thought, fortifying himself for the ordeal to come. Her "leaks" had made him the best-informed political correspondent at Westminster. She took risks he had no moral right to ask of her. If he could, he thought he would give her the best fuck of her life. But he couldn't even promise an erection. And it had been a long time. She would be hungry, deprived, as demanding as hell. He groaned again and slipped lower in the bed. He still wore only his pyjama bottoms and he was ashamed of his unmanliness, the merest rash of golden hairs on his chest.

"Good morning, Mr Scoops." She was framed in the bedroom doorway, smiling brightly and eagerly. She wore his dressing-gown and he knew what that meant: beneath that, she was in the nude. The image of her nudity revolted him. She withdrew the hand which had been behind her body and presented him with the *Daily News*. "I thought you would be interested in this, Edwin."

She stood at his bedside while he absorbed his triumph. Christ, he thought, we made it big. The death of Hargreaves was splashed all over the front page; under the masthead were the words in red: 2 a.m. Exclusive. *Edwin Battle*. There he was in big type. In the middle of the page was the picture: Sir William Lawson, the Prime Minister's doctor, face frozen in shock, looking up from the car door, Edwin Battle also in the frame, to mark his triumph. They had used all his stuff and buttressed it with the Prime Minister's obit, from the morgue in the library.

She leaned over and kissed him on his wide-open mouth. He must have shuddered because she withdrew to look at him. But he smiled falsely, he had enough decency to know that he must never let her down. He must make the sacrifice. He worried that his body would fail to respond. He started to think of erotic images. She leaned over the bed to kiss him again and he saw the cleft between her big, drooping breasts, the red marks left by the bra, where they had been squeezed.

"How is the journalist of the year this morning?"

"Never felt prouder. But I'm worried. I don't like you taking all these risks. I feel guilty." He was surprised to find that it was true.

"Let me be the judge, Edwin. I know the risks I run. I only want to make you happy."

"By God, happy isn't the word. I'm over the moon. So will my editor be." He was still trying to stifle the guilt. It wasn't corruption. It wasn't as if she did it for money and that he had the guilt of paying. She did it for love, the most powerful motive of all, and there could be nothing so all-consuming as the love of a spinster, and not a particularly attractive one, passing the equator, so to speak.

"Ready for it?"

"It?" he asked, desperately.

She giggled flirtatiously, like an adolescent.

"Breakfast, of course. *It* comes later."

He wondered how it could be that someone so smart and

efficient, speedy and business-like in a responsible job, could be such an absolute idiot, so desperate for cunt. He pitied her.

"Back in a minute," she said, and he watched her move, with what she no doubt thought was a sexy sway of her rump, to the kitchen. She returned, and placed the breakfast-tray across his lap, pumped up the pillows at his back. He felt rotten through and through.

He ate and she watched him adoringly from the side of the bed. He had no appetite and choked on the greasy bacon, but he needed time to try to evoke some response from the reluctant body. As he finished the breakfast she continued to absorb him with her eyes as avidly as soon she would absorb him physically. When he had finished the meal, he drank the coffee.

"Edwin," she said, hesitatingly, "it isn't only *that*?" "*That*" was his work, spread across the whole of the page. "You do love me?"

"Of course," he lied. He hoped she had not noted the pause, but his response had been almost immediate. He realised he was always half-ready for the question, it was so predictable. It astonished him that she could believe him. But, with absolute trust, she took the tray.

"Back in a minute," she warned him, and he watched her on the way to the kitchen miserably. What a couple they made! A middle-aged whisky-sodden snoop without a scruple, a man who didn't care whether he ever had another shag; ugly, fat, out of condition, slowly drinking himself to suicide. And Stella? A figure squat and ugly, defaced by a large wart on her chin, tits dangling like pendulums, armholes in which one could still see the stubble left after shaving, shadow of a moustache on her upper lip. He felt disgusted and panicky because he wasn't ready for the inevitable sacrifice.

He tried mentally stripping Princess Grace of Monaco but the impression was all saccharine and no sex; he tried the coloured ads. of the television girls, with glistening lips closing slowly and languorously on the chocolate bar (undoubted phallic hints), Eartha Kitt reclining on her settee (he didn't like dark skins), the Soho belly dancer he had once seen, olive-skinned, undulating belly, jerking pelvis, tassels rotating on bare nipples like Catherine wheels (too athletic and sweaty). All failed, and he began to feel the shame already. It was a schoolboy memory which did the trick, a brewer's dray stallion mounting the mare in the field near school.

She came back sinuously. He was now proud of his erection and he even watched with some anticipation as she dropped the dressing-gown and climbed into bed. Her breasts swung low across his eyes and she thrust one of the large nipples into his mouth. Christ, he thought, it's as hard as a ball bearing.

She couldn't wait. She mounted him at once, erection slipping easily into her because of her genitalia's sexual saliva. She swallowed him up. He thought: Christ, she'll take my balls as well. She was galloping ecstatically away as though in the saddle, gripping his flanks with her knees. Her breasts dangled and swung; he was beaten by her bouncing pubes, he was helpless under the assault, just able to breathe. But he consciously struggled physically and mentally to maintain his stiffness within her: she deserved the very best he could give her. But now, she was still bouncing away in an empty saddle. . . .

They recovered their breath. He saw she was weeping. Out of an unexpected sympathy he put out his arm and drew her into it.

"I'm so happy," she said.

"A funny way to show it." She put her face against his.

"It made you happy, too?"

"Of course." He lied out of habit: he was a journalist. He was more that a journalist; he was a political hatchet-man. He felt her fingers tickling his chest amongst the sparse, golden hairs. He began to fret. He knew she was unsatisfied, that she might try to mount him again. He'd done his stint, he thought. She'd been paid off. He also felt disquiet at her apparent indifference towards the risks she ran. It had been a mistake to give her a key to his flat.

"You're sure no one saw you come in?"

"Positive. I used the service lift. There wasn't a soul about in the flats." She dismissed the fear of awful sanctions which discovery would bring. The fingers in his hairs had become more wheedling. Mentally, he was already backing away; physically, he separated their bodies.

"Edwin?" It was almost a coo. Like a bloody pouter pigeon, he thought.

"Yes, Stella?"

A significant pause. He couldn't imagine what was in her mind.

"Would it be better if I moved in?"

Shocked, he reared up in the bed.

"Christ, Stella you must be mad." The sweat had burst out of the pores all over his body. After thirty years of drink, Battle sweated easily. "It's risky enough at all with you coming in at midnight or dawn. But all the time – You *must* be mad," he said again.

He looked down at her disappointed face and the full extent of her desire struck him another blow. It was worse than he thought: she wanted marriage. She was his best contact, his golden key to the secrets of Whitehall. To her, Battle was a lover: under-sexed, perfunctory, unenthusiastic, mediocre, perhaps; but she had no other standards by which to judge; he was her one and only experience of sex.

She was still hopeful of a repeat; she was totally unsatisfied. He felt her fingers searching beneath the sheets and was conscious of shame. She would never get it up. He just wasn't interested. The nearness of her body repelled him.

Quickly he got out of bed.

"I'm sorry, Stella. I've had it. Too much whisky for too many years. It destroys the sex urge."

She pouted. God, how he hated her little girl responses.

"I know it means more to me than to you," she said without acrimony, accepting he was *pas capable*.

"But you *do* understand we can't live together because of the risk?" He couldn't afford to lose her, he had to placate her at almost any cost. "These liaisons leak out too easily."

He knew that his movements at Westminster were closely watched by Hayling, and Joe Hepworth. His exclusive stories gave away the fact that he had a "leak" in official places. "Someone will find out and put two and two together."

He wanted the "leaks" to go on, he didn't want to become a martyr. As to Stella, he had a horrified vision of her stumbling down the steps of the Old Bailey dock, to the cells below.

He asked, putting on his trousers: "When are you on duty again?"

"Four o'clock."

"Keep in touch. But for God's sake, be careful."

"I will" she said, obediently. He knew that she would gratify his every whim. It was like a dog being followed around by a bitch. Her absolute adoration frightened him; he knew the safety of their relationship hung by a thread every day and night. He completed his dressing quickly, running the electric razor over his thin, fair stubble of beard. If she moved in despite the risk, it would be nothing but bed, and his needs were drink, not sex.

"You must be tired after being on duty all night," he said, offering her sympathy when she wanted a red-hot prick.

She yawned voluptuously and deliberately sat up in bed so that her two great flabby breasts hung down. They were like archery targets, he thought: an outer circle of mammary flab, an inner ring of ugly brown pigmented skin, and a bull's-eye of large pinky nipple. He looked away with a shudder.

"If you don't mind," she said, "I'll get some sleep here." He supposed she would get some vicarious thrill from sleeping between his sheets if she couldn't sleep with him.

"Go ahead," he said. "I shall not be in until late tonight. But you will be careful when you leave? And don't answer the telephone or show yourself at the door."

He looked at his watch ostentatiously. "Thanks for the breakfast," he said. He was ready already for the first Don't be Vague of the day.

Fascinated by the ugliness of her breasts he did what she expected of him, bending down and kissing them one by one, managing to conceal his disgust.

She drew him down and held him fiercely for a moment until he felt it was safe to break away. Still sweating, he waved at her from the doorway, and made his escape.

Joe Hepworth looked up from his desk in the Government Chief Whip's office and watched Hayling limp to the empty armchair, upholstered in expensive green leather, and decorated by the portcullis symbol of Parliament. Hayling's war wounds were obviously playing him up.

Hayling pointed to the clock. "In twenty-four hours nominations will be closed. And I think you're wrong, Joe."

"I've never claimed infallibility. What am I wrong about?"

"Prestcote. I think you guessed wrongly about him not standing in the leadership ballot."

"It isn't a guess. It's an intelligent deduction. You can't be Government Chief Whip in this place for ten years without developing an instinct for character. He's scared stiff of being kicked in the unmentionables by the comrades. He remembers what happened to Morrison. He hasn't had the stomach for a real fight since he fell down at the Treasury. Hargreaves deliberately made him what he is today – a jelly fish."

"Jelly fish can sting."

"Not this variety."

"In any case, you're going to have a big enough fight on your hands to get enough votes for Pam Bruce to nail Westwood. You might have to play it dirty."

"Politics is a dirty game. A clean politician would drown up to his ears in shit."

"Some might take it amiss – using the Whips' office as a candidate's campaign headquarters, and the Whips as campaigners. They should all be neutral."

Joe Hepworth spread his arms wide, a caricature of innocence. Hayling thought: he has the nerve of the devil himself. Technically, Hepworth was not his boss. He didn't authorise his miserable salary, which was a disgrace to the Labour Party; but there was a bond of respect between them. He inhaled the smoke and expelled it so that Hepworth, a non-smoker, smelled the tobacco's pungency.

Hepworth said: "If I were you I should be afraid of the shape my lungs were in. You smoke like a bunsen burner. You're as bad as Hargreaves used to be."

Hayling pointed upwards with the stem of his pipe: "He's

probably having a drag up there."

"Don't speak facetiously about your dear, departed leader."

"After what I escaped in the war, I've never been afraid of death," said Hayling. His right leg was still full of souvenirs. He'd survived several operations. "I've used up my allocation of luck already."

Poor bugger, thought Joe Hepworth, affectionately. He hadn't much to show for his devotion to M.Ps needs and the Cause.

"It's a rough old world," Hepworth said.

"Pardon?"

"Forget it. I was thinking."

"What were you thinking?"

"That you have something on your mind. You think it's important." They were bound together by invisible links, as reliable as radar.

"Let's get back to Prestcote."

"All right. What are your readings?"

"Since early on I've heard and seen his sympathisers at work. They must have been called in."

"They were."

"But why? If Prestcote isn't standing?"

"I wouldn't tell anybody but you this, Nick, but I have my spy on the Downing Street switchboard."

"The supervisor?"

"I never disclose my sources."

"No one else would have the nerve."

He didn't know about Stella's bondage, her love for Edwin Battle.

Joe Hepworth said: "Remember how it was in the war – ?"

"I'm not likely to forget."

Hayling massaged his right leg and winced.

"Well, the telephone-lines were busy after we left the Downing Street meeting. Remember how the increase in signals traffic used to give away when an offensive was coming?"

He opened the top drawer of his desk and took out a piece of foolscap paper. He slid it over the desk top to Hayling.

"There are about twenty names. Prestcote rang all of them before dawn."

Hepworth waited for Hayling to study the list. Then he said: "Well?"

"Very impressive indeed. It bears me out. He intends to stand and was ringing round to rustle up support. Getting in early." Hayling grinned. "I notice one important name is missing. Yours."

"Oh, I know I should be for the chop if ever Prestcote went to No 10. He'd want his own man, not Pam Bruce's."

"Especially after you stymied him so successfully last night." Hayling slid the list back to Hepworth. "There's also something very significant. The half-dozen who have been patrolling the lobbies, grabbing the ex-M.Ps as they come back are all on the list."

Hepworth shook his head stubbornly. "I still can't believe Prestcote intends to stand."

"Well, that's all I know. Prestcote's men are whipping up support. For what? It's nothing to do with me but I should put your boys on to it."

"Don't worry," said Hepworth, grimly.

"Why don't you go back to your supervisor? They always listen in. She would know exactly what Prestcote is up to."

"I'm a bastard," said Hepworth. "*You* know I'm a bastard, the whole House knows I'm a bastard. But I can't ask her for further favours on this. She's taken a big enough risk. Above all, I don't want to foul up a useful source. I might need her for a really big one."

"I can understand that." No one was in a better position than Nick Hayling to know how difficult it was to keep a secret or protect a source at Westminster. News, especially bad news, spread like a forest fire.

Suddenly something flashed in Hepworth's mind, like a streak of lightning. He slapped his knee.

"I must be slipping," he said. "We should have thought of it before."

"Then what *is* Prestcote's game?"

"I don't know what he intends." He gnawed a lip. "But I'd

bet even money he's planning something for the party meeting tonight."

"A last-ditch stand?"

"Could be." Joe Hepworth stood up. "I must get busy," he said. "I've got time to find out."

Pam Bruce stood at the head of the staircase leading down from Great Smith Street to the basement restaurant of Church House, searching for her daughter, Elizabeth. Almost immediately she saw her, waving from the bar.

She waved back. The closer she got to Liz the more she felt a motherly pride. They had the same red hair but Liz was more than just a good-looker. They kissed warmly.

"You're tired," Liz said, sympathetically.

"Up half the night." She yawned.

"So I gather."

Beneath Liz's elbow was the *Evening Standard*.

"You've been reading all about the jockeying for power?"

"The Political Correspondent has got you marked down as a candidate for the leadership."

Laconically, giving nothing away: "Has he now?" She made an elaboration of pretence. "I admit there is some genuine pressure. I'm still thinking it over. Have you any views?"

"Discount me altogether. I'm proud of your Cabinet rank already. But I wouldn't push you for my benefit. Let me get you a drink. You look as though you could use one."

"You're right, Liz. A gin-and-tonic, please."

She watched as Liz ordered a gin-and-tonic and bloody Mary. She ached with pain and resentment when she thought of a Westwood taking her naked in his arms in bed, stroking her breasts, fondling her buttocks, enjoying a Bruce body of such delectable beauty. It seemed an alliance against her.

Pam Bruce, she told herself, you're just bloody irrational and jealous – of their youth, of their freedom, of their sexual happiness. Of that happiness she had no doubt: it glowed on Liz's face, and in her body. In any event, she told herself, she had always recognised her daughter's right to her own sovereignty and independence. For instance, she remembered, she had never sought an explanation when Liz had been sent down from Girton. That had been an exercise in self-control. But, she had told herself, at twenty-one, Liz had been a woman.

"Cheers, Mother." They drank. "I have a table booked."

Suddenly, Pam thought she detected an unusual trace of nervousness in her daughter. It showed when she took the packet of Castellos from her hand-bag, dangling on her arm by its strap.

"Please don't," pleaded Pam.

"I'm sorry, Mother," Liz said, with instant contrition. "I didn't mean to embarrass you."

Liz's first of many, many appearances in the gossip columns had been her cigar-smoking. Originally the cigars were intended to shock. They had now become an addiction.

"I can see," Liz said, "I shall have to be on my best behaviour for the next forty-eight hours." She put the carton back in her hand-bag.

It was just high spirits, Pam tried to reassure herself; high spirits and a touch of recklessness. She was notorious for some of her dangerous activities – driving the circuit at Brands Hatch in a Lotus, a Guinness book of Records entry for the longest free fall by a woman parachutist. And the most notorious exploit of all. Invited by the Prince of Wales to spend a week-end at a Royal house party at Windsor Castle, she had declined on the grounds that it would be compromising her republican principles. She had always sworn she had not given the story to the Press, and Pam believed her. But she was as celebrated for her eccentricity as her beauty.

"Shall we take our drinks to the table?" Liz led the way.

Pam was still thinking: she couldn't complain. There had been no bastards or abortions; no court appearances for drug possession; no drop-outs in Piccadilly; no communes, stained jeans and filthy, bare feet. She did not doubt that there had been plenty of sleeping about. Liz's sexuality was blatant and inviting. But parenthood was always a risk. She was partly responsible for what Liz was because of neglect; she had devoted practically all her life to politics. As they approached the table, Pam saw it was laid for four and had a reserved sign.

"You are making quite a name for yourself."

"As a playgirl?"

"Well – "

The word, then the silence, was only a mild rebuke, no assumption of authority.

"You mean the gossip columnists? Oh, it's you they're after. They follow me about."

"Hoping for indiscretions? Of course. Well, I'm sure you know it's a sensitive period."

"They're *agents provocateurs*." Liz put out a hand, covering her mother's on the clean napery. "Don't worry. I'll be especially careful. No more Press cuttings until after the general election. Are you going to win the ballot?"

"According to Joe, I could."

"All morning, I've been trying to get used to the possibility of moving into No 10 with you."

"But you'd keep on your flat?"

"Of course."

For Richard Westwood, of course.

"But take it step by step. First the leadership. Then the election!"

"How's Joe?"

"Over-worked. Scheming his head off. For the good of the Party."

"Which means for the good of Pam Bruce."

"Naturally." She had never regretted being frank with Liz about her parentage: after Jim, she could never have married another man but she had wanted a child, the natural fulfilment. She had always been glad she had turned to Joe. "He would like to see you, he told me to tell you."

"I'll give him a ring and fix up something. Promise." Liz had never born any grudge, or suffered psychological damage, from Pam's confession that she was born out of wedlock. She and Joe were father and daughter but it was their secret. They got on together famously. Of the two, Joe Hepworth was the one most affected: he could never stand up and show his pride. Joe always remembered how Pam had looked at her age but found pleasure in the features which he had given her daughter. She had his tallness; she was a head higher than Pam.

Liz said: "I know it's going to be a hell of a hectic time for you, and it's no good asking you to take things easily. But you look so tired."

"I'm a bit frayed." The truth was she was fifty-eight and was facing the most important decision of her life. She envied those with faith who could take comfort in prayer. She found it difficult to concentrate her mind on the coming weeks: the past kept intervening, memory blotting out the present and future. In her past she was on the platform at Victoria, waving Jim off on his journey to Barcelona, the International Brigade, and the useless sacrifice. Their last act together had been sexual intercourse without precautions, a conscious decision on their part that she should conceive. If he was to die she wished to retain a part of him, a son or a daughter, flesh of his flesh, blood of his blood. But she did not conceive and it had been sixteen years before Liz had been born.

"You're thinking of Joe," said Liz quietly.

"Yes. He's been marvellous." He had loved her but Jim's shadow had always been in the way. Pam could give Joe nothing but comradeship, and the pride that she had deliberately picked him to father her child. She put out a hand and placed it over Liz's on the table.

"Do you remember what you said when I told you?"

"Yes, I remember exactly. I said: 'I feel as if I had been let out to contract.'" They both laughed. Then Liz went quiet. "Poor Joe, he had to be satisfied with second best."

"He has a good marriage."

"Pam, you know he worships you." He had honoured her stipulation – no further sexual intercourse after conception. There had been two men only in her life. Harrowed by the past, she struggled mentally to reach the present. She studied her daughter frankly. It gnawed like tooth-ache that she was having an affair with Tom Westwood's son. She again realised that, beneath her apparent calmness, she was on edge. Some presentiment turned her eyes to the staircase. She stiffened. Without looking at her mother, Liz waved; the man waved back. Pam Bruce recognised the enemy at once. He came towards them, improving in appearance at every step: he was tall, dark, masculine, soberly dressed in an expensive suit of dark grey. Only his smile was tense as he reached their table.

Pam looked at him, bitterly. "Mr Westwood, junior, I presume. Richard, isn't it?"

"To that, I plead guilty, Mrs Bruce."

"I don't think we should pursue the topic of guilt." She felt her own crime, that she should be so civil to the enemy. She turned her anger on Liz. "This is false pretences, Liz. I thought it was a tête-a-tête. It's not a pretty plot."

Liz was pale but calm. "Mother, I'm the daughter of a politician. All right, I resorted to the tricks of the politician. It was the only way I could get you two to meet."

"That guilt you spoke about, Mrs Bruce." Richard Westwood was firm, but calm. There was nothing ostentatious, nothing objectionable, about him. "It's been around a long time. It hasn't done anybody any good. As far as Liz and I are concerned, it ends at our generation."

Pam Bruce made as if to rise. Westwood put out an arm and detained her. The grip was painless, but firm. She sat down in surprise, and Richard Westwood took the empty chair next to her.

"Please don't go. I don't want Liz to be upset. Can't we talk? How much longer is this feud to divide you and the old man? You're in the same Government, working towards the same objectives – He paused, realising that if the evening papers were accurate, the Westwoods and the Bruces would tomorrow be locked in a struggle for power: first the leadership, then the Premiership.

"It's not just a case of ancient guilt, Mr Westwood."

"No?"

"I don't happen to like your type."

"What type am I, Mrs Bruce?"

"Money-grubber. Parasite. Speculator. Materialist."

"You forgot the most objectionable – candy-floss man. But I'm also a Socialist, Mrs Bruce." She was angered by his coolness, his masculinity, his obvious ability to influence Liz; but most of all by Liz's obvious pride in him. She felt robbed when she saw the glow on her lovely face.

"Not my kind of Socialist, Mr Westwood."

"There are many kinds. Why don't you call me, Richard, Pam?"

She ignored his nerve, his arrogance. She said: "You have exploited your fellow men, traded in their bodies. You organised take-overs, using paper money, closing factories and losing jobs." She saw, with inward pleasure, that she had at least damaged his self-esteem. But he fought back.

"I also helped, in a small way, to restructure British industry. God knows it needs it. Sometimes my activities were actually beneficial."

By now she knew she had established that he felt secret guilt. That was something in his favour.

He said, defensively: "What can I do to make you approve of me, Pam? Endow a new Ruskin College? Would that save my soul from damnation?"

"I leave your salvation to your conscience." By now she knew he had a conscience. It might have been dormant but she had reawakened it, she knew. "My Socialism comes from a generation which went down the pits under the starvation regime of the private owners. There's blood on the nation's coal, Mr Westwood. Tell that to the City of London and the gnomes of Zurich."

"I know you won't like this, Pam. But you are exactly like my father – bloody insular, bloody near-sighted, bloody antediluvian. I'm not his kind of Socialist either. He hates the idea that I make money speculating in futures. Most of all, he hates my Jag as a status symbol. But I happen to believe there's room in the party for people like me. What are your relations with Harold Lever?"

"I don't exactly clasp him to my bosom. I respect his financial expertise."

"You must accept that sunken baths, gold-plated taps, and flood-lighted statuary in the garden, are just idiosyncrasies. They offend your old-fashioned image of the Party. The Tory Press taunts you with them and you fear it loses you votes.

You're against profit. You'll soon be against a mixed economy. It's time the Party opened its mind."

"I'd like to see you stand as a candidate in a mining constituency."

"Why not? Donovan, another dilettante Socialist, represents Boswell."

Deep down, struggling to rise, was an inner admission that she liked him – for his audacity, for his intellect, his impudence. Most of all for his honesty. But she mustn't allow liking to overcome prejudice.

"I wouldn't want what you represent in my son-in-law."

"Very few mothers really get the son-in-law they want. Usually, when they get what they thought they wanted, it turns out he's not what he seemed. What do you want, Pam Bruce – a miner? Or a freak from Essex University?"

So far, Liz had been tactically silent, head moving from one to the other as the exchanges went on. But now she protested: "Who said anything about marriage?"

"Liz, if I proposed marriage, it would be to you, not your mum."

"In the meantime, you sleep together."

"Mother! Don't play the puritan. Don't tell me you never had pre-marital sex. After all, the Bloomsbury set wallowed in it."

Pam Bruce felt the truth rising hotly up her neck and to her cheeks. She hadn't anticipated an invasion of her past privacy. With pain, she remembered the night Jim had taken her virginity, their first mutual disappointment with sex, the feeling was that *all* there was to it? Jim's first reaction was to complain of the bruises on his knees from the bare boards. She had been eighteen. They had borrowed a friend's room for the initiation, but the furniture hadn't been moved in and there was no bed.

"Pam," said Richard, still deliberately and defiantly using her first name, "in less than forty-eight hours you may be going to the Palace. On the other hand, it might be my father. Whoever wins will need the votes of Socialists like me, admittedly the minority."

He was right. She hadn't moved with the times. Nor had the

Movement. She must have the rich, the merchant bankers, the entrepreneurs, the professional classes, the public relations and advertising men. She must remember that, all over Britain, there were secret Socialists, some living in houses where the windows were plastered with the blue Tory posters.

"As for marriage," said Liz, soothingly, "he's really in love with his Jag. I come a bad second."

"He can't take a Jag to bed."

She smiled. She felt the first thaw, the small floe of ice breaking loose.

Westwood took his chance. "What about ordering lunch?"

"You're pretty sure I'm staying," said Pam Bruce, putting up a token resistance to the end.

"That's because I know you're an adult, with well-developed common sense. Besides, we have planned a big surprise for you."

Pam Bruce looked at him suspiciously. Liz had buried her face in the unfolded menu. Their guilt was almost tangible. Instinctively, she turned her eyes towards the entrance and saw the surprise. Tom Westwood was standing at the head of the staircase, looking down into the restaurant. As soon as he identified them, he turned sharply, and walked back to the street.

"Thank *you*," said Pam Bruce, bitterly. "Thank you *very much*."

She stood, and began to leave the table, throwing off Richard Westwood's restraining arm.

"All right," he said, angrily. "But it's tribalism, pure bloody, medieval tribalism. It's time you two silly old buggers grew up."

Deliberately taking Richard Westwood's hand as her mother left, Liz shouted: "You're as antique in the mind as your Party's bloody penny-farthing bike."

Pam Bruce hardened her heart and went towards the stairs.

Immediately he had received the telephone-call from Eric Bassett, Edwin Battle knew it was going to be his day. Bassett, who had always been one of the Commons temperance group, was doubtful about Battle's choice of meeting-place, but all Battle's meetings were in bars, and Bassett finally agreed to meet him in the upstairs cocktail-bar of St Stephen's Tavern, in Bridge Street, opposite Big Ben tower.

When Bassett came in, Battle was already sitting on a high stool at the bar, still euphoric at the memory of the front page of the morning's *Daily News*. Bassett was never seen without his bulging brief-case. He put it down at his feet and greeted Battle with a nod.

"I see you were busy in the small hours," said Bassett. He read the political news in all the newspapers before breakfast. Not a minute of his day was wasted.

"Yes. I see you have your portmanteau with you," said Battle, facetiously. "Stuffed full with State secrets?"

"I never carry State papers about with me," said Bassett. "Remember poor Dick Crossman?"

"Yes, he left confidential papers in Prunier's in Soho. But then Dick was always falling flat on his face."

"This," said Bassett, tapping the bulging case with the toe of his shoe, "contains the usual bumpf – White Papers, Blue Books, and Labour Party policy documents."

"Including some of your own mad-brained schemes?" Battle, waiting for the favour he was certain he was about to receive, wouldn't have said it if there was any fear of insulting Bassett. But Bassett was immune. When he was ready, at the moment of his own choice, Bassett would speak. He was now looking round suspiciously, like a conspirator.

"It's all right," said Battle, soothingly. "I've already checked. There's no one here to identify us. I know you are conscientiously opposed to alcoholic drink but let me get you a soft one." He was already on his second double Haig.

"No thanks. They're full of sugar and colouring matter." Bassett was also a food crank, a great believer, as Cripps had been, in the curative value of shredded carrot, vegetables and nuts. Battle waited for the revelations.

"Mr Battle, you are probably the best-informed political correspondent at Westminster, as this morning's paper proves. What do you think of my chances in the ballot?"

"No bullshit?"

"No – " Bassett's church training balked at the word. "An honest opinion."

"You will be eliminated in the first ballot."

"Humiliatingly?"

"I didn't think you recognised the word." One of Bassett's strengths was his indifference to setbacks. Once decided, nothing would deflect him from his course. "I should think you will get thirty or forty votes. You have the Workers' Control group in your pocket."

"Forty is an over-estimate," said Bassett. "The group is not more than twenty-five strong. I fancy I shall wean away another five or ten votes not at present committed. Total, about thirty."

"What is going to happen to Prestcote?"

"At the moment he's sitting on the fence."

"He's been sitting on the fence so long the iron has entered his soul."

"I doubt whether he will be nominated. I suspect Mr Prestcote has other fish to fry."

"Tell me about Mr Prestcote's fish-frying."

Bassett closed his lips. "You had better ask him. It is one of my principles never to discuss a colleague with the media."

"Would Wedgie have done better than you?"

"I doubt it. Like me, Wedgie was thirty years before his time. Like me, he would have been left at the starting-line if he hadn't had that regrettable accident."

"You really think your time will come, don't you?"

"Of course. Don't be so sceptical and incredulous, Mr Battle. You and your colleagues make a big mistake in calling me a young man in a hurry. Actually, I'm a very patient man. I can afford to be. I am young enough to wait. I have a base. A small one, it is true, only ten per cent of the Party. But, one day, it will all be rearranged. The leader will be elected by the annual conference."

"Over Joe Hepworth's dead body."

Bassett shrugged. "So be it. He doesn't get any younger. The youth is running the party more and more."

"When youth's real day comes, you'll be an old man."

Bassett said, convincingly: "In thought, I shall never be an old man."

Battle looked into the staring eyes. They had a mesmeric effect. He thought: The young bugger actually believes he will one day get to No 10. Battle felt touched at what he regarded as Bassett's crazy belief. But he was touched also by a reluctant respect. He had the intellectual ability. His energy was inexhaustible. He had guts. It was his judgment which Battle doubted.

The conversation had flagged and Battle was all the keener to hear the secrets Bassett obviously wanted to convey surreptitiously. But he knew better than to barge in. He signalled the Spanish barmaid for a refill.

"Who's your campaign manager?"

"I am. I do everything myself." What he meant was that he wouldn't allow anyone close enough to examine his brain and unveil its secrets. Battle thought: I suppose he's no better off than Jesus. He *had* thirty disciples, but the odds were just as heavily against Bassett as they had been against Him. He saw the look of disapproval on Bassett's face when the drink came up.

"You know you're signing your own death warrant?" Bassett asked. "It's written on your face."

"I know. I also have it in writing from my doctor. And the insurance quack just laughed when he saw my whisky veins and I told him I was a newspaperman. But it's the most pleasant way of committing suicide. At least let me get you a plain tonic. With ice."

"There's quinine in tonic. Quinine's a depressant."

Battle said, with heavy irony: "How *do* you indulge your frolicsome little nature? Come on, be a devil."

Despite his valiant and defiant words, Battle felt a maudlin self-pity at the thought of his self-inflicted cirrhosis, the brain damage the hospital tests had shown. The graph of his life expectancy was already on a swift downward curve. Then he took a gulp at the Haig and cheered up. At least death wasn't imminent; meantime the Haig was an antidote to thought. The verdict would be death by natural causes, not death by Don't be Vague.

"You know, Battle, I like you." Battle thought: Here it comes, at last. "Despite the basic differences in our life-styles and temperaments."

"Perhaps because of them," said Battle. "But, thanks ever so." He made a mocking bow from the pinnacle of the high stool. It was a hazardous enterprise. "Is that why you're going to do me a favour?" He did permit himself the risk of an interrogative tone. Bassett was ready to talk. But he still ignored the bait.

"I genuinely mean it. You're always haunting the Lobby, or in some secret den like this, digging away like a ferret."

"When I'm not in Annie's bar, slurping the Haig. There are several ways of doing the Lobby job, my dear Bassett. You can get fallen arches standing around in the Lobby, get corns on your bum sitting on the high stools in Annie's bar; or you can sit at a desk rewriting Government and Opposition hand-outs. I call that lot the 'hand-out fusiliers' That's not for me."

"Who is going to win the ballot, Mr Battle?"

"Tom Westwood or Pam Bruce."

"That's evasion, not an answer, Mr Battle. You said 'either' and 'or'. I asked for the winner. Try again, and be braver. For instance, what will decide it?"

"Writing off Arnold Prestcote, if he's absent on his fish-frying, the answer is how your vote will split up between Westwood and Bruce."

"Anything more?"

"I can't think of anything."

"Come, Mr Battle, where is that professional skill and clairvoyance of yours? I'm going to give you a small item of intelligence."

"We call it news. And that's what I was hoping. Not too small, I hope?"

Bassett continued to tease, like a bather poised at the very tip of the diving-board.

"You mustn't quote me, of course, but you can say in tomorrow's *Daily News*, quite decisively, that I would not serve in a Cabinet which Pam Bruce led as Prime Minister."

Battle's glass was at his lips and he nearly choked on the whisky. Then he swallowed it in one. When he had recovered, Bassett asked him cheerfully:

"How will you describe me in your story – a man of principle, a man who ought to be in the madhouse, or a wrecker of Party unity?"

"I thought the fundamental rule for an ambitious politician was – never resign, never apologise, never explain."

"If it's the wrecker line, Mr Battle, you might like also to point out that no politician ever became head of state, Prime Minister, or took over power, without, at some stage in his career, having been a wrecker. At one time, all the gaols in the colonies seemed full of potential presidents."

"Are there any other Ministers taking the same attitude?"

"You would have to ask them."

"It looks to me as though you're handing the election to Westwood on a plate."

"Pam Bruce would be under Joe Hepworth's thumb. He is so far to the Right he is a menace to the advance of Socialism. He should be in the Tory party. If I served in Pam's Cabinet I should be faced with a crisis of conscience every week. I prefer a big bang now, rather than the long drawn-out mutter of gunfire."

"I can promise you a big bang tomorrow," exulted Battle.

"Westwood would at least try to keep a Government pointing Left, implementing as many conference decisions as possible."

"You really believe in that conference bullshit. You really believe in workers' control, don't you?" Once again, he looked at the give-away eyes, firmly fixed on a distant horizon no one but Bassett could see.

"Of course. Up to now the leading figures in Left Wing politics have been seduced into compromise, either to get or retain what is left of power after it had been emasculated by the Civil Service. Take Nye, the hero of the Left. He was seduced by good food and drink and the company and treacherous flattery of the rich power maniacs like Beaverbrook. How did he end up? In harness with Gaitskell on the nuclear independence issue, whining about being sent into the conference chamber naked. Take Michael, once the modern-day darling of the Left. Whoever thought he could serve in a Labour Government which allowed over a million-and-a-half unemployed?. You can say that Bassett doesn't compromise."

"Then you're bound for the political scrap-heap, like Enoch. The only way a politician achieves power in Britain, or even survives, is by going round obstacles, not by meeting them head-on. You're heading for the political wilderness for the next five years."

"The next Government won't last five years, Mr Battle. As for going into the wilderness, look at Churchill, even Eden – however he ended up. And Enoch exerts as much influence over the Tory party as the Opposition Leader."

"This isn't a conspiracy? A carve-up with Westwood?" He apologised at once, seeing the glow of anger deep in the staring eyes at the suggestion of a political expediency.

"If I could anticipate your next question, Mr Battle, no, I shall not give any guidance to my supporters who to vote for in the second ballot."

"But a nod is as good as a wink." The Left would want Bassett in the Cabinet. But how would the floaters go? Bassett would play the silent role of the traffic policeman, directing his supporters into the Westwood Lobby.

"Well," said Bassett, dipping his hand down to lift up his bulging bag, "those are the facts. I think I can safely leave the embroidery to you."

"You did say this was exclusive?"

"I didn't. But it is."

"Bless you." First the Premier's death, now the Bassett revolt against the Right Wing. Bassett went as unobtrusively as he had arrived: for one split second a smile lit up his eyes, like the fleeting glimpse of a sun-ray on the icy peak of a mountain.

As soon as he was alone, Battle began to write his story mentally. He was a master of his craft. He never used a note-book or pencil; he abhorred modern electronics such as the intrusive television and tape recorders; he despised the University graduates, who had taken over the key Fleet Street jobs, as intellectual thugs.

Battle could go straight to the telephone on the very deadline and dictate from his trained mind. He had a spasm of regret for his own wasted life when he remembered Bassett's undismayed confidence, his calm untroubled face, the brain clear and pure, not alcoholised, motivated quite simply by ambition and lust for power.

By Christ, thought Battle, signalling for a refill; the bugger will do it and I shall not live to see it: not this time, not next time, probably not the time after. But the time after that, Bassett and workers' power would take over. And, without even taking a glass of water for his throat, Bassett would spend the intervening years, preaching the gospel of Socialism according to Saint Eric.

By the time he had reached Frith Street, and *L'Epicure*, Tom Westwood's anger at his son's bungling contrivance to bring about a meeting with Pam Bruce, had dissipated. He had a decision to make and he knew, like the shrewd politician he was, that decisions taken in anger usually turned out to be wrong. Donovan, the dilettante Socialist, who had staggered him by volunteering to be his campaign manager, had already started his lunch.

"Thought you'd had cold feet," he said, with his disarming grin.

"No. A slight family complication," said Westwood. Despite Donovan's obvious readiness to hear more, Westwood closed the subject and ordered a prawn cocktail. Donovan went on eating his *moules mariniere* with the elegance of a *bon viveur*. "Perhaps we should have gone to the Ritz," said Westwood, with heavy irony.

"Why not? It's my treat," Donovan said. "You still think it's a gimmick, don't you?"

"What?"

"My original membership of the Workers' Control group at the House."

"You must admit it was a bit bizarre while it lasted."

"There's a perfectly natural explanation. Basically, it was an act of revenge on my old man. Not only was he an insufferable high Tory, he was a tyrant. He was a colliery owner in the bad old days of private ownership. One of the worst. He was a sadist watching the miners starve. I was brought up in the lap of luxury without realising his crime, when kids my own age outside the manor gates and wall were eating crusts."

"It's all in the Party's history," said Westwood. "The Socialist motivated by his middle-class guilt complex."

"I couldn't understand it at the time, but the day I got the nomination of the Boswell constituency as a Left Wing Socialist, he had a stroke. It never caused me a qualm of conscience that I was the cause."

"Boswell used to be a miners' union preserve," said Westwood. He had decided to let Donovan do the talking. He would judge him on his words.

"I changed the pattern," said Donovan.

"So you changed the pattern. That doesn't explain why you want to be my campaign manager and your desertion of Bassett, your old group leader."

Donovan was silent while he concentrated on removing the mollusc from the shell. He swallowed it, then wiped his mouth delicately on his serviette.

"I've already told Bassett the reason. He isn't ready. He hasn't got a strong enough base to build on. His time will come but he cannot win now. He knows it, you know it, all Westminster knows it." Donovan shrugged. "You and I may not still be around when he does win, but he's probably right in thinking it's his destiny."

"I wish your constituents could see you now," said Westwood, as Donovan cleaned up his plate, and drank fine wine.

"It wouldn't make a scrap of difference to my majority," said Donovan calmly. "I am just as much at home with them at the miners' welfare club with a bloody, great, dirty pint in my hand."

Westwood went on thinking of reasons for Donovan's surprise offer. He finished his prawn cocktail. Even that gave him a sense of guilt when he thought of the millions of empty bellies all over the world. To him, even a prawn cocktail was a compromise with conscience. So was the wine he tasted despite himself, and felt it appreciated by his taste buds.

"The big rumour is that Prestcote won't stand," said Donovan. At least his ears were to the ground, Westwood thought.

"It wouldn't make much difference. He and Pam Bruce would be fighting for the same vote. The moderates. The fence-sitters, the safety-first men. Prestcote knows he would be humiliated. The fight is between Pam Bruce and me." At the thought the past stirred within him like a cess pool. Victory would bring him revenge as well as pride.

Donovan pushed his plate away. "Should we get down to business?"

"You start."

"We both know you need Bassett's Workers' Control votes to win the final ballot."

"I'd feel better if I could win without them." He did not want to be a Prime Minister with the albatross of Workers' Control on his shoulder, ready to bring him down at every leadership election. Re-election had to be accomplished every November.

"The figures don't add up in your favour without them."

"And you think, even as a defecting member, you can get them into my camp?"

"Such was my intention," said Donovan, affably.

"Right."

"During the time I've been in the group I've studied Bassett's character from close quarters. He regards the group as his scouts and he is the scout-master. He wants to demonstrate that while he can't make big claims, he has his own army, an army which at present depends on sabotage, not numbers."

"Very interesting," said Westwood, digesting the words, and recognising their truth. "I have always thought there was a sharp head on that hundred guinea suit."

"You've forgotten the price of inflation, old man," said Donovan. "Old man" was the first faint note of mocking patronage. "One hundred and fifty guineas. Savile Row's best.

I'm glad you recognise I'm not just a tailor's dummy. I join in all the activities in my constituency – pot-holing, which I don't recommend; riding pit ponies at the miners' gala. They all like a bit of class. Poor buggers, they're snobs at heart. Now you, Westwood, are an inverted snob."

"If that means I hate all pretension in a world of poverty and want, I am."

"Well, I like to have it both ways. But don't make any mistake. I carry out my constituency obligations sincerely. I serve Tories, Communists, Socialists, Maoists and Marxists, to the extent of my influence. And I've pulled some powerful strings in my time."

"I know you've got it made. Now you want to pull strings on my behalf.?"

Already his attitude towards Donovan had secretly changed. He was a subtle and skilled manipulator, that had become clear. But calling up a dilettante Socialist of Donovan's type, stuck in his gullet. Whatever hate divided the Westwoods and the Bruces, they shared the same background, the same form of Socialism: the memory of the small colliery community, the terrace of miners' homes, back to back, with access for the shit carts. His worst memory of all was watching his father after the inquiry, sitting in the darkened parlour behind blinds which were never opened, never leaving the room until he had died slowly and suffocatingly from a disease called guilt. Socialism was the death of his brothers the day the emergency hooter had blown, appealing for succour. Socialism was pride, the donkey-stoned front step. Dirt was a social disgrace.

"What do you run?" he asked, emotionlessly. "A Jag or a Bentley?"

"A Jag. Why?"

"Like my son. You have a lot in common."

"Like money? Like me? I never inherited a penny. The old man cut me out of his will the day I was nominated for Boswell. You think money is indecent, don't you?"

"I thought the creed of Socialism was that it should be spread more equally. I don't like to see it being cornered.

Especially by my son." He hated the idea so much that he regretted his son had been smart enough to escape ruin when the property bubble burst. It might have reopened a relationship with his son. Only his son's ruin would restore Westwood's basic Socialistic dignity. He realised he was getting more and more deeply involved in the possibility of accepting Donovan's offer. At least, it no longer seemed ridiculous.

"You know," he said, "this might be a good leadership ballot to lose."

"What kind of scenario is that?"

"I've just come from Transport House. All the statements so blithely made that Labour is ready for an election are a myth. It's chaos, nothing but bloody chaos. The unions aren't coughing up the money, not enough has been done in the marginal constituencies. The postal vote is a shambles. But they're ready across Smith Square. The bloody Tories are always ready."

"Whenever we win, we've had to overcome the same handicaps. But you mean we're going to lose the election?"

"It's a probability."

"Then you mean, let Pam Bruce carry the can for the lost election and challenge her for the leadership in November's ballot?"

"The possibility had crossed my mind."

"But you quickly crossed it out again," Donovan scoffed. "You're too much of a political animal to go into a fight intending to lose."

The waiter took away their plates and served the next course – *Lamb Bretonne* for the elegant Donovan, minute steak for Westwood.

"It's true the polls show them miles ahead," said Donovan.

"The polls?" Westwood turned down a thumb expressively. "They're as often wrong as right. In any case, you don't have to worry at Boswell. I hear they don't count the votes up there. They weigh them."

They ate in silence for a few moments, then Westwood said: "You've put forward the Workers' Control group's votes as a reason for managing my campaign. Are there others?"

"There are."

"Such as?"

"The Labour M.Ps you might describe as Donovan's little lot. The Harold Levers. The rich. The Social conscience group. Among them, I would be your best vote-catcher, and you know it."

"So far, you've given me two good reasons. Any more?"

"Yes. You know it isn't Pam Bruce you'll be fighting?"

"Of course. It will be Joe Hepworth."

"You know what kind of a campaign that means?"

"I know Joe can play it pretty rough when he likes. Especially when he's losing."

"You know he would stop at nothing to get Pam Bruce in?"

"So you're suggesting I should play it dirty?"

"I'm suggesting you should be ready to retaliate. With me. Not you."

"Where would that leave me?"

"As pure as driven snow and top of the poll. I would make it clear you were not responsible for any dirt. You could repudiate me."

"That would mean giving you a free hand from the start. In other words, place my political future and good name in your hands without a safeguard. A man I don't really know. A man who is no more than a political novice."

"Novice I may be, but I learned a lot from Bassett when I was in the group. And I learned in the toughest school of all. Old Etonians always make the toughest political thugs."

"I'd forgotten you were at Eton."

"*Floreat Etona.*" Donovan placed the palms of his hands together and bowed in mock homage. "How I hated thee."

"Tell me, Donovan, how long have you been a member of the Labour Party?"

"Seven years."

"And you think that's a long enough apprenticeship to mastermind a leadership campaign? You're a poseur, a dandy, and you think politics is a circus. You're just a playboy at heart, getting kicks out of the Party."

"But you like me."

"I know you're not half as big a fool as you pretend. I admit I like your nerve."

"Enough to trust me with the job?"

"Trust? The word isn't in my vocabulary. I know it would be taking a big chance. A lot of my close friends are going to feel hurt." He looked closely in Donovan's eyes. "Tell me, what's in it for you?"

"Just the excitement. The prospect of a gladiatorial contest with Joe Hepworth. You see, I think I'm the only man who can outmatch him in politics."

"You're mad. Everybody has a grievance against Joe."

"I'm offering you a bargain on the two things which matter – the Workers' Control vote, and the guilty rich. It's up to you to decide. There are two ways we can play it: one, you give me *carte-blanche*, and I take full responsibility for whatever happens. You could publicly repudiate me. Or *you* can dictate the campaign, and I'll just carry out your instructions. I would prefer the former." He went on, doggedly challenging Westwood's inclination to gamble. "I really think I could be useful."

"You must admit you hardly have the qualifications to run a Left Winger's campaign for the leadership – no poverty, no drudgery, no years on the dole or social welfare. A scion of one of the monsters of capitalism."

Donovan spread his arms wide. "I know it's your risk. Drink up."

"You think I need Dutch courage?"

Despite himself, Westwood found himself inclining more and more towards acceptance. The man could charm. Who better to charm the Parliamentary Labour Party? He turned his glass round and round by the stem. Eventually, he obeyed Donovan and emptied it. Donovan immediately filled it up again.

"In the first place," said the relentless Donovan, "The main plank in your campaign should be anti-feminist. We're facing international as well as economic troubles. Oil and energy. Common Market crisis. Danger of NATO's dissolution. Growing menace of the Warsaw Pact. This is no time for

Britain to turn to a woman."

"And have Elizabeth I quoted against us?"

"Anything that pre-dates 1945 is dead as far as the Labour party is concerned."

The wine had begun to flush Westwood's cheeks. He knew he was falling for Donovan's charm. The man must be Irish with his blarney. In his inner mind, he knew he was already condemned to Yes. The direct challenge came.

"Well, what do you say?"

"All right." He wondered at once whether he had just made the biggest political mistake of his life, whether he had locked and bolted the door of No 10 against himself.

"On which terms? My responsibility, with a free hand? Or your hand on the tiller all the time?"

"You're out on your own. Transport House is round my neck." He still had the feeling that fate had committed him to this man. Could he, faced with political death, wash his hands of responsibility like Pilate? To administer the quietus to his conscience, he thought of Pam Bruce. Then he thought of Joe Hepworth. Finally, he thought of victory – first the ballot, then against all the apparent odds, in the general election. The question now was: victory for whom? Westwood or Pam Bruce?

Across the table their eyes met in uncertain comradeship. Tom Westwood knew it would be an exaggeration to think of it as trust. Donovan signalled the waiter.

"I should think your chances are about even," he said. It was Donovan who paid the bill.

3

"So much for the great reconciliation plan," said Liz Bruce.

"We must have been crazy," said Richard Westwood.

"Yes."

Tactfully she omitted to make the point that the idea had been his. He had never fathomed the depth of her mother's feelings, she thought, without resentment. She was sitting in the passenger seat of the Jag as he drove along Parliament Square, past the statue of Churchill, gathering its daily quota of grime. The gates of New Palace Yard were open, and cars and taxis were entering to set down the returning balloteers, in readiness for the evening's Party meeting.

"You know," she said, tentatively, "you were pretty grim and silent all through lunch."

"I had a lot to be silent about," he said. "Your mother laid the lashes on pretty hard. I thought I was immune on the conscience front, but she got through my skin. What was it she called me? A parasite? She made me feel more like a slave trader." All through the lunch he had been taking a deep look into himself: he hadn't liked what he had seen.

"On the subject of parents," she said, "you never talk about your father. What are your real relations with him?"

He said, dryly: "In view of my life-style, I suppose you could say the best possible for both of us – we just don't communicate any more."

There had never been a blazing row, an open breach, a banishment or an abandonment. It had happened as a gradually widening estrangement, as he went deeper and deeper into his orgy of money-making. But things had now changed overnight, he realised; the death of Hargreaves and his father's inevitable bid for the succession put Richard Westwood's dubious Socialism into the firing-line, made him one of Tom Westwood's biggest burdens.

Suddenly parts of the past he had thought permanently paralysed were awakened. He remembered his father as a human-being, not a figure-head, a loving parent who had tried to place his son's first faltering steps on the road to Socialism by the birthday presentation of *The Ragged Trousered Philanthropists*. Flashes of warmth and love: his father taking him by the hand and leading him to the reserved seats to watch the miners' gala procession behind the proud bands and swirling banners, strong arms lifting him to the massive shoulders so he could see over a forest of heads at the Celtic–Rangers match at Ibrox. Suddenly, he had found his peace of mind jeopardised.

He said: "I don't know who is the more deeply committed – your Pam or my old man." He couldn't foresee how, but he had a deep presentiment that the ballot was going to bring a drastic change to his life-style. "Liz," he put out a hand from the steering-wheel to cover both hers which were resting on her knees. He felt the immediate response in her blood: she was always ready, either to initiate or respond physically. "This leadership campaign isn't going to last many hours, but a lot of shit is going to be flung. Things may never be the same between us."

"Then we'll have to see that we don't become personally involved." She slid closer to him across the seat, emphasising what he already knew: her instant availability. "I'll take care of any worries you've got. I know the formula." The meaning was clear: she had one answer to everything, the solacing cure of sex. To her the sexual act was instinctive; she thrilled to it as she thrilled to motor racing, parachute jumping, or a high dive – a pleasure in which she had created consummate skill. To her sex satisfied a constant bodily, not emotional need. Unlike others, she separated the two.

"I just don't want us to get involved in the cross-fire." He concentrated on his driving as the Jag joined the processional queue of traffic down Millbank; on the left the Thames, on the right the commercial monstrosities and Government offices, palaces of glass, concrete and steel.

"Then the simplest thing is for us to opt out."

"It might not be as easy as that."

"You mean blood is thicker than water? We're too sophisticated for that kind of crap. We live our own lives now. Pam and Tom are generations apart. Why should we involve ourselves in a dated quarrel?"

He realised she hadn't the capacity to fathom that he had suddenly encountered the obstacle of guilt, his culpability of what his father regarded as a betrayal, a family treason.

She went on, happily ignorant: "All we've got to do is to maintain our own neutrality whatever and whoever flings the shit. One day they'll see reason and kiss and make up. Who knows? This ballot might do it, the need to unite the Party."

He listened, but without belief. He tried to burrow back and find the origin of his present shame. How long had it remained buried in his sub-conscious, just waiting for the happening to drag it to the forefront of his mind? He defended himself silently: hadn't he the right to live his own life? He had broken no laws, he had played the money game according to the current rules. His only offence was to make money. By what right had his father to impose on him his own rigidity, the responsibility to avenge the cruelties inflicted on the working-class before he was born?

He said, recklessly making a commitment against his better judgment: "All right, Liz. Let's make a pact: if, in the next forty-eight hours, we feel any urge to take sides on family grounds, we will reverse the normal. You take Tom Westwood's side and I take Pam's. In that way we shall be certain of true neutrality."

The truth was, he confessed to himself, he was safe-guarding his future against the stupidity of the sudden sense of loyalty which was sweeping back into his mind. He feared it. He had to take steps against it.

"Done," she said, without a thought of the possible implications. "It's a bargain." She hadn't a political instinct in her body. He envied her the immunity: without it, he would have been a happier man at present: she was just the pleasured repletion of her own flesh, not the tormented victim of a mind. Despite himself, his blood quickened at the thought: she was an utterly desirable sex-bomb, there just to be used, for she asked no more. But she had at least noticed the intentness with which he was watching the driving mirror.

"What's the matter?"

"It sounds crazy, but I think we're being followed. A green Cortina."

"He just can't help it. It's a case of follow-my-leader."

"No, it's not just that. He's behind us now. He followed me into the parking-space outside the Abbey when I drove in for the lunch. He followed me out. He'd been waiting for us. He's definitely tailing us."

"What in hell for? The police aren't after you? The Fraud squad?"

"Liz," he said patiently, "don't you realise that one of us is going to be a V.I.P. after the ballot."

"You mean . . .?"

"That perhaps it's the Special Branch." Through the driving-mirror he examined what he could see of the occupants of the green Cortina – two men, dressed in nondescript grey. "It seems a bit early for a bodyguard."

"God," she said, "I hadn't realised just what it would mean. Special branch men peering into every orifice."

"Not *every* orifice."

"God, no. I'm not going to change my sex life."

"You couldn't."

"Since when have you grumbled?"

"Never. But I don't like the idea of a plain-clothes man with big feet and a leering eye, listening outside the door to the squeaking of the bed-springs."

He knew that she wouldn't mind. In fact, he suspected she would like an audience. To him, sex was an act which should be shrouded in secrecy and shadow. But his involvement with the thought of sex did not last: he was still preoccupied by his new sense of guilt, the guilt he would bear either way: if his father failed, or if he won and went to No 10 Downing Street.

Either way, Tom Westwood would have to bear the odium of his son's unacceptable face of capitalism.

"I can't imagine you a ragged-arse socialist," she said. He had underestimated her intellectual capacity: she had accurately read his thoughts. "*This* is you. I can only see you at the wheel of an E-type or a Rolls-Bentley."

She indicated with a sweep of the hand his expensive suiting, shirt and tie, and then slid the palm of her hand on the polished leather of the upholstery. He had to slow and stop behind the long line of traffic converging on the Lambeth Bridge roundabout. Her right hand began to stroke his thigh gently and he felt the familiar, primitive response in his loins. She moved her hand closer to his core to register his response.

"Randy, randy," she mocked. He was at the mercy of her peerless body, and he knew from experience her own insatiable need as he throbbed in response to her practised touch. She took her hand away as he moved into gear and the Jaguar inched ahead.

"There is something I've been meaning to tell you," she said. "The ballot makes it necessary. Now that you've met Pam, you'd better know the truth. I'm what is usually called a love child. Not adopted."

"I'd already figured that. I've never heard of a Mr Bruce."

"Pam kept her own name for political purposes. In such an enlightened man, I shouldn't think this would affect our – " she paused before she released the word – "relationship."

The question hung in the Jag between them. Was there a relationship? Or was it just sex, a successful coupling which would pall? At present he didn't care about the answer.

"Of course not."

"You haven't heard it all. My father is Joe Hepworth."

He expelled a breath of surprise. "That must be one of Westminster's best-kept secrets. Not even a breath of scandal."

"They were not so important politically when I was born. Pam's husband had been dead for years. He was killed fighting in the International Brigade in the Spanish civil war. He was the one love in her life. She would never remarry."

"But she wanted a child? And Joe obliged."

"You make me sound the sordid result of a deal."

"If sex is sordid, we're all sordid," he said. "Us especially." He reflected. The news hadn't helped his peace of mind. "So my old man will be battling against Pam *and* Joe?"

He had always used the words "my old man" with a self-defensive irony, convincing himself they were a form of endearment, a salute to a high-principled integrity which erred on the side of self-righteousness. Now there was no room for kindly contempt. He felt cheap and small. He feared the little cloud of remorse which had entered his mind on the consequences of the death of Hargreaves. Now the cloud was ballooning aggressively.

"Joe Hepworth has always idolised her. He would have divorced his wife to marry Pam, but she wouldn't. All she wanted was a child. I know there has been no sex since Pam conceived. That was the arrangement."

"It all sounds so cold-blooded."

"Good politicians are cold-blooded. Now, I'm different."

"You're always on heat. As I well know."

He knew she wouldn't take offence. She was proud of her sex prowess. Her hand was searching him out again. Her eyes were gleaming with a mixture of lust and power: she knew she had only to curl a finger and he would harden. He could only ignore the give-away throbbing and say, self-consciously: "I suppose we're taking the rest of the day off?"

"Where should we go?" she asked, mockingly.

"We could spend a couple of hours at the Imperial War Museum." They were passing the Tate. "Or we could go in there and inspect the nation's treasures of abstract art."

"You mean any old iron? Goering – or was it Goebbels? – might have said something about culture before me, but when it comes to the big C, I prefer cunt to culture."

He flinched mentally, as he always did, at the frequent passage of foul language from such beautiful lips. "I rather thought you might. So it's to be cunt in the afternoon?"

"I had promised myself I would wash my hair this afternoon."

"Liar. But if it's not convenient – "

"You know you can hardly wait."

"Well, it's certainly not your hair I'm especially interested in."

They had both known from the first that he was driving to her flat. They were already at the approach to Chelsea Bridge.

"So the orgy is to be at my place?"

"It's nearer than mine."

"And you are so impatient. What a delightful compliment."

"You know what the merest proximity of your body does to me. So you can imagine – "

"I don't have to imagine. I know from experience the wonders it can perform."

He had stopped the car outside the block containing her flat. He waited deliberately for the green Cortina to pass but failed to identify its two occupants, men wearing low-brimmed hats. How did one distinguish the Special Branch? He supposed it was deliberately made difficult. Shrugging, he removed the ignition key.

"All change," he said, dismissing the mystery of the green Cortina and its two occupants. They climbed the familiar stairs. At the first landing, she took the key from her hand-bag and opened the door to her flat.

"Coffee?" she asked, archly.

"With this beat on? You must be joking."

"It would be a pity to waste it."

He followed her into the bedroom, lay on the bed, and watched her with both love and lust. She began to undress with tantalising slowness and languor, undulating her body provocatively.

"In Soho, you'd have to pay for this. I do it for free, just for the hell of it."

"You strip like a professional. All that's missing is the music."

He sat up and removed his jacket, never taking his eyes off her.

"And the fake booze and dirty old men in raincoats."

"Don't you think it was time you were totally emancipated?" Her hands were behind her back, unfastening the clasps. She tossed the bra on to a chair.

"You think I couldn't burn it?"

She thrust her breasts forwards so that they tilted up firmly, rosette tipped. He caught his breath.

"You know perfectly well you've the finest pair in Christendom."

"And what about the rest?" Slowly and seductively, she removed her tights and panties. At last she posed for him, hands clasped high above her head, supremely proud of her unflawed nakedness. He had never seen her so lovely, so lovely that for the moment lust faltered at the altar of such perfection. It would be a crime to maul it.

"I hope you don't mind," she said, "but Chichester wants to paint me in the nude for this year's R.A."

"I dare you to pose like that. No fragment of material to hide away that golden fleece."

"Well," she said, "perhaps we'd better let the whole world know. I'll insist on no concealment at all. But I know what Chichester will say: art lies in the concealment of artifice." She looked in the dressing-table mirror, modestly proud of her body.

"I'm just thinking of the head-lines your nudity would make if Pam becomes Prime Minister."

"I never thought of that," she said. The reminder of the importance of current events brought a shadow to their fun. It could be that life would never be the same. She forced herself back into the mood, jerking her pelvis towards the bed, where he still lay recumbent. "Why are we wasting time?"

"Why indeed?"

"I suppose you're waiting for me to undress you. Then move over." It was the ritual. She stood over him and began to undress him in the same slow style. When she came down to the singlet, she stroked the bulge.

"Richard," she said, as she rolled off his underpants, "I'm a nympho, aren't I?"

"Liz, if you're a nympho then I'm a satyr."

"No," she said, "we're different. The temperature isn't the same." By now, her experienced hands had revealed him totally, erect and tumescent, engorged with desire. She bent down and kissed it. She took him in both hands. He stretched out a hand and encountered a breast. He pulled her on the bed, all the time gently kneading: the nipple came up hard. They went through their customary love play until desire burst the barriers of restraint. They both trembled in anticipation of the moment of union in the favourite of their postures, her buttocks firmly fitted into his thighs.

With a moan of anticipation, she lifted herself on to him, and was impaled. He thrust until penetration was complete. By now they were experienced in each other's needs and he remained still, erect and strong within her, while she thrust and thrust, and moaned and moaned . . .

He continued to play his passive role until she had her first orgasm. They waited a few minutes and then began an orchestrated movement until they climaxed simultaneously. Once again it had been perfect. His arm went round her neck and stroked her breast. She guzzled his ear.

When they parted they lay side by side, spreadeagled on the bed, naked. She said, drowsily: "Richard, I think my mother behaved like a bloody *prima donna*."

"For God's sake, don't apologise. My old man behaved like an ignorant pig."

Hands clasped in the acknowledgment of their pact and the words which had just confirmed it, they fell into a repleted doze, naked and contented on the bed.

Long after Bassett had departed, Battle continued his lonely drinking and meditation in the cocktail-bar above the Dive. He enjoyed his solitude; he had no great respect for his fellow-beings, especially Lobby correspondents, most of whom he despised as incompetent competitors. They were down below, he thought, picking each other's brains. All of them would have given a lot to have the one contact such as Stella.

It was Stella he was thinking of with tipsy gratitude. She was asleep in his bed, still sexually hungry. He remembered with distaste the eager way she had mounted him, gripping his flanks with thick, powerful legs, using his body as a vehicle for the short, short trip. Soon, he feared, what with his drinking and his original low sexual potency, it would be even worse: he wouldn't be able to get it up at all. Yet the unwritten bargain must somehow be fulfilled.

His lack of virility, and even distaste for sex, might one day prove a disaster. He was no bloody good in bed, he thought, despising his lack of manhood: even at the onset of puberty, he had only occasionally felt the need to jerk himself off.

He thought of the old wive's tales, the mystic powers attributed to the aphrodisiacs of millionaires: monkey glands, powdered rhinos' tusks, Spanish fly; and the oysters and Guinness for the proletariat. He knew of no treatment under the National Health, even if he had been prepared to submit to a confession and the indignity of a physical and psychological examination. But even money couldn't buy a hard-on.

He thought of buying a supply of hard porn on which he could feast before she came to his bed, anything which could sustain an erection beneath her suction. He owed it to her to oblige, but not enough to cut down his drinking which, he knew, would stimulate his sexual desires. The situation wasn't as desperate as that, he thought, picking up his Haig.

At three o'clock, the time to withdraw from the comfortable cocoon sheltering him from life as it carried him away to his premature but pleasant death, he still reflected on Stella and the importance of gratifying her appetite.

The telephone on the wall behind him rang just as the barmaid called: "Time, gentlemen, please." But for him, the bar was empty and he knew instinctively that the call was for him. His News Editor knew where to find Edwin Battle in the last resort. He hadn't been in touch. He slid off the stool, picked up the receiver and banked on his News Editor being in a good mood, that his ulcer wasn't playing him up.

"Battersea Dogs' Home," he said, facetiously, and barked into the mouth-piece. He was back in high spirits, some from the bottle, some left over from the morning's exclusive, the rest from Bassett's tip-off.

"Blóody funny," was the News Editor's unamused response. The ulcer was in volcanic eruption. "Just because you happened to get an exclusive of the Prime Minister's death doesn't entitle you to take the piss out of me. Where the bloody hell have you been, as if I didn't know."

Battle soft-soaped down the line. "You will be very pleased with me when I tell you what I've got for being out of touch. I've been with Brother Bassett. He's given me the exclusive story that he would refuse to serve if Pam Bruce became Prime Minister. So, you see, I haven't been idle."

"Oh, I know you're never idle. I can see you now, lifting the right arm from the elbow."

"The bar's closed."

"It hasn't been closed for the last two hours and I haven't heard a cheep out of you."

"But you knew where to find me in case of emergency." Suddenly, he was interested. "Is it an emergency?"

The News Editor deliberately kept him dangling in suspense. "Oh, everyone in the News Room knows where to find you if you don't ring in. How's that Spanish piece of crumpet behind the bar?"

"You know that isn't my vice. I'm totally dedicated to my job." He mourned the lack of vice, the low level of sensuality which handicapped him in the repayment of Stella. He laughed for the News Editor's sake: he wasn't a bad sort when his ulcer let him; he initialled Battle's huge drinking bill every week without the flicker of an eyelid, without a question. He knew Battle was worth it, every penny.

"You're not so indispensable that you can stay out of touch as long as you like." But the News Editor didn't sound really angry, he was just keeping Battle on the hook of suspense. "You're not the age."

There was an ominous reminder in the voice of the danger of redundancy in the economic blizzard now blowing down the Street. Battle thought with a chill of the onset of age, the creep nearer and nearer to the day when he would be over the hill, and his drink bills would be challenged and found unacceptable. Then he remembered his insurance: he would be dead before that happened. But it might be a bloody close-run thing. A specialist, like a political correspondent, could be a blue-eyed boy one day, and out on his ear the next.

"Well, I didn't ring up to be kind and sentimental to you," said the News Editor.

Edwin Battle took an enormous risk on a hunch that the News Editor was in as good a mood as he sounded. "I thought you'd maybe rung to say you were giving me a rise."

"Fortunately, we can't because of the Government's pay policy. In any case, you know the paper's losing millions. There's a long list in the Editor's top right-hand drawer, the names marked for the chop."

"You want me to be grateful? Okay, I'm grateful."

"Sorry, old man," said the News Editor, and he sounded genuinely contrite. "I've had a bastard of a morning. I've got news for you. Someone has been asking for you, someone important."

"My tailor? A debt-collecting agency? A deputation of jealous Lobby correspondents? An opposition paper wanting to buy my contract off the *News?*"

"Battle, you must bore your informants to death. Why don't you let me tell you? Janet Hargreaves has asked to see you."

They both participated in a long, puzzled silence down the line.

"The Prime Minister's wife? Widow, I mean." Battle, who prided himself on his poker face in times of surprise or stress, saw his face in the mirror behind the bar, dramatised in an expression of wonderment.

"I thought that would jolt you out of your whisky-haze."

"But what the hell does it mean? I suppose she wants to read me the riot act about my obit this morning?"

"I don't think so. In fact, I'm sure from the way she treated me. She said the paper had always given Hargreaves the treatment he deserved."

"Christ, Hargreaves would regard that as a back-handed compliment. I thought it was one of the best hatchet-jobs I'd ever done."

"Perhaps that's why she was so pleased. All the public

gossip and dirty jokes about his sexual exploits must have shredded her self-respect for years. The fact that he was a sex maniac read between the lines in your piece. Now, Battle, be honest with me. What sort of a drunken state are you in?"

"Absolutely sober."

"You liar. I can almost smell the whisky back here."

"I confess I have had a little tipple to celebrate my successes." He regarded himself in the bar mirror and so admired his success that he did an impression of W. C. Fields. But the News Editor was persistent.

"Have you got a clean shirt on?"

"Certainly," he lied. He had always refused to let Stella do his washing. Sometimes he missed the laundryman, who wouldn't climb the stairs to the flat when the lift was out of order.

"If you take my advice, you'll go to the toilets and put your head under the cold water tap for a few minutes. There isn't time to have a hair-cut, but at least comb what hair you have left. We don't want her complaining to the Board. Remember, you represent the *Daily News*."

"You make it sound like a vocation. Perhaps you're mistaking us for the *Times*."

"If you are as full of Haig as you sound, for Christ's sake, don't vomit all over her carpet."

"A gentleman can hold his drink."

"I don't see the gentleman connection. Now, I'm going to put in a call to No 10 to warn them that you will be there in ten minutes. Use five of them to make yourself presentable. Report back as soon as you've left her. And don't forget it, but God knows, I like you, you fat slob."

"And up yours," said Battle. "Bring out the violins." He basked tipsily in the rare sunshine of editorial affection.

He hung up, said good-bye to the Spanish barmaid, and went to the toilets, dutifully following out his News Editor's instructions. He emerged from the cold water douche pink, breathless, but stone-cold sober. I mop up the stuff like blotting-paper. He thought proudly of his steady, relentless, accomplished drinking as a skill.

He went carefully down the stairs into Bridge Street, then into Whitehall. This is my patch, my beat, he thought, as he entered Downing Street, using the road because the pavements on either side were packed with tourists and sight-seers. The nation's insatiably curious. Last night was revived in his memory, especially the outraged face caught in the camera's flash. He felt uneasy suddenly. Had Lawson reported him to the police for impersonation?

He had no need to knock, to say Sesame: the door was silently opened by the inside doorkeeper as soon as his foot touched the step. They saw each other like this practically every day when the Lobby was briefed.

"Mrs Hargreaves is expecting you, Mr Battle. In her sitting-room."

"I know the way," said Battle. "I'll go straight up."

He crossed the hall and went along the red-carpeted corridor, past the table with its Visitors' Book, towards the fawn, felt-lined double doors leading to the Cabinet Room. As he reached the foot of the staircase, the doors opened and Arnold Prestcote half-emerged. They froze in the act of recognition.

Edwin Battle lifted a preparatory hand for the approach as he remembered Eric Bassett's significant words: *Prestcote had other fish to fry*. He had already pieced together the jig-saw bits of last night's emergency meeting and knew how Prestcote's bid for power had been foiled. He would have liked nothing better than a swift talk with Prestcote on Lobby terms.

But Prestcote snubbed him with no more than a swift nod of recognition, then immediately turned back into the sanctuary of the Cabinet Room, where Battle could not follow. The doors closed. Battle shrugged, thinking: You can't win them all. Prestcote had every reason for being a shrinking violet after last night's fiasco. Meantime, he himself had other fish to fry. Janet Hargreaves was waiting for him upstairs.

He began to mount the staircase. With each step, he became more conscious of the history along the line of route: on the wall, flanking the staircase, were the photographs and engravings of past Prime Ministers. He was passing the dead who had glibly believed they were ruling an empire upon which the sun would never set.

With every step he mounted, the years rolled by until he came to the end of the stairs and Hargreaves. With Hargreaves, Britain had seen the end of empire and was now an offshore island, militarily defenceless.

Ring down the curtain, he said to himself as he went on to approach the sitting-room. He knocked and the voice of Janet Hargreaves invited him in.

Battle remembered at once how the Steinway dominated the room. The last time he had been there was for a tête-a-tête with Hargreaves when the Prime Minister wanted to use him secretly, and it suited Battle to be used. Beyond the Steinway, he saw Janet Hargreaves sitting on the settee. In front of her was a low coffee table with a tray, tea-pot, cups and saucers, sugar and milk and a plate of pastries. Just like home, he thought. Somebody wanted a favour.

"Tea, Mr Battle?" She watched him, tea-pot poised interrogatively over his cup. She must have known about his habits because, at his automatic flinch of revulsion, she said: "Or perhaps you would prefer something a little more stimulating? Please help yourself."

She indicated the drinks cabinet and Battle obeyed like an automaton, but a puzzled one. She spoke brightly, there was no evidence of grief, and she was wearing a gaily coloured frock.

He turned with his whisky and she indicated the chair opposite the settee. He sat. There was a drink tremor in his hand. He couldn't hide it. She turned her eyes tactfully away.

He tried to break the ice which was forming. Condolences were necessary, whatever he felt about Hargreaves. "Please accept my sympathy, Mrs Hargreaves, in your shocking loss." He went on in the traditional manner: "Words can't help at a time like this. I can only say that we in the Lobby are deeply sorry."

She sipped her tea – once, twice, thrice – and put down the cup and saucer.

"I'm not, Mr Battle."

He thought his hearing was at fault. Then he saw her face, wondered whether she was still in a state of shock. It couldn't have been pleasant to find you had been sleeping with a man already dead.

"There have been messages of condolence from all over the world, Mr Battle. All insincere, of course. The few Kings and Queens who have not yet lost their thrones, Presidents we once kept in gaol, once-backward countries which have now passed us in the survival-of-the-fittest race. As far as I can see, there have been none from his fancy women. But then, I never knew all their names."

Calmly, while Battle sat with mouth open, she sipped her tea again, finally put down her empty cup. When she laughed it was a musical, but not a pleasant sound. "You look appalled, Mr Battle. I fear I have shocked you."

In an extremity of embarrassment, Battle observed one of his trusted moves: a diversion. He pointed towards the Steinway. "You'll always have your music, Mrs Hargreaves."

"Yes," she said, but she changed the tenses and, for the first time, there was bitterness in her voice. "I gave it up for him, to stand at his side. The faithful dummy during the long years of hypocrisy. I never dreamed when I married him, almost an unknown, that it would lead me to No 10. I never wanted it. I have hated every minute of it." She flexed her fingers, then clasped her hands in front of her, on her lap. "You see, don't you? They have lost their suppleness. No practice. I rarely play a note now, and then only for my own comfort. Music is a kind of balm against pain and sorrow."

Her words were evoking all his professionalism. Let her talk, experience told him; she wasn't in shock, she wasn't a hysteric, there was something big in this for Battle and the *Daily News*. So he allowed the silence to linger. The initiative had to be hers; she had to be allowed to approach the reason for the meeting of her own volition.

"My husband often spoke of you, Mr Battle." She had begun to skirt the edges cautiously, as a disposal expert approaches a bomb, with outward calm.

"Favourably, I hope?"

"Not always, I'm afraid."

"No? I was something of a thorn in his side. Basically, our aims were incompatible. It was my job to get the unpopular news, and it was his interest to keep it secret."

"Or falsify it?"

"Well – he liked to put his own gloss on it." Battle, the bachelor, realised that no husband was a hero to his wife. Not even when he was dead. But this went deeper than that.

"Sometimes he feared you especially, but always the power of the Press. He said you were the best digger of them all, and he was always afraid of what you might dig up. And there were a lot of skeletons to dig up, were there not, Mr Battle? The names of his women, the locality of their meetings, the short reigns of each mistress. I assume we're talking on Lobby terms? You see, Mr Battle, I have picked up the jargon."

"Then there mustn't be any mistaken understandings, Mrs Hargreaves. Lobby terms means I can use the material but not attribute it to any source." He had to warn her whatever she had to tell, he couldn't afford a retraction. "Lobby terms means mutual trust." He wondered: confessions? Indiscretions? Revelations?

"Help yourself to more whisky, Mr Battle."

"Not at the moment, Mrs Hargreaves. Can I get you one?"

"You think it might help to loosen my tongue?"

"I am still wondering – " Was she about to use him to cleanse herself from a lifetime with Hargreaves, all the wounds, the insults, and the public pity. But the hand which she used with the serviette to wipe away the stain of tea from the corners of her mouth, was perfectly steady. She returned the initiative to him.

"Tell me, Mr Battle, what was your honest opinion of my husband?"

It was the last question he would have preferred. But she had demanded absolute honesty and she was watching him through eyes which had suddenly turned hard, even ferocious. She was a many-sided woman. "Don't be afraid of speaking evil of the dead. Above all, don't try to spare my feelings."

He still tried the tactical escape. The most he could do was to proffer a bromide. "Everybody in the Lobby recognised his shrewdness as a tactician, an opportunist, maybe; not at his best in strategic terms, absorbing the totality – " Christ, he thought, mouth drying up; he could have been writing an editorial.

"Shrewd, Mr Battle? Isn't the word inadequate? Wouldn't you care to substitute devious, unscrupulous, hypocritical, disloyal, treacherous, ungrateful – oh, surely you could find more picturesque adjectives than 'shrewd' Hargreaves would have been disappointed in you."

"I was trying to look at him in terms of politics. Every Prime Minister has to compromise, even manoeuvre, take decisions he personally finds distasteful or even degrading. He often faces situations brought about by events over which he had no control. More than ever, Britain today is the victim of external influences – "

His voice dried up again in the face of the contempt in her eyes. For Hargreaves? For Battle, his defender?

"Are we talking of the same person, Mr Battle? I asked for absolute honesty. We both know that he was straight as a corkscrew."

Battle squirmed. He felt himself in the beam of a great spotlight, pouring down a stream of honesty, bright and gleaming. Janet Hargreaves was behind the light and Edwin Battle was no longer just a professional spectator: he was a participant in a macabre game of flaying a dead man with a widow's whip: his protective carapace, built layer by layer over the years, was penetrated by a demand for honesty now burning him like a laser.

"Forgive the cross-examination," said Janet Hargreaves, apologetically, as if she had suddenly realised even Edwin Battle was capable of embarrassment, of human feeling. "But your true feelings came through between the lines of your obituary this morning, Mr Battle. I regard you as an ally. I know you despised him."

"Most of it came from the library morgue. I only brought it up to date. We didn't expect him to die like that."

"It was sudden. He was the first to know," she said, callously, thinking of the few last conscious minutes. He knew what she was thinking: Hargreaves didn't deserve such as easy death. Her attitude was straining his nerves.

"Mrs Hargreaves – " He did not finish, but she must have known he was pleading: why was he there, enduring her macabre pleasure?

"You're getting impatient. Then tell me, Mr Battle, who is going to win the ballot tomorrow?"

"I wish I knew, Mrs Hargreaves." Sometime, in the hours ahead, he would have to make a forecast for the readers of the *Daily News*. "There isn't a cat's whisker between Westwood and Mrs Bruce. Even the bookies aren't taking bets. Even Joe Hepworth isn't sure."

"Ah, yes, Joe. The all-powerful Joe. My husband's executioner." Once again he was shocked, this time at the hatred in her voice. "Mr Battle, why did my husband cling to office in order to fight this election? Everyone expected him to retire."

"Well, there is a sort of insinuation – " He paused on the threshold of impugning the dead. It didn't suffice.

"Don't be afraid of hurting my feelings, Mr Battle. We both know it was to keep Arnold Prestcote out. He delayed deliberately, so that Arnold would be too old."

Her use of the Christian name, the sudden trembling of her hands, supplied the answer to the enigma. It burst into his brain like a rocket, spreading into a chandelier of allied thoughts. Arnold. Arnold and Janet. The triangle.

"If Arnold fails to convince the Party meeting tonight, Hargreaves will have succeeded." Her hands were now clenched into fists. "If so, I'm glad he never lived to see his triumph."

Now he waited with patience, knowing that soon he would walk away with another sensation. He smelled the cyanide already. Bitter almonds.

"I won't attempt to hide my disgust at the way Mr Prestcote has been treated. It's abominable. First by my husband, then by the Cabinet, and, I've no doubt, tonight by the whole Party."

He applied a calculated balm, shaking his head dolefully:

"I'm afraid, Mrs Hargreaves, that the Labour Party has a long history of treating its leaders badly. But all political parties are basely ungrateful. Their only criterion is success. The price of failure –" He cut his throat with a jerk of his index finger. "Mean and shabby. The worst are the Tories. But it's democracy of a sort."

"He never told me, but I sensed what his plans were. Having kept Arnold out to repay old scores, he intended to retire in two years' time and write his memoirs. He was already negotiating with publishers. Can you imagine how the truth would have been distorted?"

"Truth is a many-sided thing, Mrs Hargreaves. Even Winston doesn't appear as the colossus his memoirs suggested, now that a few years have allowed other versions to appear . . ."

He kept the conversation going back and forth, like a tennis match: he waited, now with patience, for her to make her volley. He knew it would not be long delayed when she got off the settee and went to the window overlooking Downing Street, hands nervously clasping and unclasping.

"The great British public," she said, pointing down, "enjoying its curiosity." He realised the ordeals she must have endured, a naturally shy creature for ever in the spotlight of publicity. When she turned to face him again, he was taken by surprise at the sudden change in her voice.

"Tell me, Mr Battle, would you think I could be a vindictive woman?"

"Well –"

"That was unfair. I won't embarrass you, Mr Battle. All women can be vindictive if they are hurt enough. For years I have been on the rack." But he knew her vindictiveness was a proxy thing. It was Arnold who had been wounded, Arnold's pride which was being dragged in the dust of the political arena. She sat down again, and quickly regained her composure. He realised again he was dealing with a formidable woman, someone tougher than her reputation.

"I have found it difficult to approach you, Mr Battle. Unlike my husband, I am not a natural conspirator. But what I am going to suggest is that you enter into a conspiracy with a vindictive woman. In other words, I can give you an item of news involving leading politicians. The question in my mind is whether your paper would dare to print it?"

They had reached the point of no return. He knew she could not turn back. He felt the excitement growing within him, the unquenchable excitement which the imminent possession of news could still evoke after all the years.

"If it's true, not obscene or libellous, my object, and the paper's policy, is to publish and be damned."

It didn't even have to be true, he thought. Sometimes it was a half-truth, sometimes it was a monstrous lie, dressed up as speculation. Had Fleet Street ever been a calling, an Estate?

"I can vouch for its truth. I can even furnish the visual evidence. I am not qualified to pronounce on libel."

"That's all right. We have a tame lawyer. We can usually agree a compromise which gets into the paper. The main thing is: does it have readership value? Does its public interest justify publication?"

"Without being an expert I can reassure you on that point. And no other Prime Minister took out more writs against the Press than my husband." He was afraid she was going to have second thoughts. But all she said was: "Now his litigation days are over."

She still withheld the words he anxiously awaited. She was still having to force the vindictiveness up to the surface. How she had tricked the public! he thought; she had the reputation of being kind, tender and shy.

She said: "I can see how you've made your name, Mr Battle. He always thought you had a 'leak' in the Cabinet, or the Cabinet secretariat. I ought to warn you, Joe Hepworth is trying to track down your 'leak'."

"Thanks for the warning, Mrs Hargreaves." It brought him back to his growing worry, his increasing difficulty in satisfying Stella, his sex-starved golden goose. He saw from her face the revelation was coming.

"It's about Joe Hepworth and Pam Bruce. We all know that Joe Hepworth is working for her. But no one in Westminster knows –"

He listened with growing amazement as the voice went on, draining a mind and body of venom while the slender innocent-looking fingers restlessly turned the apostle spoon over and over. Battle listened in silence until she had finished. Then she showed him the proof. Their eyes met and he interpreted her anxiety: she hoped he wouldn't despise her. She was ashamed of her role of informer.

"Well, Mr Battle, what do you say to my proposition now?"

He cleared his throat. The low table, the cups and saucers, the untouched plate of pastries, the Steinway, the Environment Department's furniture and pictures on the wall – everything testified to the validity of the happening. . . .

"Professionally speaking, I should say it will be the most sensational gossip column lead of the year. Politically speaking, it could be a bombshell."

"So you are willing to conspire with me? You are not disgusted?"

"Disgusted?" He laughed at the outrageous idea. Disgust was an emotion he couldn't afford. He said, sadly: "It's a long time since I felt disgust, Mrs Hargreaves. After all, this is politics we're engaged in. We didn't invent the rules of the game, nor did the Marquess of Queensbury. As for my personal feelings, I know that in Fleet Street, you're forgotten the day after your by-line drops off the front page. Yes, I'm willing to conspire."

In any case, he thought, no one would be able to blame him. It was one he wouldn't get the credit for because it was clearly destined for the gossip page. Next to the Court Circular, he thought maliciously, washing his hands of venom and vengeance. In a moment, he thought, knowing human nature, she would try to justify herself, silence the voice of conscience.

"You can't share life with a politician without some of the dirt rubbing off," she said. Her voice quavered but, he knew, it was a momentary weakness. Feeling for Arnold would win the battle.

She rose, just as he had expected: she wanted him out of the room, he was the evidence of her guilt. He held out a hand for the evidence, took it, and they said a formal good-bye.

As he closed the door he thought: This as good as gives the leadership to Westwood. The Labour Party was still old-fashioned enough to hold strong views on adultery. Yet Pam Bruce wasn't the real target. The real target was Joe Hepworth, who had executed the plan for the ditching of the precious Arnold but, like Lady Macbeth, she had put the dagger in another's hand. As for Edwin Battle, he could afford to smile and he did, all the way down Downing Street, as usual, on his way to the nearest telephone.

It was all in a day's work to Edwin Battle.

4

Joe Hepworth sat at his desk in the middle of the Government Chief Whip's office. His great joke was to describe it as his torture dungeon, but to many of the M.Ps who had been summoned to meet him there, it was not a pleasant joke. Throughout the ten years of his rule, he had maintained discipline, sometimes like a martinet.

But, he reflected, there was more to his job than just putting the boot in. He had a full armoury of weapons for peace and war: he could roar like a Regimental Sergeant-Major, he could coo like a dove; he could spread flattery like butter, provide a shoulder for M.Ps to weep on, and hand out presents to the dutiful like a Father Christmas with a bran tub.

It all added up to one thing: the power of patronage. Joe Hepworth knew he was the best and most powerful Labour Chief Whip since Attlee's Willie Whiteley. But, like all good Chief Whips, he didn't expect to be loved. Respected regretfully, yes. Feared, yes.

There was nothing distinguished about the office, an inner sanctum shielded from unwanted visitors by an outer system of defensive offices occupied by the Whips and their runners. Round Joe Hepworth were the filing cabinets containing the voting records and dossiers on his M.Ps, wall notices showing the last state of the parties before dissolution, the final division lists of the dead Parliament. He had no time for fun like the Opposition. In the Tory Chief Whip's office, across the Lobby, there hung on the wall a symbol – the huntsman's whip of a Master of Hounds. Sometimes, he was baffled by the Tory mind.

He identified Hayling from long experience of his special knock on the door. Hayling came in uninvited, limping towards his favourite armchair, sinking into its comfortable depths. He was smoking his abominable pipe. Hepworth wrinkled his nose in distaste.

"I've been watching your agents at work," said Hayling.

"Yes? It has been rather a busy day. A lot of traffic through the Lobby."

"Profitable?"

Hepworth paused before answering. His men had been on the prowl all day. It had been everything but the thumbscrews: listening sympathetically, suggesting, insisting, inspiring, treating in the Dive Bar, promising, threatening. Now, thought Hepworth, he had the picture. Had it been profitable?

"Yes," he replied, smugly, "I think you could say it has been profitable."

"Prestcote's going to use Adam Bolt, isn't he?"

"So, you haven't been idle yourself. Yes, Adam Bolt," he said, derisively, "the Father of the House."

In one way it made sense, he thought. Bolt was one of the most venerated men at Westminster. The qualification for his title was that he had been the M.P. with the longest period of uninterrupted service. He had a fine presence, with a leonine head, a mane of totally white hair which gave him a Lloyd George resemblance. Bolt consciously aped the dead warrior, using a voice of fine timbre and all the tricks of the famous orators of his time.

His time? That was a little obscure, since all the reference books lied about his age. Hepworth calculated he was at least seventy-five. He had served in Attlee's Cabinet. Wilson had flung him out of *his* Cabinet just before the 1966 election, simply to reduce the average age of its membership.

Joe Hepworth said: "His first ploy will be to claim that, since the dissolution, the Parliamentary Labour Party does not exist."

"So that's Prestcote's game?"

"Yes. And Golding will be here soon to let us into what he thinks is a well-kept secret. You're the expert. He will have to consult you on the constitutional position." Hepworth smiled his wicked smile. Golding, chairman of the Parliamentary Labour Party, was a Prestcote man, and Hepworth intended to make sure his fangs were drawn. Golding had served under Prestcote at the Treasury as Chief Secretary, until Hargreaves kicked him out. Well, it had been Hargreaves' boot, but the foot inside had been Hepworth's. He could expect little co-operation from Golding tonight. He asked, casually: "What will you tell him?"

"That the Parliamentary Labour Party has not been formally dissolved. Ex-M.Ps now continue to draw their salaries during the dissolution. It is still the only forum for electing a leader. In this emergency, a ballot ordered by tonight's meeting would be entirely in order." Hayling said, emphasising that he was above the political arguments or merits: "That is the advice I shall tender to the chairman."

"And, naturally, you're right. But that isn't all. Prestcote is putting more fight into his last stand than I expected. I'm told by my spies that Bolt intends, if he fails in his first ploy, to move a motion. He's given written notice. I'm sure you can guess what the motion is?"

"That a ballot for a new leader should be left to the newly-elected Parliamentary Labour Party, and that the deputy-Prime Minister be authorised to fight the election campaign."

"Dead right. What's your opinion on the legitimacy of such a move?"

Hayling said, stolidly: "I'll have to tell Golding he must accept the motion and put it to the meeting for debate. You must have guessed that."

"Of course. You can assume I've already arranged to have my troops positioned." He had been on the telephone all day, delegating to a dozen of the more influential and experienced of Pam's supporters, the task of deflating Bolt. His out-dated oratorical tricks would be harmless against today's brutal logic, ridicule and directness. He would play his silent part – sitting beside the suspect chairman to make sure Golding called speakers fairly: one Bruce man for every Prestcote man. Or, if he could frighten Golding enough, two Bruce men, for every one of Prestcote's.

Hayling knocked out the embers of his dying pipe in the ash-tray, blew up its stem, and put the pipe, bowl still warm, in his pocket.

"Winning this means a lot to you, Joe, doesn't it?"

"More than just a lot." He wondered if Nick Hayling knew the depth of his feelings for Pam Bruce, whether he suspected that Liz Bruce was his daughter, a young woman who was going to fill even more of the gossip columns soon.

"It isn't just for the high office you'd get?"

"Christ, no. Oh, I'm sure Pam would offer me a choice of the top Secretaries of State if I pull it off and she wins the election. But no, I should come back to this same office, this very desk, and my old spider's web."

What he was saying, Hayling thought perceptively, was that Pam Bruce would be as strong a Prime Minister as Joe Hepworth made her. This barely furnished room would be the centre of power, the origin of patronage. Silence was all Joe Hepworth asked, silence and secrecy: no majesty, no pomp and circumstance, no public adulation; and, most of all, no Press ferreting: just the total control of the puppet-master, out of sight, hands working all the strings.

Hepworth asked, reflectively: "What sort of turn-out do you expect tonight?"

"Not too bad in the circumstances. But a lot of candidates might decide their own little patch needs more cultivation and is more important than the leader."

"Especially those in marginals."

"Especially. You can't blame them. Self-preservation."

"The first instinct. But it might help Prestcote."

"The argument being that most of the Left wingers are in the marginals?"

"Right. But Bassett will see his Workers' Control men are here." He had already decided that the decisive element in the ballot would be the ultimate destination of Bassett's first ballot vote. "What sort of a percentage poll can we expect?"

Although Hepworth possessed the power, Hayling was the true expert on the Parliamentary Labour Party. Hepworth had to admit it, albeit grudgingly, because it was a reflection on that power and sovereignty. Hayling had all the records, back to the days of Keir Hardie.

Hayling shrugged. "It could be as low as 70 per cent. On the other hand, because of the general election campaign, all the candidates were in their constituencies, not swanning about all over the world. So, we might even get an 80 per cent ballot."

"Well, no one can say he didn't get notice. The B.B.C. have been relaying back-to-Westminster broadcasts all day."

In addition, his staff had telephoned his personal summons to Pam Bruce's supporters. It had been the equivalent of a three-line whip and not many, if any, would chose to defy Hepworth on the threshold of a new Parliament.

Hepworth went on thinking mathematically while Hayling watched the face for some signal of the result of the sum: on an 80 per cent ballot, Pam would need at least 140 votes for an overall majority. Failing that, if she was to be certain of success, at least some of Bassett's rabble must be persuaded to abstain after Bassett had been beaten. She certainly wouldn't get any of their votes.

Then how to work the trick? He could rule out a direct appeal to Bassett. He would give the stock reply that every vote was a matter of personal conscience.

He terminated his line of thought. The Parliamentary Party meeting still had to be negotiated. First hurdles first. Hepworth still had to complete his demolition job on Prestcote. If the twenty cronies Prestcote had rung last night had each gathered a cell of five, Prestcote could raise a hundred votes which might be just enough, in bad turn out, to win the Party over without a ballot. He gnawed his lip. He couldn't believe it was on.

Hayling had been reading his mind. He said: "It looks as if tonight is the end of the road for Prestcote."

"Could be – " indifferently.

"I suppose Pam could send him to the Lords to run the second chamber."

"That's the usual procedure." If Hayling was asking him to shed tears over Prestcote, he was wasting his time. It was like putting the pit ponies out on the meadows in the fresh air after they had had exhausted their strength, their muscle and tissue, in the darkness underground. Unexpectedly, Hepworth discovered an honest part of his mind still alive and it turned like a ray, lighting up an unsuspected sincerity. "What a hypocritical lot we are as a party," he said, with a self-disgust which wouldn't last long in the jungle of his mind. "How many times has the Party conference committed a Labour Government to abolish the Lords? But Hargreaves used the place as a dustbin, a receptacle to receive all the cast-offs and old friends. Some of the choices were an offence to human dignity. Now, as a result of the abandonment of the hereditary principle, and enactment of the Life Peerages Act, there are fewer aristocratic bums and more working-class arses bulging on the red benches."

"Yes, I've seen it all before. They come down from North, East and West, preaching revolution, and finish up signing the Lords attendance book, drawing the working-class Peers' dole."

"I wonder if Michael Foot will ever end up in gold and ermine."

"Stranger things have happened to people who preached abolition in their youth. Sometimes it doesn't take long for the firebrands to slake their fire. Abolition merges into reform; reform merges into plans for a more legislative body; strengthened power at the expense of the Commons. More legislation is first introduced into the Lords now than ever before. It was the first House to be televised."

There was a knock on the door.

"That's Golding," said Hepworth, briskly. "You know the drill?"

"I *am* the drill," said Hayling. It seemed important suddenly to assert his independence.

Golding put his head round the door.

"Ready?"

"Let's go."

"Two things came up," said Golding, clearing his throat

which, with Golding, was usually a sign of guilt. They were walking along the Ways and Means corridor towards the lift, going slowly because of Hayling's wartime souvenirs. "It's Bolt."

"Oh, yes?" said Joe Hepworth, innocently, with just the perfect note of curiosity in his voice. He hadn't wanted Golding, the Prestcote man, to know prematurely that his code had been cracked, and that Hepworth already had his skilled troops at battle stations in the party meeting. "What's the old goat up to?"

"I tried to get you on the telephone earlier." Golding coughed again, choking on the lie: Hepworth hadn't left the telephone all afternoon. "First, he argues that there's no authority for the meeting and that it should dissolve itself without considering the motion before it."

"Then we'd better consult the constitutional expert, hadn't we? What do you say to old Bolt's theory, Mr Hayling?" He flashed Golding one of his special smiles.

"The meeting is in order, Mr Chairman," said Hayling.

"So that's that," said Hepworth. "What else is troubling Bolt and his sponsors, whoever they be?"

He was playing a game which amused him, but it had a serious side: did he concoct, conspire, plot, prevaricate, because intrigue was a necessary characteristic for his job, or was it already born in the man he had become?

Whatever the answer, he knew what was running through Golding's mind this very moment: *his* only hope of office again was for Prestcote to become Prime Minister. That's why Golding was either a man to watch, or a man to fear. He weighed it up as Golding spoke again.

"Bolt has also served me with a notice of motion – " Golding paused, coughing guiltily again.

"You ought to take something for that," said Hepworth, tranquilly. "It sounds nasty."

"Nerves, just nerves," said Golding. "I always get them before an important Party meeting."

"I'm sure you'll conduct the meeting without fear or favour," said Hepworth. His voice was soft but sinister: it served warning on Golding that he would be under Hepworth's scrutiny, and that he would be watching Pam Bruce's interests.

"Undoubtedly," said Golding: the uneasiness in his voice indicated that he had detected Hepworth's threat.

"Would it be a motion to reject the liaison's committee's recommendation to ballot for the leadership and the time-tables submitted?"

"You knew all the time?"

"It wasn't too difficult to imagine that Prestcote would put up some sort of a fight." It was now a good time to let Golding know that dispositions had been made, that Hepworth had deployed his troops to ambush Prestcote's men.

The lift carried them up to the committee corridor. As they emerged, they encountered a score or so of Lobby correspondents encamped outside the doors to the Grand Committee Room. One man in the group interested Hepworth more than any of the others. *Edwin Battle*. He was giving Hepworth and his phobia for secrecy the run-around. But Joe Hepworth didn't doubt they would locate his "leak" and block it up as one did a rat run. It was simply a question of how much damage Edwin Battle did first.

As soon as the door to the chairman's entrance was opened by Hepworth, the hubbub of a mass meeting of 200 burst out, together with clouds of tobacco-smoke. He saw that their three places had been left empty in the middle of the platform.

Prestcote, Westwood and Bassett – three possible contenders – had also seated themselves on the platform. Displaying themselves like the goods in a shop window, Hepworth thought. Pam Bruce was sitting among the men and women whose votes she wanted, acting on instructions from Hepworth: even in a short campaign, there was always the danger of over-exposure: politics was a lot like horse-racing, the early pacemakers rarely passed the post first. Modesty was the role tonight.

They sat down in the three empty chairs on the platform, Hayling on Golding's right, and Hepworth on Golding's left. This brought Hepworth next to Prestcote and he favoured him with one of his cheerful, deadly smiles. It was as if a spark crossed the small space between them, carrying Prestcotes's message of nervousness and tension.

Swiftly, Hepworth cast his eyes round the faces down below. It took him no more than a few minutes to count that all his men were present, but for two absentees. Grimly, he made a mental note: if Pam won the ballot and then the general election, two senior members of the Parliamentary Labour Party would wonder why they had not been invited to serve in the Government.

Golding rose and commanded silence by vigorously knocking his desk-top with the chairman's gavel. The hubbub died – first to a mutter, then to complete silence, except for Golding's nervous cough.

"Comrades" said Golding, "before I declare this meeting open for business, it is the Party's sad duty to pay its respects to the memory of the late Prime Minister." He coughed and Joe Hepworth knew he coughed up bile. No one had better reason to hate Hargreaves than Golding, who had been peremptorily fired from the Treasury.

But Joe Hepworth knew what to expect. Another Mark Antony oration. *If you have tears, prepare to shed them now*. He stared out cynically into the mass of solemn, receptive faces waiting for, expecting and accepting the hypocrisy of Golding's tribute to a man they all knew had been a fixer and a twister, a man who had polluted, poisoned or devalued most things he had touched, a man of whom it could be said he had hoped to solve problems by slogans.

So Joe Hepworth did not participate in the silent farce. He knew the truth of the man because he had been his twin in political double-dealing. To sanctify Hargreaves because he was dead was cant. The only vice he had not shared was sexual licence; unlike Hargreaves, he was not a compulsive fornicator.

When Golding called for the formal recognition, the minute's silence, and all stood with heads bowed, Joe Hepworth closed his eyes and chuckled in his throat: against the screen of the closed lids he saw the picture of the day he had literally caught Hargreaves with his trousers down, when he had innocently walked through an unlocked door into the Leader's suite at the Imperial Hotel during the party conference, and had been greeted by the spectacle of the two bare cheeks of Hargreaves' backside, high in the air as he dipped his wick in the Transport House Secretary, who lay under him with skirt up over her bare thighs and her panties round her ankles. It was the comicality of that scene he would remember Hargreaves by, not the entries which would subsequently appear in the *Dictionary of National Biography* and the *Encyclopaedia Britannica* under the H's. . . .

The minute passed, boots scraped, the meeting sat.

"Now brothers," resumed Golding, in a more business-like manner, glad that the dutiful obsequies were disposed of, "I have to make a ruling. Mr Bolt has challenged the right of the party officers to summon us after a dissolution on the grounds that no Parliamentary Labour Party exists. He argues this meeting should be wound up without conducting the business on the agenda. Is that right, comrade?"

Adam Bolt rose, bristling with aggression, small of stature, head magnificent with its mane of hair. Hepworth thought: The old bugger only wants a cloak and he could be the Welsh wizard himself. He certainly had the same sexual appetites, even at his age. A lot of secretaries had passed through his hands. They called him the "groper". Bolt opened a sheaf of notes.

"I'm sorry, comrade," said Golding. "I have taken advice" – the chairman flipped his hand to indicate Hayling, by his side – "and my ruling is against you. Like a ruling of the Speaker it cannot be challenged or debated. The meeting will proceed."

"Move next business," said Hepworth, knowing that his intervention would aggravate Prestcote's initial defeat. Bolt sat, glowering at the failure of his opening venture. Round one, Hepworth thought; now for the knock-out. He actually felt Prestcote's tension across the gap between them. The chairman was on his feet again.

"Brothers, I have also received from Brother Bolt, a written notice of motion, which I have accepted as a legitimate subject of debate. Brother Bolt."

Joe Hepworth watched the old warhorse rise through cold, calculating eyes. Bolt read the terms of his motion: "Mr Chairman, I beg to move that this meeting instructs that the election of a new leader of the Parliamentary Labour Party be deferred until the end of the general election campaign." It was short, deceptive, made no mention of Prestcote in his role of caretaker. Well, it wouldn't succeed; and he had seen to that.

Bolt was already launched into his repertoire of oratorical poses. Behind his style were decades and decades of speech-making: in the Chamber; in the Grand Committee Room; at ill-attended meetings in cheerless, unheated Labour halls; and, deep in the past, at street corners.

In his own way, Hepworth thought, this time with a measure of reluctant respect, old Bolt was a bridge with both the glorious and inglorious past. Well, it was on Bolt that Prestcote was defending his dignity. By now, his pallor was almost waxen. God help Britain if he won. Then, with an honesty which was repeating itself too frequently for his peace of mind, he thought: God help Britain even if Pam won.

Throughout all its history, he lamented silently, the Labour Party had sought self-destruction; tonight, he was only trying to frustrate its death wish. Listening to the skilled voice, the rise and fall of the cadences with only one part of his mind, he allowed the other to stray into the past . . .

This was the smoke-filled room, the cockpit where the spurs went deep and the blood and feathers flew, not the Chamber. It was here, in this room, that the history of the Parliamentary Labour Party had begun. Through its thick oaken doors, Keir Hardie had walked with his heavy lace-up boots, a mark of his class: Keir Hardie, the first of many, the standard-bearer for the rest.

By now, the voice of Bolt was a mere accompaniment. It had ceased to be important because he already knew all the arguments he could put. Until the vote, he had merely to see that Golding preserved the balance of speakers. His memory was free to roam over the victories and defeats which had happened in this room: here the rebels had heard the denunciations and suffered the excommunications. . . .

No, Hepworth hadn't had to deal with Nye, Cripps, Mosley, Strachey and Strauss, the rebels of the 'thirties. But silently he boasted that he would have negotiated a peace. It was the leadership of the day which was weak, not the rebels who were exceptionally strong. He would have used the classic formula, divide and conquer. Now, today and tomorrow, he would have to find a contemporary form for the historic formula: how to divide Eric Bassett from his Workers Control. . . .

Bolt was going on too long. Hepworth knew it; Prestcote certainly knew it, but it had been the risk he had to take when he selected Bolt as his battering-ram. But, at last, Bolt had finished his peroration. Now he was sitting, discarding his notes in an inside pocket. And although the cheers were inconclusive, it was clear that many in the room were Prestcote men. It was a good thing he had taken insurance out, Hepworth thought, remembering his unofficial three-liner. Hepworth made sure Golding kept the scales even; it was a Bruce man who caught his eye. . . .

He looked out at the massed faces through the fog of smoke as the new voice droned on. Fodder, he thought, Lobby fodder. His troops. The poor bloody infantry of the Parliamentary Labour Party. Some of the faces would be missing after the election, but there would be new ones. The system would go on, grinding hopes and aspirations into the dust: they all came down to Westminster to build a new Jerusalem. But even before they were accepted as candidates they had already signed away their freedom, acknowledged perpetual obedience to the Party's decisions.

True there would be the protection of the conscience clause. To a limited extent, a rebel could shelter behind that. A collective conscience clause, the only one which mattered, was denied them. But then, democracy was a word which could mean anything. In the case of the Parliamentary Labour Party it was the name Joe Hepworth stamped by an underling on the Party whip every Thursday, demanding obedience, reminding the mutterers of the power behind the name to enforce decisions taken by the Cabinet.

It didn't matter a damn to Joe Hepworth whether those decisions were right or wrong. He did his duty, driving the herds, rebellious or not, into the correct Lobby. The truth was there could never be peaceful co-existence between Parliamentary liberty and Party discipline.

Every now and then, some of those meaningless faces before him had fought back. He actually enjoyed his arguments with a rebel or two. So far the force of his arguments, the obedience clause, the waving of a bad voting record under noses, the mere threat of writing to the rebel's constituency management committee had been enough.

No, an awkward squad was not so dangerous to the Labour Party as rows and rows of uncritical, acquiescent, non-dissenting back-benchers. They were the kind of people who would watch the party die of inertia before they did anything about it. It had happened before, not only on the back benches. . . .

Joe Hepworth looked at the clock. Throw a bone into the arena and the Parliamentary Labour Party would gnaw on it for ever, however few the arguments to plead. He had already arranged a way to end the debate but everything was going fine and many more still wanted to speak. He could afford to wait a few more minutes for the inevitable – the humiliation of Arnold Prestcote, now sitting like stone at his side, chin resting on clenched fists.

Of Westwood he thought with respect. He would be hard to beat. He hadn't the wit, the brilliance or the devastating style of Nye. But he had teeth which didn't let go. Westwood was a man he could have worked with it if hadn't been for his utter commitment to Pam.

Once again he looked at the clock. The knowing faces amongst those massed in front of him were watching him expectantly. He sensed the fraying of Prestcote's nerve and knew he was doing his own arithmetic and their answers coincided. Was he going to throw the towel in? The current speaker sat down and Joe Hepworth gave the pre-arranged signal, rubbing his index finger round his collar.

The result, by all appearances spontaneous, was an eruption from every quarter of the room: "Vote . . . vote . . . vote. . . ."

To Joe Hepworth, the arrangement was so effective, and Prestcote was so immediately jeopardised, that he considered it crude, not up to his normal standards of subtlety and delicacy. But it brought Prestcote to his feet, the towel predictably fluttered in. Prestcote was surrendering. His judgment had been absolutely right.

Golding, face set in anticipatory sorrow, seeing the end of his Ministerial hopes, was banging angrily on top of his desk with the gavel.

"I call Brother Prestcote, order for Brother Prestcote."

Cowed inwardly, but professionally calm outwardly, Prestcote stood there silently a moment, about to concede defeat with a crooked smile and a simulated sportsmanship. In his place, Hepworth thought, he would be resolving to repay with interest every hurt, every wound, every poisoned verbal dart. When he spoke his voice hardly trembled.

"Mr Chairman, listening to the debate, and considering the views expressed, it has been apparent to me that the general consensus is in favour of the immediate ballot. I concede there is a strong case for it.

"I would like to thank Brother Bolt for his loyalty and for the kind personal things he has said of me. But, in the light of tonight's meeting, I would not wish a vote to be taken which would, almost on the eve of the general election campaign, suggest a split in the Labour Party on what is after all, a procedural matter. The Party must be our first love and our first consideration. A vote tonight would be a bad omen. In the interests of unity, therefore, I would ask Brother Bolt and his seconder to withdraw the motion."

What he really meant, thought Joe Hepworth, was that he didn't want the television and the newspapers to report a vote which would have irreparably damaged his ego, just as Morrison's had been permanently damaged. He couldn't afford to be eliminated before even the preliminaries began. In his own way, Prestcote could pose as the man who had given up the pursuit of power to unite the party. Behind whom? It wouldn't be Pam Bruce who would get his support, it would be Westwood. That was the counter-productivity of his plot. Prestcote would still have to be watched, the last possible spark of danger from that quarter eliminated.

Bolt had risen to signify his agreement, his seconder had complied, the motion was withdrawn. Round two had been decisively won. Knowing his Party with sad love, Joe Hepworth guessed the rest would be a formality. The bars were open outside the Palace. The chairman was on his feet.

"Brothers, that seems to be a happy outcome. I now suggest that in the interests of unity at this critical time, we take the liaison's committee's alternative time-tables formally. Mover?"

Arms were raised all over the room.

"Seconder?"

Other arms were raised. Hayling could take his choice of names for the minutes, which would record Prestcote's political demise for posterity. Joe Hepworth realised that he was intoxicated by easy victory. He sobered up quickly. The real fight hadn't yet begun. Before this time tomorrow night, some shit would hit the fan, someone was going to get smeared.

Golding said: "You've all had the terms of the proposed time-tables. All those in favour?"

Arms shot up all over the room. Hayling had no need to count.

"Against?"

One lonely, but resolute, hand was raised. Adam Bolt's. The meeting, which could have been such a danger to Pam, dissolved in laughter.

"Then I declare this meeting closed."

Joe Hepworth rose and stretched his arms. Decency demanded that he should make some gesture to Prestcote, who had risen at his side, simultaneously.

"Sorry it had to happen like that."

It was the best he could say without stigmatising himself a bloody hypocrite. It was not sorrow he felt, it was pity. The man had just been broken politically and it was Hepworth who had planned it all, down to the last detail. He took refuge from his conscience: it was for the good of the Party, for the good of the nation.

He put out a hand for appearance's sake, Prestcote touched it formally, with cold fingers, turned on his heel and, with a tattered cloak of dignity, walked out of the Grand Committee Room.

The moment Joe Hepworth stepped out into the committee corridor he was surrounded by a crowd of Lobby journalists, oppressed by the approach of dead-lines for the first edition.

"Boys," he pleaded, arms raised, eyes sweeping the circle, facile face muscles relaxed into guile, "just be patient. In a few minutes the chairman will give you a full briefing in there." He had his special technique for dealing with the Lobby – charm not muscle. He remembered the soporific days when the institution was a nice freemason – like collusion between Ministers and minions. Now the cry from Fleet Street was for more open Government and investigative journalism.

Joe Hepworth could only meet cunning with deeper cunning. He was on Christian name terms with them all, he drank with them socially in Annie's bar. When drink loosened their tongues he probed for the identity of sources – and gave them bugger-all, unless he was flying Government kites.

Scanning their faces, his smiling eyes momentarily turned baleful: out there on the fringe of the circle was his biggest menace; deceptively languid, obese, and professionally sceptical – Edwin Battle.

Over their heads he saw his quarry, Eric Bassett, moving swiftly and effortlessly along the corridor with the speed of a skateboarder. He set off in pursuit, almost running until he reached the corridor's corner. Fortunately, the lift was one of Westminster's antiques. Bassett opened the metal grill. Joe Hepworth followed him in. He knew that charm wouldn't work with Bassett.

"Hello, Joe." They exchanged their smiles; equally saintly, equally deadly.

"Could you come to the office a moment? There's something I'd like to discuss with you."

Bassett looked significantly down at his wrist-watch; his life was neatly proportioned, minute by minute.

"Just a few minutes," insisted Joe Hepworth, feeling the secret anger he always felt in Bassett's presence. It irked him, having to plead with such a shit, but it was the only way. Bassett knew he held the victory card.

"So long as it doesn't end with me in the Tower." Their heels clicked on the marble floor of the Members' Lobby: They passed through the perimeter wire of the outer offices. Inside his private office, Joe Hepworth pointed to the leather chair facing him across the desk. The only light in the room came from the table-lamp, situated on the desk so that the illumination fell on Bassett's face.

Without a word, Bassett leaned over and turned the base of the lamp so that the light coned on to the desk-top between them, in the neutral zone.

"Joe," said Bassett, gently, "I was an interrogation officer in intelligence in the Army."

"Thought you were a bit young for the war."

"National Service. Cyprus. The intelligence corps seemed pleased with my results."

Yes, thought Hepworth, grimly; I'll bet you were a cunning little bastard.

"We know each other well enough. Shall we dispense with the civilities?" he said.

"I was never one for the civilities. Let me have it, Joe."

"You know what I want, Bassett." But Bassett didn't help him on his way one iota. "I won't insult you by trying to buy your votes when they're running free in the second ballot." He held up his hands, like a conjuror trying to convince an audience that his trick was genuine.

"I know, Joe. Nothing up your sleeve. Just a cobra. But I'm grateful Joe, that you rate my intelligence more than those who regularly submit to your wiles, your bribery, flattery, blackmail and all the other tortures in the Chief Whips' rule book." Bassett smiled coldly. "Forgive my little joke, Joe."

"All right, Bassett." Enjoy it while you can, Eric. You won't look so grand when you collect thirty votes tomorrow. "We've both done our sums, and we know what they all come to in the end."

"Remind me," said Bassett, insolently. "You want my votes the second time round?"

"Not me. Pam."

"But you know what they are all saying?"

"No. Tell me."

"That a vote for Pam is a vote for Joe. How popular are you, Joe? This seems an ideal time to find out."

"If you're right, it will cancel out the anti-feminist vote."

"Perhaps. But you're letting the audience see the strings which make her dance to your tune, Joe. I detect a certain amount of disillusionment."

"The last thing I expect from you, Bassett, is concern about my image. But while we're on the subject of Chief Whips, how did you rate me? Be honest, Bassett. I'm never afraid of the truth."

He knew Bassett would be honest. He could never be anything else, and he waited with an anxiety which surprised him. He had always flattered himself on his complete immunity from the fear of public or private opinion.

"You have my sincere respect, Joe, for the way you've done what is essentially a dirty job. You've always known when to apply pressure, the extent of the pressure necessary to do the trick, and on whom to apply the pressure."

"Then you'll agree with me, when I say I've given you and your lot more latitude than I needed to. I could have closed you up. Put up the shutters, stopped your secret meetings, group decisions on voting, running a party within a Party."

"I could have argued the case before the National Executive. I think I would have found that a sympathetic jury."

"What matters to us is the Parliamentary Labour Party. I could still have put your shutters up."

"Then why didn't you?"

"Because it was in the Party's interest to let you run on an easy rein." Make Bassett a martyr; how he would have loved that, face on the box every day, the victimised.

At that moment Bassett administered his shock.

"What you're trying not to say is that you had a fifth columnist in our ranks all the time, Joe. You know, I wasn't in the least surprised. I can even guess at his name."

Joe Hepworth's telephone rang. At first, he thought it had come to his rescue. Saved by the bell.

"Yes?"

Facing the slyly smiling Bassett across the desk, Joe Hepworth said: "Ring back in five minutes. I'm tied up at the moment."

Bassett said, smiling: "Talking of Donovan. . . ."

"Who's talking of Donovan?"

"All right, Joe. Then let's talk of Donovan. I'm glad you pulled him out of our group when you did. You see, I'd rumbled him and I didn't want all the publicity which would have followed his expulsion from the group. I knew he was acting for you within three weeks of his application for membership. I expected that, knowing you, Joe. I can even accept that it's all in a day's work for a Chief Whip. But to get him installed as Tom Westwood's campaign manager – that Joe, really is a coup. Now you've got a line directly plugged into the enemy camp. Yes, Joe, when it comes to the dirty tricks department, I take my hat off to you."

"You're talking rubbish."

Bassett solemnly shook his head slowly from side to side. It was the action of a bell tolling out the truth. "Joe, Joe, you're incorrigible. It doesn't matter to me, but I feel a bit sick for Westwood. He's a man I've always respected. Give my respects to Donovan when he phones again. Ask him how his middle-class social conscience is getting on. As for poor Westwood –"

Without feeling guilt, Joe Hepworth was concerned. Bassett was sufficient of a puritan, that he might consider it his duty to warn Westwood. He said, casually: "The only way Westwood could find out is if you talked." He shuddered away from the idea of pleading for Bassett's silence. He wouldn't give Bassett *that* satisfaction.

"Joe, it isn't my job to wash your dirty linen in public. Your secret is safe with me. As for the ballot, I've no more faith in

Westwood than Pam when it comes to policies to save Britain."

"Well, you owe me a favour. I had ample evidence to close your group down." If he couldn't bribe, cajole or successfully threaten Bassett, he could with decency present a bill. It wouldn't be degrading or arse-licking, there would be no loss of pride. "The next Chief Whip might not decide to turn a Nelson's eye. He might liquidate you. I have all the evidence of disloyalty on paper."

"Oh, I know that if Westwood wins you'll be out of a job. That's why I'm making allowances."

"The prospect doesn't fill me with alarm. The only person I'm concerned about is Pam Bruce. But, as for you, surely the better the devil you know. . . . ?"

Bassett rubbed his aquiline nose reflectively. "It's a very appealing plea."

"It's not a plea."

The young bugger was trying to rub his nose in the shit. Well, they would see tomorrow. Meantime, Bassett would be disappointed if he expected Joe Hepworth to lick his boots. He would be licking Joe's arse when the portfolios were being dished out.

"I can see the force of your argument, Joe. But you're assuming I lead a homogenous group. Whatever you say about a party within a Party, we have no discipline, no Whips. We all act individually. I have never told them how to vote. That's a man's own responsibility. The essence of democracy, Joe. But you won't want me to preach democracy to you."

"They've all signed the obedience clause in their constituencies." How did one deal with a man like Bassett? It wasn't often Joe Hepworth felt helpless but he did now, staring at the young face, young enough hardly to need a razor. As he looked, a glacial calmness came over the demented-looking eyes. He knew the sign: Bassett was secretly admiring some mischief he was planning. Hepworth saw Bassett's jumbo-sized brief-case propped up against one of the legs of the desk. He remembered the historic failure, the bomb, Von Stauffenberg, the assassination cock-up. Bassett's eyes had resumed their normal glitter.

"I'll go as far as I can, Joe," he said. "I won't directly suggest they should plump for Westwood."

"Thank you *very much*," said Hepworth, with heavy sarcasm. "That wouldn't prevent Westwood winning."

"Was *that* supposed to be my objective?" asked Bassett, innocently. "Anyway, it's as far as I intend to go."

"Bassett, you've a lot to learn. I'm afraid you're going to learn the hard and rocky way. Those men you think you lead aren't in politics to give public service. They don't give a sod for the public welfare. They're here to burrow beneath the foundations of Parliamentary democracy. They're wreckers, and when they've finished with you, they'll throw you away like an apple-core."

"Thank you for this belated interest in my career," said Bassett, completely unaffected. He rose, picked up his bulging brief-case, went towards the door. "I'll let myself through the minefield," he said, cheerfully. "See you at the declaration of the ballot. And good luck."

He went.

Joe Hepworth angrily restored the table-lamp to its strategic position, ready for a more pliable victim. He despised himself when he was bested, especially by Bassett. The bugger, he thought, with grudging respect. But he, Joe Hepworth, hadn't started the game yet. The telephone rang. Once again it was Donovan, reporting from the enemy lines.

When he reached his office at No 12, the doorman had a message. Would he see Mrs Hargreaves whatever the time he returned? She would be waiting for him in her sitting-room. He crossed the intervening rooms to the red-carpeted stairs to No 10.

He didn't like what was coming. He was sorry for Janet; he knew how she felt about Prestcote's failure. He prepared himself to comfort the victim of his work. It would need all his professionalism. He couldn't expect her to understand why Prestcote had to be butchered and he couldn't expect her to appreciate the fact that Joe Hepworth had done it as painlessly as possible.

On the left-hand wall as he mounted the stairs were the portraits of British Prime Ministers. He intended the next one to be Pam Bruce. *This space reserved*, he thought, elatedly. He heard the sound of the piano. It was a long time since he had heard Janet play.

He knocked at her door and went in. She got up at once.

"Please," he said, "go on. Brahms, isn't it?"

"His piano concerto. I didn't know you were familiar with his works, Joe." The inference was obvious: Joe Hepworth was a philistine.

"I'm not. It was just a hunch. The Palm Court Orchestra and Rhapsody in Blue are my cultural limits."

"It's a beginning." She indicated the settee and he sank into its comfortable depths. She sat in an armchair opposite. Her attack came out of the blue.

"Was Brutus an honourable man, Joe?"

He absorbed the blow before he replied.

"You know?"

"Yes, Arnold rang me from the House. He sounded as though he'd been cut to ribbons. My husband started it by overstaying his time of retirement until Arnold's age was a barrier. You finished it tonight with your dagger. Oh, I knew it would happen, Joe. You have the politician's most powerful weapon, haven't you? The knowledge of human weakness. And that knowledge is power."

"It was a fair fight, Janet. He had every chance last night when he called the Cabinet, and he had every chance at tonight's Party meeting. I know the truth is hard to face, Janet, but he has nothing more left to give. There's no more fire in the belly. All he could lead would be a coalition and there's no chance of that. He only wanted the job out of natural pride. He could never have done it."

"You decided that, Joe. You always play the part of God."

"I had to do my duty as I saw it. It was my duty to see that Arnold did not get the premiership out of mistaken loyalty. I've told you: he isn't up to the job."

"Don't lecture me on patriotism, Joe. I gave up everything

for Hargreaves' version of patriotism. To me it's an umbrella: every time anyone wants a defence for a dirty trick they raise the umbrella of patriotism. It covers every evil act. Like tonight's."

"You accused me of being a Brutus. Why don't you face up to the weaknesses of Caesar?"

"You all ganged up on him."

"I know you care for him, Janet. It must be a painful moment. But it was in the interests of the Party and country. Please see it through our eyes."

He felt that hurt pride on Prestcote's behalf had stiffened her. She had some secret, some hidden resolve. He suddenly felt that he had under-estimated her reaction and wondered if there was any way in which she could retaliate for the degradation of Prestcote. He had no illusions about women: when they desired you for physical or any other reasons, they could make themselves vulnerable. But when it came to calculated hatred and vengeance, they were more dangerous than men. What did Janet really want of him?

"You talk of caring, Joe. You're in love too, Joe, aren't you? You're not fighting for yourself, your own self-aggrandisement, although that will be a by-product. You are devoting that devilish mind of yours to making Pam Bruce Prime Minister at any cost. Well, it might surprise you, Joe, but I have the weapons to see that you don't succeed."

"Janet, you're upset –"

"Oh, I know you've always thought of me as a non-political wife, an adornment, someone to grace No 10 and Chequers, to play hostess and soothe his guests by Chopin or Strauss." She was quite calm, but quietly venomous.

"Chief Whips can't afford the luxury of a conscience, Janet."

"You've proved that over and over again, Joe. You'd be Rasputin to Pam's Czarina."

"It isn't the end of political life for him, Janet. The pressure will be off. He'll live twice as long. I can guarantee him a secure job if Pam wins."

"A job which will turn the dagger in the wound? I can see it in your mind, Joe. A little glimmer of consideration: Lord Privy Seal and Leader of the Lords."

"With a seat in the Cabinet. And a life peerage for you."

"Still dishing out the patronage, Joe? Perhaps it won't be at your disposal after the ballot and the election. I have a feeling Pam isn't going to win."

"If it's any consolation, I understand your bitterness. Hargreaves swallowed you up in his political life. I hope you enjoy the remainder."

"The only thing which sustains me, Joe, is that I think you are going to lose. My guess is that you'll be on the back-benches in the next Parliament." Once again the threat. "I should laugh like hell if Pam was beaten."

"I'm sorry you take that attitude towards Pam, Janet; she's entirely innocent of any conspiracy. I had to push her to stand for the leadership."

"No one who was married to Hargreaves for half a life-time could come out of it without a bit of political guile, Joe." He sensed another dart was on its way. "You loved her, didn't you, Joe? And Liz Bruce is there to prove it. You're her father, Joe, aren't you?"

This time the attack mortally wounded his confidence. He felt himself lurch on the settee.

"How did you find out?" He knew the futility of lying. She was so sure, the truth must have been evident from his crushed demeanour.

"I knew the moment I saw you standing together at one of our No 10 receptions. I confirmed it at Somerset House. She has her mother's red hair, Joe. But she's got your features. I knew she was a Hepworth, all right. Somehow it pleased me."

"Pleased you?"

"The thought that you had a beautiful daughter like Liz you couldn't claim. Her parentage had to be secret for political reasons. You were only the stud. To be used. That amuses me, Joe. The thought of someone using *you*. It also gives me a hold."

"Janet, you're overwrought – " He had to coax her into common sense. She could do him damage. Worst of all, she could do Pam more serious damage when the doorstep of No 10 was so near, so desperately near.

"Joe, you know I'm not overwrought. I'm just enjoying to the full the kind of power you've exerted. The kind of power which pushed Arnold over the edge."

"Janet, it wasn't my fault you were born to be barren. I didn't rob you of children."

He felt his pulse beating erratically; there was a pain in his chest. In all his machinations he had overlooked one of the principals. He saw suddenly Janet was a dangerous woman, an enemy to deserve his highest skills. He had come with solace; she had replied with hemlock.

She pointed with arrogance to the pile of newspapers lying on the piano-top.

"The early editions, Joe. As you know, Hargreaves had an arrangement with the proprietors. He got them all at eleven o'clock. I think you had better take a look at them."

He rose and lifted the papers, turning towards the door. "I'll say good-night, Janet. There's nothing left to say, is there? I'm sorry we have to part bad friends. Perhaps you'll feel better when the shock has passed."

"Read them here, Joe."

For some reason she was mocking him. He knew at once. There was something in the first editions to Pam's disadvantage. He opened the bunch of papers uneasily.

The *Daily News* emerged first and he saw the banner heading: He shuddered with shock.

The bugger, he thought; that treacherous young bugger, Basset. *Edwin Battle again*. He looked through glazed eyes at the head-line:

BASSETT: WOULD NOT SERVE UNDER BRUCE

It could just mean the difference between victory and defeat, he thought, reading the text of Edwin Battle's communiqué from the Westminster front. Pam, we're in for a real fight. A lot depended now on how many of her supporters would be induced to defect by Bassett, the strength of the young bugger's influence would have on the bulk of the moderates who would decide the issue. She was speaking.

"If I were you, I should turn to page 12, Joe."

"I never get as far as the gossip columns," he said, contemptuously. "I'm usually too nauseated by the leaders and the selective readers' letters."

"I assure you you'll be interested in this."

He turned the pages with a new premonition of evil. He had made a grievous mistake he now knew: he had thought of Janet Hargreaves as a retired concert pianist. She was a politician. A dangerous politician he had left out of account. Well, he was paying now; more important still, Pam was paying.

Aghast, he stared at the leading story on the gossip page. Together, inset side by side, close together so there could be no mistaking the resemblance, were the pictures of Liz, Bruce and Joe Hepworth. The whole story of her parentage was there. Stunned, he read: . . . "*always regarded as an adopted child . . . Westminster never suspected . . . effect on today's ballot . . . dislike in the constituencies of scandal . . . Party still notoriously puritanical view of extra-marital sex . . .*" The evidence was conclusive, the photostat of the birth certificate.

He held on to the door-knob, fist clenched in anger. He looked at her with bewildered eyes. The triumph glittered back at him, hard as agate.

"You, Janet? But why? You did this to Pam and me, and worst of all to Liz?"

"The sins of the fathers, etc. etc., Joe. You know now I'm not as gentlemanly as Arnold. Needless to say, he doesn't know anything about this."

"But at least I gave Arnold a fair fight. In the Cabinet. At the Party meeting. The better candidate will still win in the end."

"Only the ballot will show that, Joe."

He had needed a little time to recover his nerve. Like the boxer with legs of rubber he had waited for his brain to clear. He had his own campaign planned. Nothing would stand in his way. He still had ways and means. He summoned up a smile from the wreckage, anything to shake her damnable gloating. He could at least be civilised and treat her like a lady and not a virago.

"Pleasant dreams, Janet. I'll say good-night."

"Good-night, Joe. Sleep well."

She was no lady. He turned as he opened the door.

"At least, you've taught me something tonight, Janet."

"What's that, Joe?"

"That I'm glad I'm fighting Arnold, and not you."

"But you are, Joe," she said, exultantly, "you are."

He closed the door on a gloating enemy and only then allowed himself to admit the depth of his anxiety. Somehow, he suspected he hadn't heard the worst. Slowly, he wiped the sweat off his brow.

5

Her mind stupefied by sleep, her body satiated by sexual gratification, Liz Bruce slowly and reluctantly emerged from the depths. The telephone on the bedside-cabinet was jangling.

What the hell, she thought, regaining mental balance slowly. She disentangled her naked body from his, and picked up the receiver.

"'Lo," she said, sleepily. Richard had awakened too, and was turned towards her, sleepily curious. She looked at the luminous clock-face, then pulled the cord to give them light.

"Miss Bruce? Miss Liz Bruce?"

"That's right." She was suspicious of the voice immediately because of its professional cutting edge, the sense that it was accustomed to telephoning victims at all hours. It carried an indefinable menace. "Who's that? It's after eleven-thirty." The premonition grew. She was old enough to have discovered that's life's blows were usually inflicted at the end of a telephone-wire.

"The *Daily Express*."

"Oh, Christ, no." She laughed. She ought to have guessed, accustomed as she was to the attentions of the Press. They were an irritant but she was good-humoured and even co-operative, accepting that she was "good copy", that they had to earn a living. So, she bore their attentions philosophically, neither seeking publicity like Liz Taylor, nor assaulting and prosecuting her pursuers like Jackie Kennedy. "What can you bastards want at this time of night?"

She turned towards Richard, who was watching her, arms now folded at the back of his head.

"The *Daily Excess*," she said.

"So I gathered."

"They want to read me a gossip lead in the first edition of the *Daily News*. They say I would be interested." She turned her face back to the mouthpiece.

"Read on."

Richard saw her face slowly harden, her lips draw tight with shock, the jaw bones clench. She listened for a while, then turned towards him, hand over the mouth-piece.

"Some bastard has been putting the boot in for Pam and Joe," she said, stonily.

He sat up in bed, suddenly wide awake at the tension in her voice.

"The story is all about my parentage. What bastard could have done a dirty trick like that?"

He saw her eyes widen and, for the brief moment it lived there, he identified the accusation. Who would be the beneficiary? Then the accusation diminished into the bewildered question: could Tom Westwood really be that mean-hearted bastard?

"Tell me exactly what they said."

"Oh, it's all there. Photographs of Joe and me together so that the resemblance is striking. A poisonous text. But worst of all the clear evidence – the birth certificate."

The accusation was forcing its way back. A perfect coup. The morning of the ballot. The smear of a lifetime. Before he could prevent her, she had returned to the telephone.

"You asked for my comments? All right, I'll give you them. And you can quote me. I know who my father is. Pam Bruce knows, Joe Hepworth knows and, as for the British public's right to know, I don't give a fuck for the great British public."

Angrily, he wrenched the instrument from her hand as she tried to hang up violently.

"Liz," he said, quietly, "I don't think that was very clever."

He leaned across her naked body and spoke into the mouthpiece persuasively: "Are you still there? Good. Look, old man, I'm sure you appreciate that Miss Bruce was very upset. I hope you'll be understanding."

He listened without hope.

"No," he had to admit, "of course, I couldn't deny she said it. What do you think I am? A politician?"

It was an unwise thing to say. It produced the inevitable follow-up.

"All right, who *are* you?"

He sensed the eagerness, the deep suspicion as doubt, hardened by the Press cuttings on the desk before him, publicising Richard Westwood, the City's whizz-kid, as the sexpot's most recent escort, became near-certainty.

"Does it matter?"

"That all depends on who you are. For instance, if you were Richard Westwood sharing her telephone – " the prurient pause – "and her bed. . . ."

"Yes," he said, heavily, "I am Richard Westwood, and we're just good friends."

He slammed down the receiver and, somewhere, he imagined, a cock crowed as he betrayed his father. Very soon the tumbrils would be rolling as Fleet Street sharpened the blade of its guillotine for Liz Bruce and Richard Westwood. Calmly, completely unaffected by her folly, she leaned over to the bedside-cabinet and lighted one of her aggressive cigars, as if following a stage direction.

She was, he reflected furiously, dynamite; a woman completely without conscience. All she ever felt was in the flesh, the heat of her loins. Her bare breasts he had so recently nuzzled were above the sheets, and it was the first time her nakedness had left him feeling degraded. He was nauseated by shame. She thought that all she had to do to snare him was to lie back with her legs open.

"He didn't do it. Not Tom Westwood. He's above that sort of thing." Oh, he knew he hadn't honoured, hadn't obeyed, had been a disgrace to the Westwood brand of Socialism. But, all at once, it was necessary to defend Tom Westwood against innuendo.

"I never said –"

"You didn't have to say. I read it in your face. Tom and I have had nothing in common since I went into the City but I know him *here*." Passionately, he stabbed his heart with a finger. The truth was he had found the burden of his father's reputation and rectitude too hard to carry. He had fallen down under the load. The thought seared his conscience like acid: all the years of his adulthood he had shut out memories of love and tenderness in the Westwood home of his youth. Part of that love was that Richard Westwood had never been down a pit. Meanwhile, he thought violently, bare-tits beside him had no real conception of the damage she had done, she was just waiting for the well-worn approach, the laying-on of hands in the erotic zones. What had happened was that the simple implementation of their non-involvement pact had extended the Bruce-Westwood feud down to the present generation.

The telephone was ringing stridently again.

"Let it ring," he said, brusquely. "All it means is that the other bastards in the Street have found your phone number."

"They're a lot of merciless buggers."

"It's the politicians who give them their ammunition."

"Talking of politicians, I wonder who really put the poison in for Pam?"

"Whoever it was, is safely in his funkhole. Or hers."

He slid his bare body from beneath the sheet, stood up, felt her eyes feeding on him hungrily, and covered himself with sadistic slowness in his dressing-gown. It was a victory, the knowledge that she needed him and he didn't need her. Torn as he was by remorse, he could have done without her for ever. He walked to the windows and drew the curtains. The moonlight came in.

"Well, I'm buggered," he said. In the street below, parked on the opposite side of the road, was the green Cortina. The same two men he had assumed were Special Branch, were still in the front seats, tirelessly smoking.

"What is it?"

"The Cortina. And the Gestapo's still there."

As he spoke, a car came speeding up the road from the distant roundabout, stopped outside the flat with a screech of strained tyres.

"Get ready to smile for the dicky-bird," he said, grimly.

"The *Daily Excess* photographer has arrived."

For a few moments Joe Hepworth swam up like an unconscious man emerging from an etherised limbo. As soon as he broke surface, he remembered the disasters of the night. He lay silently for a few more minutes, convincing himself that all was not lost and the figures of the voting hadn't yet been affected. But, he thought, grimly, he would have to act quickly: it was going to be a long, hard and dirty day.

Once he was out of the camp-bed he moved swiftly, shaved with the electric razor in the bathroom, came back and neatly folded his blankets. Joe Hepworth had always been one of life's warrant officers, he had never had a batman. He knew his station, he wasn't officer material, not the pukka thing, too much of a thug.

There was a knock at his door and the happy face of Mrs Kershaw, No 10's housekeeper appeared. There was not a line on the face to indicate the political tragedies and catastrophes she had witnessed throughout the regimes of four Prime Ministers. Today, he noticed, she treated him without curiosity, just as if she hadn't read the *Daily News*.

"Mrs Hargreaves asks whether you would like to take breakfast with her, or whether you would prefer a tray on your desk?"

Remorse? He knew better. Janet simply wanted to savour the full flavour of her revenge. He knew his women now. Even Pam. She had carried her hatred for the Westwoods in her heart for a quarter of a century.

"I'd like a tray here, Mrs Kershaw, please. Just toast and marmalade. But bring a jug of coffee for two. I'm expecting Mrs Bruce."

He watched her face. It never twitched, he saw with affection. She knew more secrets, and spicy secrets, than many of Whitehall's mandarins. But she had signed the regulation document; she would never be able, unlike members of the Cabinet, to write her memoirs under the guise of a treatise on the Constitution. She would never be able to disclose the truth about Hargreaves' sex life, although she must have known some of the juicier parts. The Official Secrets Act had a more secure bite than the Privy Council oath.

Mrs Kershaw had hardly delivered the tray before Pam arrived. As he expected she was in a state, the night's events showing on her face. She badly needed stiffening up for the day ahead. She had the bloody newspapers under her arm.

"Coffee?" he asked, casually. He could see she hadn't slept a wink. "They pestered you? The Street?"

"What do you think?"

"Two lumps, isn't it?"

He knew, of course; had known for a quarter of a century.

"How can you be so calm, Joe? The roof fell in."

She tossed the *Daily Express* and the *Daily News* on the desk. He looked at the front page picture in the *Express* dispassionately.

"This I haven't seen. The other I saw in the first edition."

He opened the top drawer of his desk, took out the flask, poured a liberal dose of cognac in her coffee.

"Something to boost your morale," he said, when she protested. He must show her, at least, that he was in full command. She threw up her hands in despair at his glacial calmness. He examined more carefully the pictures of Liz and Richard Westwood. Clearly they had been dug out of library's files.

"That won't compete with the *Sun*'s page three injection of lust today," he said, quizzically. "And everyone must admit they make a handsome couple."

"Joe," she said, seriously, "I suspected from the first I should never have allowed you to persuade me to stand."

"Drink up your morale," he commanded. "You're still going to win."

She laughed harshly, in open disbelief.

"After what I have to face today? The sneers, the open joy of our enemies, the contempt of the prudes. And there are plenty of those in the Party."

"Correction. What *we* have to face. You couldn't have produced the captivating but infuriating Liz without my ardent co-operation. We never expected to have it easy."

"Who did this to us, Joe? Who hates us so much?"

"Fasten your seat-belt, Pam." He paused, giving her time to accumulate strength. "It was Janet Hargreaves. She even boasted about it to me last night."

"Janet? But why, for God's sake, why?"

"Because of what I did to her idol, Arnold Prestcote. Because of *your* Liz and *her* barrenness. Perhaps the last stages of the menopause. Because she suffered so much indignity at the hands of Hargreaves. Who knows? But it's done, and we have to fight it."

"I'm most sorry for your wife. Having to face this embarrassment after all these years. I feel terribly guilty about her."

"I spoke to her last night to break the news before the newspapers got her. She's taken it well. She's gone away where they won't find her."

"It's a foul thing when the innocent have to suffer."

He felt a tremor of impatience. For years his relationship with his wife had been one of peace and contentment. She was a Westminster widow, surrendering her husband to the day and night duty calls. Ever since he had met Pam Bruce theirs had become a marriage of convenience, a façade for the public, a protection for his career.

"Pam," he said, gently, "the situation hasn't changed in all the years. She knows that if you would have had me on any terms, I should have left her for you. She consented to my fathering Liz on the understanding it would be secret, that there would be no sexual affair as such, and that her marriage wouldn't be broken." That's how it had been: coitus by consent. "Well, we've kept our part of the bargain, and she recognised it."

"She's a very fine person, Joe, and I'm sorry it had to happen like this." She finished her laced coffee. It brought colour to her high cheek bones. His first task was accomplished, the restoration of morale. "Joe, be honest with me. I know you only tell me what you think is good for me to know. This time the truth: have we a hope in hell?"

"Jesus," he said, simulating exasperation, "A hope? We're going to win." He had to quell his own inner doubts and fears.

"Let's analyse the facts coldly and calmly. First, Bassett's repudiation. What is the worst it could mean? The possible loss of a few dubious supporters, afraid his defection might raise disunity as an election issue. We would never get the bulk of his votes – the Workers' Control mob – in any case."

"I wouldn't want them, Joe. To me that mob is as big a menace to the Party as the Tories. All right, Joe. Rub out Bassett. That's one cheer."

"Point two, the revelation that Liz is our child. How many people at Westminster are going to be shocked in this day and age? Twenty years ago, perhaps. My guess is it will hardly affect the voting at all."

"There are still bigots and Simon Pures in the Party, Joe. But all right. Two cheers."

"Point three. Richard Westwood must have been tight, but he came to our help at the expense of his father. He's identified with her, as implicated as Liz, in sexual permissiveness. It will also remind the Party of the other skeleton in the Westwood family cupboard – the son's solidarity with the rich. Now you can give three cheers."

She said: "I've failed as a parent. Liz needed a father, Joe. She's totally irresponsible. She even promised me she wouldn't get up to any of her escapades in these forty-eight hours."

"Pam," he said, "they are kids still. It's a generation or two's gap. They never knew the hungry 'thirties, the Jarrow march, the war. They blame us for the chaos. And who are we to say they're wrong? Our Party was as responsible as the Tories for turning a blind eye on Guernica and the shame of Munich. Our generation was responsible for the extermination camps and the incineration of Dresden, Hamburg and Berlin."

"Joe," she said, surprised, "you're showing passion."

"If I am," he said, "the sad thing is that it's so unusual. Sometimes I think I'm just a machine, a man with a computer mind. Or a man fossilised by Westminster and the Whips' Office. But we haven't time for philosophic discussion, Pam. I'm telling you, we can still win."

"I want to win, Joe. But above all, I want to win fairly. Not by methods such as this."

With disgust, she indicated the newspapers on the desk.

"I'm thinking purely in terms of figures, not dirty tricks," he said. But he felt his heart flutter with guilt. He couldn't tell her the truth, that in a clean fight they would be beaten. There was nothing clean about the Byzantine plot evolving in his brain. But his face was a mask, his guilt submerged, when he said: "Leave the figuring to me, Pam. Go about as if nothing had happened. Remember, they will be measuring you up for the job."

"You sound like an undertaker, Joe." She made a grimace as she realised again she might be facing political death.

"It's Tom Westwood we're going to bury," he said. He meant it, despite the risk he would run of totally alienating Pam. The guilt persisted, the fear of her scorn if the facts ever leaked. He was already deeply involved, having suborned Donovan, first planting him in the Workers' Control rebel group to spy on Bassett, and then the real coup, installing him as Westwood's campaign manager. He looked at his watch: Donovan was due to report.

But Donovan would be his minor crime. If she knew what he was planning in alliance with McBrane, she would be really sick. In his years as Chief Whip, Joe Hepworth had pulled off many coups, had been forced by circumstances into many questionable acts, but he knew the deceit he was now planning would take him to the very edge of disgrace. When he saw her beloved face, clean and innocent of vice, he feared for her. If he was betrayed, her repudiation would be the hardest burden of his political destruction.

He thought of the odds against him – Bassett's cunning, Janet's hatred, Edwin Battle's mole-like digging, patient and dedicated. He could only make the silent promise – *her* hands would be clean.

"What should I do about Bassett? Make an appeal for unity?"

"Ignore him. Don't waste your fire. Tom Westwood is our target."

Westwood was his worry, not Janet, not Prestcote, not Bassett, not Edwin Battle. It was Westwood who had to be beaten.

And to be beaten he had to be analysed, his strengths undermined, his weaknesses displayed in neon. He was supreme in his own field – organisation of the mass; he was good on ideas and policy-making; he thought with rugged simplicity without depth. But he was not sufficiently patient with people and people were Joe Hepworth's strength. He studied them from the secrecy of his bunker. His brain was compartmentalised into people's files and he knew the minds of over 300 M.Ps. In particular, he knew the things to their discredit. Most of all, at the moment, he knew about McBrane, that he would keep his mouth shut if *the* bargain could be struck. He had one last thought on Westwood: his greatest weakness was his incapacitating honesty. He brought his attention back to Pam, who was still fretting about her questionable ability to unite the Party.

"Unity?" he asked, divining her fears. "Unity is what we're always talking about but it never seems to exist for more than a week at a time. It's always been the same, Pam; if we were united it would only mean that we were dead."

He drained his cup and rose to his feet, the signal for her to leave.

"This is where I begin the eventful day's work," he said, briskly. "I have the feeling it will be historic. To show you how confident I am, I have already laid the champagne on with the Government Hospitality Fund." He knew it was a kind of fraud; celebration would be a Party, not a Government matter. He put his hands on her shoulders. "Be confident," he said, tenderly, and tenderness was an emotion he rarely felt.

"It will be hard," she said. "But I'm obedient."

"I've got big money on you to win. With Ian Mikardo. Good odds, too."

"I know he runs a book on these events. And what is he offering against me."

"Don't worry," he said, evasively. "Just believe I've safeguarded my investment."

He continued to smile his encouragement falsely until the door closed. Then he sat at his desk and picked up one of the telephones. In a moment he was through to the office of the

Government Whips, issuing orders.

"These are strict instructions. There has to be at least one man attending the ballot-box all day. I want a list of those who have voted at hourly intervals." With his knowledge, and uncanny instinct combined, he would be able to gauge failure or success in advance. "But, most important of all, I want to see McBrane when he comes in to collect his first ballot paper. And give me the tip when he is on his way to my private office. Is all that quite clear?"

"Quite, boss. And I'll leave written instructions for every man on duty here."

"I'm relying on you." It was more than a command; it was a threat. There would be no mercy if there was a foul-up. And his staff knew how brutal he could be. But now he sat in sombre silence, still experiencing the bile of guilt.

It was not too late to give up the plan and rely entirely on the power of Pam's personality. The plan meant trusting McBrane, and Joe Hepworth did not believe in trusting a fellow man. But if trust could ever be condoned, it could be condoned in McBrane; an extremist, yes; but a man of honour, too. Honour? He was a politician and every politician put a different valuation on honour.

Joe Hepworth got up and began to prowl his office, still in doubt. He had never been so indecisive in his life. Then he remembered that what he would be doing he would be doing for Pam and not for himself, not for personal gain. The moment he made the decision, fear dropped away from him like a discarded cloak. He went back to his desk and began to study the names on a division list.

Against those whose support was already firmly promised, he made his mark. At last he was functioning normally. He no longer feared the long, hard and dirty day which remained before him.

6

By the time McBrane had penetrated the outer defences of the perimeter of offices and reached Joe Hepworth in his headquarters, Joe was already at the drinks cabinet pouring out the whiskies.

"I reckon you wouldn't turn down a wee dram." He put on his jocular routine in the hope of de-freezing some of McBrane's natural frost. "Without inducement, of course."

"Of course," said McBrane. His eyes remained hard and suspicious. "On that understanding ah wouldna say No."

Hepworth knew it would have to be perfect navigation to steer through the shoals of McBrane's rocky conscience and rectitude. He was an honest extremist making no concessions, completely uninterested in the fruits of office, or in accumulating material possessions. The trouble was that his mind was closed. Hepworth had to prise it open. Had he enough jelly to crack the crib?

McBrane took the glass held across the desk, and sat down in the chair strategically placed for Hepworth's victims. He had nothing to hide: he didn't object, as Bassett had done, to the proximity of the desk-lamp illuminating his facial expressions.

"Cheers," said Hepworth, raising his glass. There would be others before the process was over, successfully or not.

McBrane tossed back the double Scotch all at once, head back. He put the glass on the desk-top, between them. It was a challenge to Hepworth's duplicity. He put it into words.

"Why, Joe?"

Hepworth registered his best expression of surprise.

"Why what?"

"Why this sudden invitation and hospitality. Don't forget I have my reputation as a revolutionary to consider. I can't hob-nob with Chief Whips."

"Everyone would know that Joe Hepworth wouldn't be fool enough to believe he could influence the incorruptible McBrane with a few Scotches. No, don't fret, I'm not asking any favours, Mac."

He used the diminutive as casually as he could. The first necessity was to get rid of McBrane's natural suspicion. So far, McBrane's scepticism was undiluted.

"In any case, it's too late to influence me, Joe. Twenty years too late."

Joe Hepworth slid his copy of a division list across the table. "I've already got you down for Bassett. But it saddens me, Mac, to see a man of your calibre marching solidly to an empty landscape behind Bassett's banner."

"If you want to cry, Joe, you can borrow my shoulder or my handkerchief."

Joe Hepworth laughed. He was on the way to the warmness that came from mutual respect, not the glow of whisky. But it was still too early to get at the safe he had to open: the loot was McBrane's willing co-operation. As Chief Whip for ten years, Hepworth was a master in the role of a disarmer of suspicion. He did not believe McBrane would hold out against the prize he was going to offer.

"I haven't been able to show it Mac, because of my job. But, unofficially and secretly, I've always admired your utter independence."

"Come off it, Joe. You're not talking to a newly elected Member. I must have got something you want. You're approaching me as if I were a frightened virgin. You want something pretty badly. We both know that. But I don't know what."

Joe Hepworth congratulated himself silently. Curiosity showed in McBrane's eyes. It was the first stage completed.

"You're wrong this time, Mac. I want to do *you* a favour. You and your native Scotland."

He knew at once, by bringing in McBrane's beloved Scotland, he had deepened curiosity and interest. He kept the bait dangling. "I'm worried about your seat, and the whole of Scotland. What are the prospects in your constituency?"

"Dicey. Bloody dicey. You know that, Joe. I've got the Nats, the Commies, and now the Independent Labour man to split my own vote. I should be there now, fighting."

Joe Hepworth shrugged his shoulders, but sympathetically.

"I know the picture. It's grim."

"It's more than that."

"Another dram?"

McBrane hesitated. Hepworth thought exultantly: He's nibbling. He paid his second visit to the drinks cabinet. McBrane's new double was passed across the desk and, this time, treated more circumspectly. McBrane left half in the glass after his first taster. He was prepared to listen, at least.

"In view of the tough job you've got there, I was reluctant to bring you down for the ballot. But I couldn't make exceptions. And I knew I could rely on you despite your constituency troubles. I'm sorry you'll be wasting your vote on a crackpot but that's your affair. He's chasing a mirage like a thirsty man in the desert. You and I know that Workers' Control will never come."

"Not in our life-time perhaps, Joe. But, unlike Wilson, I don't think a week is a long time in politics. To me ten years is a short time. There's a difference between us, Joe. You're a machine-man. The machine created you and now you drive it. You're given orders and carry them out. Well, I take orders from no one, and that includes the Cabinet and my constituency management committee."

"Not even Bassett?"

"Least of all Bassett."

"So, if he ordered you, or asked you, or pleaded with you, to vote for Westwood in the second ballot, you wouldn't feel obliged to do so?"

"Please don't insult me, Joe. Westminster isn't my kind of democracy but, even here, no one tells me what to do. Bassett knows better than to try. Mine is the only influence I listen to."

McBrane finished his second whisky and Joe Hepworth watched it vanish with silent approval: That's it Mac, he thought; it's time you had a little lubrication in that mind of yours, a little oil on the hinges so the door will swing more easily. But the job wasn't even properly started yet.

"I've been thinking about this recall, Mac. Perhaps I ought to have made certain exceptions."

"I simply obeyed the summons."

"For once," said Joe Hepworth, with a wry smile. "I'm still wondering whether I could make a few exceptions in special hardship cases once the first ballot is over. They would have to be Bassett men, of course and it would have to be kept quiet. Everybody in a marginal would think he was a special case."

"Joe, I never thought the day would come when you invited me to play truant. What's behind it?"

"There's no point in concealing my deep anxiety about Scotland. For years we've been able to rely on Scotland to give us a majority. Those days have gone, thanks to the Nats. This time we could easily lose the election over the Border."

"For Christ's sake, Joe," said McBrane, with the first hint of emotion, "I've been trying to tell Transport House that for the last five years."

"It's penetrated, Mac."

"Now is a little late. Every seat is vital."

"I remember you voted for the Government at the third reading of the Bill setting up the Scottish Assembly."

"Yes, for once I voted with the Government. That doesn't mean I was satisfied."

"How do you feel about it now? Can you sell it to your constituents on the basis of the manifesto?"

"I told you at the time. The assembly is emasculated from the beginning. You've given us a political eunuch."

"But half-a-loaf is better than no bread."

"Given freely by a Labour Government it helps. But if we'd gone further we'd have buggered the cry for separatism. Without its myth, nationalism would have died. The shrewd Scotsman knows that separatism is just a con."

"How many of the Scotsmen in the Workers' Control group

feel the same way?"

"All of them. They're all vulnerable."

"Let's see – how many of them are there?"

"Joe, Joe, just when you're interesting me, you drop a gooley. You know exactly how many. You tell me."

"I make it eighteen."

"Of course, because there are eighteen. You're Joe Hepworth, super-salesman, trying to sell something to a rebel and you're pretending to be Old Moore."

"Eighteen constituencies. All the difference between election and rejection." He saw a glimmer of understanding beginning in McBrane's eyes. "Tell me, Mac, do you have any influence on them?"

"I'm the leader of the Scottish element. You know that too, Joe."

"Don't get impatient. They'll listen to you?"

"I don't often talk. I don't believe in the Whip system."

"Would they take your advice without wanting to know the reason?"

"That would depend on the advice. They're all free agents."

"All right. Can I be frank?"

"Well, it would make a change, Joe."

This time when Joe Hepworth smiled, it was his ice-tipped smile. "Then do this for me, the Party and Scotland, Mac. After they've cast their votes in the first ballot, get them on the first fast train to their constituencies."

He took a deep breath. He had reached the threshold – the safe was in view; whether by skill with its combination, or the blast of jelly, he had to break down the prejudice in McBrane's mind. With outward calm, he leaned back in his chair, clasping his hands behind his head, and studying McBrane's face. Silence was often more effective than words. But this silence was dynamite. McBrane still waited for him to commit himself.

When he maintained a stubborn silence, McBrane finally said: "What you're really asking is that I should conspire with you to win the leadership for Pam Bruce? By getting my friends to abstain?"

"I always knew you were a smart operator, Mac. And now you're asking yourself what I should give in return?"

"I'm not a horse-trader, Joe." McBrane got up with the obvious intention of leaving.

"Don't be over-hasty, Mac. What I'm going to offer is for the good of Scotland. Benefit for Pam would merely be a side-product." He knew that Scotland was McBrane's genuine love; he was surprised he hadn't joined the Nats. "At least be patient enough to listen to my proposition. I wouldn't ask you to do anything illegal or dishonourable."

He paused on the threshold of fear. He had lived by the creed: never trust a fellow man. It had got him where he was, at the centre of the web, manipulating all the other fools who trusted. He was being forced to turn his back on the creed, and it was like advancing into a minefield which hadn't been taped with white. A conspiracy of one was safe, a conspiracy of two was risky, a conspiracy of three invited danger; after that, the danger increased by geometrical progression: according to the numbers, the conspiracy could become political suicide.

"Don't be insulted, Mac, but before I go on, I must have a positive promise from you that you will never breathe a word of this conversation to a living soul."

He looked long and deeply into eyes which met his with suspicion, but honest suspicion. Despite the creed he was almost tempted to trust McBrane. But the real question now was whether McBrane would trust him. He had to admit that, if he was McBrane, he wouldn't trust Joe Hepworth.

"I don't like giving promises blind. I'd rather you told me more first."

"I couldn't do that, much as I respect you."

Now was the moment of danger. He was about to commit himself to a promise there was no guarantee he would be able to fulfil. He had absolutely no collateral.

"I've been talking to Pam about measures we must take if we are to win back our hold on Scotland." It was a lie, but lies were no stranger to his tongue: little white lies, diplomatic lies, big malignant lies, any sort of lie he regarded as good for Pam or the Party. "We've come to the conclusion we shall have to do something drastic."

McBrane's eyes never left his face. They were transfixed in their chairs like poker players over a gigantic pot. But Joe Hepworth was promising they could both be winners. He had built up the suspense like a film director.

"If you succeed in getting those eighteen on the train before the second ballot opens, I can promise a bargain that will shake you."

"I'm not often shaken, Joe." McBrane clung to his scepticism and Joe Hepworth didn't blame him. McBrane couldn't figure a circumstance which would benefit Joe Hepworth, Pam Bruce, McBrane and the Party, simultaneously. "What's the bargain?"

Joe Hepworth still hesitated. Danger still obstructed the vocal cords and paralysed his tongue. The words came out at last. He was committed:

"This is the deal. If Pam wins – and you might clinch it with your multiple abstentions instead of votes for Westwood – I will give you a firm promise that the next Labour Government, under Pam, will amend the Act and give Scotland really sweeping financial powers."

It was out. From this moment he was at McBrane's mercy. It was in his hands to ruin Joe Hepworth. Across the desk, McBrane moved his head sharply, but it was a gesture which took him more deeply into the cone of light from the lamp. Hepworth lost his fear. Despite his instinctive caution he began to gloat: McBrane had adopted a bargaining posture.

"Let me get this quite clear, Joe. No question of a misunderstanding. I know you, Joe. You're as slippery as an eel. What powers are you promising so firmly?"

"The right to levy local taxation. That's for starters."

"But the Government had its chance and refused. Why the change now?"

"It was held in reserve. Some of us thought it might be the election winner."

"So far it sounds vague. Can you be more specific."

"An amendment Bill would promise an allocation of not less than 25 per cent of oil revenues, specifically for Scottish industrial regeneration. Taking one year with another."

"How can I be sure of this, Joe? I don't want to offend you, but one needs a long spoon sometimes. Could I see Pam?"

"It would be a mistake. I'm keeping her clean in all this. She wouldn't like it if she knew I had given away her secret. You see, she would have to carry the plan through the Cabinet during the election campaign. There mustn't be a whisper. It must be a perfectly timed announcement so that the other parties haven't time to recover."

"What you mean, Joe, is that I've got to take Joe Hepworth's word without a guarantee?"

"It's mutual, Mac. We've no alternative but to trust each other. Remember, I've just put my political life in your hands. One whisper, and I'm ruined. But think of the prize – dishing the Nats, regaining Scotland."

"Convince me, Joe. Put it in writing."

He was genuinely shocked. "Mac, you're being fanciful. You know I wouldn't commit my grandmother's name to paper."

They were facing each other even more closely now, eye-slit to eye-slit.

"But it's hard to be satisfied by your simple say-so, Joe. I have to persuade eighteen friends."

Joe Hepworth dare not disclose by so much as the shade of an expression the enormity of the risk he had taken: one day, in the middle of the campaign, he would have to stand up in the campaign committee and demand a formal commitment to the nation that Labour would carry out Joe Hepworth's unauthorised obligation. He would have to thump the table to get his own way but he was sure he could do it because he genuinely believed: his plan was the only way to bring a Labour Government back. It was blackmail. Above all the committee must not suspect that he had promised the measure in order to secure Pam's success in the ballot. He drew a long breath. He had staked everything on McBrane's silence.

He said: "I honestly don't see how you could have any scruples, Mac." He had forgotten the qualms of the stranger, conscience. "You would be doing nothing immoral."

"You're right there, Joe. I don't give a damn who wins. Pam or Tom. They are both Conservatives to me."

"But Pam has the more genuine feeling for Scotland of the two. Westwood's only interest is Transport House. He's an organisation man, a national fixer. I doubt whether he crosses the Border more than half-a-dozen times a year." He added the little grains of denigration casually, like salt and pepper.

"Must the others be left entirely in the dark? Can't I hint it will help them retain their seats?"

"For Christ's sake, you've already promised." He watched with suspense while McBrane silently examined his damnable conscience. He suspected McBrane was deliberately putting him on the rack, repaying old scores against the Whips, the orderly life they programmed. Then McBrane grinned.

He said, maliciously: "That's the first time I've seen you sweat, Joe. It makes up for a lot of the hounding. If you deliver, I promise you the silence of the grave."

"You won't know until the campaign is nearly over. The whole essence is the timing. It must knock the breath right out of the Nats."

He found it easier now. All he had to do was to convince himself that what he had done was not for Pam but in the interests of the whole British Isles. He wasn't, unlike McBrane, a man who would die for Scotland, and very nearly had at Alamein.

"I know you have a group meeting at 12.30. That will give you a quiet chance to tackle all eighteen. The less it looks like a concerted move the better. I suggest the telephone isn't safe." He knew he was still in a minefield and would remain there a long, long time.

"Joe, you're a crook, a liar, and a cheat. But for Scotland and the future of Workers' Control I'd deal with the devil himself. Between us, we'll kill off the bloody Nats."

"That's justification enough. Can you do it? Above all, can you do it without raising suspicion in the Westwood and Bassett camps?"

"I can be very persuasive when I like, Joe. I'm pretty sure I can guarantee my end of the bargain. I'm not quite so sure you can deliver yours." There was candour but there was respect. He thought Hepworth wouldn't fail.

"I'll give you the only guarantee I can and, knowing me, you'll respect the significance. If the amendment giving the Scottish Assembly all the powers I've promised isn't the first Bill in the new Parliament, I'll refuse to serve it. I'll go on to the back-benches for a few days to make my speech, then pack my bags and go. I have never run out of a bargain, once struck."

"I hope you succeed. If you fail, it will be a sad loss to a Labour Government."

"Then you are ready to drink on it?"

"I'm ready. I congratulate you on your choice of the malt."

"For you, Mac, the best there is. Taken neat, just as it should be."

They both stood and emptied their glasses in one draught. This is what it's all about, Joe Hepworth thought. Politics. Horse trading. Shit up to the earholes. Survival of the most wicked. No place for virtue, honesty, integrity. Only nerve, cruelty, blackmail, sordidity. Westminster, the equivalent of Eton for men. He had robbed Westwood of eighteen votes, probably given the leadership to Pam.

"It's time to shake hands," he said. He was going to make it solemn, like a secret pact. It was an unfortunate simile, he thought, remembering Hoare had had to go. It was either Hoare or Baldwin. It could be Joe or Pam.

"Is there any need for formality?" McBrane said, with a mischievous smile, an all too-rare event: "After all, we're both gentlemen."

"I'd like to feel everything was properly understood."

"To me promises are informal, but binding. Written treaties are only made when one side or both, intends to break them. No one will ever find out from me. And you daren't leak a whisper."

"Not even in my memoirs."

"Are you dictating every week-end into your tape-recorder? It would show up all the Cabinet's recent efforts. Whatever *they* say, you were the real fixer, Joe."

"I believe in the principle that the Chief Whip keeps

everything secret. There will be no memoirs from Joe Hepworth. I'd be scared of the truth."

"Come, come, Joe. What have memoirs to do with truth? They are self-justification and revenge, on colleagues and the system. That's one way the Cabinet Ministers avoid the ban: they give the book a cover of fake scholarship: 'The workings of the Constitution.'"

"The last thing, Mac, I'm going to be very anxious. If you pull it off, the code word is Eureka. If, for any reasons you fail, code word G.A.F.U."

"What's all this cloak and dagger stuff, Joe?"

"There's a suspicion the telephones aren't secure. Well, that seems to be the lot."

Their hands clasped. The grip was that of two strong-willed men, almost nerveless. Each had the same thought of the other: he wouldn't hesitate to join him on a flying picket.

Fleet Street sometimes described Tom Westwood as the "organising genius of the Party". This was the reality, Westwood thought – the orchestration of chaos.

He was already down to his shirt-sleeves in the chairman's seat in the large conference room on the eighth floor of Transport House. In its other flights of fanciful prose, the Street described this room as the "nerve centre of the Labour Party's election campaign".

They could have at least let him know the date earlier (thinking of Hargreaves, gone now outside the reach of reproach, and Joe Hepworth, the living). He was the only member of the Cabinet to know the true situation about the state of unreadiness of the Party's organisation. Yet Hargreaves and Joe had fixed the date without even asking him his opinion. He had only learnt at the same moment as the rest of the Cabinet, minutes before Hargreaves went to the Palace to ask for the dissolution.

That was inconsiderate enough, but Hargreaves had compounded his folly by dying off even before the campaign began, snuffing out like a candle in the middle of the night. So, he had fucked himself to death and Westwood hoped he had enjoyed it. But he had left Westwood with the problems: the Party needed at least another half-million pounds for its general election fund, Labour had full-time agents in fewer than half the marginals, was in dire danger of losing the battle against the Nats in Scotland, was plunged into a leadership struggle at the worst possible time. Labour was in the shit. Once again it couldn't be trusted to win: it was well known that Oppositions did not win elections, Governments lost them.

He looked about him at the busy chaos. All the way down the long tables, secretaries were manning the battery of telephones, installed at emergency speed. They were taking orders for election propaganda from constituency parties: posters, pamphlets, leaflets, manifestos, points for speakers. All the usual crap. But, Westwood thought, with secret pride, despite Hargreaves' secrecy, Tom Westwood hadn't been caught with his pants down. By now, all the stuff – good, bad, indifferent, and plain bloody awful – was piling up in bales in the basement beneath Transport Hall.

He had rightly read Hargreaves' devious mind: the moment he was sure Prestcote hadn't the guns to win the battle for the succession, and the next lot of trade figures would give the economic game away, he knew Hargreaves would make his run for it. North Sea oil was the only possible saviour. Who would it save now? Pam Bruce? Tom Westwood? Or the Tories?

At his side, Martha, the grey-haired spinster, for twenty years his faithful secretary at Transport House, angrily slammed down the receiver.

"Another one," she said, angrily. "That must be the twentieth of the morning."

"Fleet Street is having a gala day," he said, calmly. The calm was fraudulent. His mind simply responded to the discipline of a lifetime. Everyone in the room had seen the *Daily Express*, incriminating Liz Bruce and Richard Westwood. He was a butt. On this day of all days. He felt bitter against his son, a deep explosive bitterness against what could only be more than an act of thoughtless folly. To him, it seemed a deliberate intention to harm.

Why? he wondered. For God's sake why? He accepted that for years they had lived at arms' length, like neighbouring countries with different policies but which had agreed to differ peaceably; diplomatic relations severed, but no war. He had accepted the right of his son to the life of his choice – the successful capitalist with accountants skilled in tax evasion, the E-type Jaguar, and all the other symbols of success. But it had always been understood that he would do nothing else to embarrass his father in his public life, his sincere devotion to the protection of the under-dog. Now, his publicised affair with that gossip-columnists' delight, the sexpot daughter of Pam Bruce, was bound to leave some ridicule attached to *him*. And ridicule was something a politician could do without. With an effort of will, he forced his mind back to the herculean task awaiting him. On his organisational skill, the future of Labour largely depended.

"Get me Moss, at the T. and G.W.," he instructed Martha.

While he waited for the call to mature, he looked round the walls of the conference room. In a few hours, the first Press conference to herald the campaign would be held, and in readiness the propaganda posters were already displayed. How many converts could they expect this kind of propaganda to attract? In any case, the Tories had long before booked up all the prime sites, ready to plaster the marginals the moment the "off" had been signalled.

The posters were the products of the public relations mind which he despised. In modern days, you tried to buy votes with the hard sell, in the same way advertising agencies sold "biological" washing powder. The con trick. Basically, Tom Westwood was an honest man. Often he shone truth like a searchlight into the recesses of his mind. Now he studied the posters with a gloomy premonition:

LABOUR HAS GOT BRITAIN OUT OF DEBT: NOW LET LABOUR LEAD THE COUNTRY TO PROSPERITY.

LABOUR HAS BROUGHT INFLATION UNDER CONTROL: DON'T LET THE TORIES RUN RIOT.

PRIVATE ENTERPRISE LET YOU DOWN: DON'T TRUST IT AGAIN.

That one he really liked because it evoked nostalgia, memories of the 'thirties which moved him most: the scenes of criminal desolation, shuttered factories with smokeless chimneys, derelict docks, grass growing in the shipyards, the workless sheltering from the wind at every street corner. That picture always made his life's work worth while. At least, it might remind the old that a Labour Government had not invented unemployment.

THE UNEMPLOYED: ASK HOW MANY UNDER THE TORIES?

Martha was handing him the telephone, whispering the name of the Transport Workers' boss.

"Moss, it's Tom Westwood here," he said, cheerfully. Good cheer was the mandatory first approach. Impassioned pleas might be necessary later, when the bills came in. He was sorry that Jack had retired; he could talk to Jack on more intimate terms than he could to Moss, more intimate than the formal comradeship between union leaders and Cabinet Ministers, which was sometimes just another word for enmity. He had been standing near Jack when he had earned his blighty in the Civil War. Together, he and Jack had begun to cobble the first social contract which, they would be proclaiming from the roof-tops in the next three weeks, had saved Britain. He said, cryptically: "I suppose you can hear the rattle?"

"Rattle?"

The tone was compounded equally of caution and understanding. The social contract was dead; it was now every union for itself, and the devil take the hindmost who couldn't claim a differential.

"The beggar's bowl. You might have heard there's a general election on." At this moment, he thought, Moss was associating Tom Westwood with the publicised sex exploits of his son and Liz Bruce, not the needs of the Labour Party. The realisation undermined his dignity. His weakened bargaining position made him aggressive. "We still need at least half-a-million."

"Tom, that's a lot of bread. You're going to have to do some arm-twisting."

"I'm a good twister."

It was an incautious comment. There was a chuckle down the line.

"You said it yourself, Tom."

"What can you do? You've never let us down."

"We've done a lot already, Tom. We're still recovering from the financial beating we took over the Tory Industrial Relations Act."

"Look, with inflation, the cost of this campaign is going to be murderous. The bastards across the road are going to pump out money in torrents of gold. The bosses know that if they are beaten this time, with the North Sea oil coming in like a flood, they are out for a lifetime."

"Tom, we have a finance committee tomorrow. I'll put it on the agenda. Would you like to make a personal appeal?"

"I'm up to my eyes in it here."

"Then I'll do my best. Are you going to win the ballot?"

"I just don't know. To tell you the truth, I haven't had time to think of it."

"Well, good luck. We all know what Pam Bruce means. She'll make an ideal front for Joe Hepworth. That means a turn to the Right."

"I'm relying on you, Moss."

"No promises, mind."

He handed back the receiver to Martha. It had hurt like hell, dragging his pride in the dust. He was a tenant, pleading with his landlord: Slater, and the City whizz-kids, were not the only people who had been shattered in the collapse of the property boom. The Labour Party's plan to build its own headquarters had been caught up in the disaster. That was why he, Tom Westwood, who might become the first truly Left Wing Prime Minister, was still sitting in the same chair in which Ernie Bevin, that Right-Wing steam-roller of a man, had bulged. Behind him, a menacing head on its pedestal, was Bevin's heavy bust.

Briefly, he enjoyed his revenge for those days, the multiple defeats suffered by the Left, annihilation by the block-buster votes cast by the Bevins, the Deakins, and the Carrons. Things were very different now, with a Left-Wing dominated Executive and Conference, and the Right Wing M.Ps being weeded out by the activists in the constituencies. Well, what had been sauce for the goose was now sauce for the gander.

He said to Martha: "Get me the Engineers." But before she could reach it, her telephone rang. This was the detestable part of his job, he thought; pleading with the Party's paymasters for more funds – down on his knees, a suppliant, a mendicant with the beggar's bowl:

Alms, alms; alms for the love of Allah.

Martha was holding the receiver out to him. She didn't seem very happy.

"The Engineers?"

"No," she said, a little apprehensively: "it's Edwin Battle, of the *Daily News*."

"Martha," he said, angrily, "I told you, no Press calls."

"He says he has some interesting information for you about a public opinion poll his paper will be running tomorrow."

"Get him to dictate the details to you."

"He says he won't speak to anyone else but you."

He hesitated. But he knew that Edwin Battle, despite his give-away nose and booze-laden voice, had him hooked.

"All right," he said, and took the telephone off a relieved Martha. "This is Tom Westwood, Edwin."

They always played out the same charade – the cooperative party organiser, the sympathetic interlocutor.

"That was a good turn we did you this morning, Tom, disclosing the truth about Liz Bruce's parentage. Pity your son had to horn into the picture and cancel it out."

"I'm not interested in your paper's gutter activities," said Westwood, curtly. "You said something to Martha about a poll?"

"Yes. I told myself Tom Westwood will be most interested in this, that he should be the first to hear."

"Edwin, you're a liar. A clever one, I'll grant you, but a liar just the same. I don't doubt that you've already given the dope to Joe Hepworth."

"I tossed a coin."

"And I lost. Edwin, I'm a very busy man. I have an ailing Party to suckle."

"Well, here it is. It seems the Tories have a ten per cent lead. It's not looking too good, I'm afraid." The fake sympathy tried to suggest that Battle, though he worked for a Right-Wing scandal sheet, was a secret Socialist. They all pretended to be under-cover Labour sympathisers, Tom Westwood thought, cynically. "As I'm sure you know, I always vote Labour."

"Pity you don't let your brain guide your pen then, Edwin." It wasn't too bad, he thought, but a bit of a jolt; he knew all about polls: when they were favourable, politicians quoted them with delight; when they were unfavourable, politicians said they were unscientific and subject to a margin of error of two per cent either way. At such times too, one recalled that Trueman, Heath and Wilson had all won against the evidence of the polls. "What about the Liberals?"

"They are being badly squeezed. Seven per cent. Even worse in Scotland."

"Tell me about Scotland." It was Scotland which would decide. Despite his distrust in polls, he waited anxiously for Battle's answer.

"The Liberals are being wiped out. Three per cent. Labour has 37 per cent. The Tories have 20. Independent Labour has 5."

"The Nats?" He made a quick calculation. "That means the Nats have 35. Neck-and-neck."

"I'm afraid so, Tom. Now I've done you a favour, perhaps you can talk. How do you think you're doing in the leadership stakes?"

"I'm too busy here trying to sort order out of chaos to bother myself. You know what the Labour Party is like?"

"Do I not! Does that mean you've left your campaign entirely to the tender mercies of Donovan?"

"How did you know that?"

The question was ignored. How did Edwin Battle get

everything else?

"With a free hand?"

"Why do you ask?"

"What made you pick Donovan?"

"He volunteered."

"That figures. I only hope, for your sake, you gave him a positive vetting."

"What are you getting at?"

"He's very thick with Joe Hepworth. In fact, Tom, I've every reason to believe Joe planted him in Bassett's Workers' Control group."

"But he opted out of that."

"My guess is that he was withdrawn by Hepworth because Bassett smelt a rat."

"Edwin, what are you insinuating?"

It could be possible that even he, Tom Westwood, the ungullible, the hard-headed realist, had been deceived by a forked tongue, and that behind Donovan, in the shadows, Joe Hepworth was doing one of his double-crosses. Did Battle *know* anything?

"It's probably all right. You know me, Tom. I'm trained to be a suspicious bastard."

"Well, anyway, thanks for the tip."

He handed back the receiver to Martha and sat for a while, in solitude despite the populated conference room. Up to thirty-six hours ago, he had never expected that Tom Westwood would be trying to climb Disraeli's greasy pole to the Premiership: this was Tom Westwood's battlefield, he thought, not the Cabinet room. He had never had that killer instinct, the overweaning ambition, the self-confidence, ruthlessness, cunning, lust for power, driving will, unscrupulous mind, that made candidates for leadership. Nor, he knew, had Pam Bruce. Yet, between them, were twenty-five years of relentless silence and enmity, and it had brought them face to face, fighting each other in a battle for possession of No 10. He knew the real enemy wasn't Pam. It was Joe Hepworth, who fought dirty, who had kept him out of Wilson's and Hargreaves' inner counsels, frozen out in the cold. In Opposition, with his base in the Party, he was more than the equal of Joe. But this fight, tonight, was the preliminary to real power, not just possession of Transport House.

He thought again of Donovan. Had he, Tom Westwood, sunk to Hepworth's level of political opportunism by enlisting a spurious Donovan for the sake of the votes he claimed to be able to deliver from the extremists of both wings of the Party in the second ballot? If so, how could he adopt a high moral tone? But high moral tones did not lead over the threshold of No 10. Now he was fighting, he must fight to win – but another way might have led to a surer possibility of victory, a refusal to campaign at all, to stand aloof above the dirt and turmoil of the contest – the statesman who refused to buy or solicit votes.

He thought he knew his weaknesses, his stolid stubbornness. Some would call him thorough – they meant pedestrian. His enemies would go further – slow-wittedness. But, despite his mistake in accepting Donovan's offer, everyone knew he was straight and loyal. He stood four-square, like the men at the coal-face. No one knew better than he the comradeship of the miners: once, men such as he, had dominated the trade union group of the Parliamentary Party; as the pits had been closed, and the numbers of the miners diminished, so their power within the Party had waned. But they had still possessed the muscle to drag Heath down into the dust. The Triple Alliance was among the dead bones of history but the future might still be an N.U.M. man in charge at No 10. He possessed one thing in common with Gaitskell, the drawing-room leader; they had both fought, and fought again, to save the Party they loved. . . .

He was still thinking of his destiny when he saw Martha was holding out the telephone again.

"The Engineers?"

Once again the agonised shake of the head. The fateful pause.

"It's your son, Richard."

They stood side by side at the balcony window, looking down at the besieging Press corps, now reinforced by a television team. He was fully dressed but she was still nude from her shower, and scented beneath her dressing-gown, slyly radiating her invisible sensuality from the distance of a few inches.

"Do you realise," she said, "that today, we are probably the world's most celebrated lovers, another Liz Taylor and Richard Burton?"

She was proud of the notoriety they had achieved. She was an immoral eccentric, a modern Mitford, with the added spice of promiscuity. But she watched him closely: she had sensed his antagonism.

"I think I've diagnosed your trouble," she said. "The still, small voice of conscience."

He tried to escape her constant presence, the temptation of her flesh. But she followed him to the bedroom, where she arranged herself on the unmade bed. He stared at the calculated exposure of flesh through unresponsive eyes.

"You're going to ring him up," she said, with sudden perception.

"Yes, I'm going to ring him up."

"Oh, he'll thank you when you wish him good luck after this morning's *Excess*. What do you propose? To beg his forgiveness?"

He did not reply. He had a plan. If he told her what it was she would think him insane. Was he insane?

"You're making a big mistake." There was a wealth of indulgence in her voice. She believed he was still her plaything. She had always been the originator, the innovator, the experimenter, in their frequent acts of loveless sex. But for him the time had come to opt out of irresponsibility. Although it might be too late, he had to repay a debt.

Standing on the brink of decision, he cast his mind back on the rare meetings of the Westwoods in recent years – never at the House, never in the City, but always on some neutral ground. He remembered the chilly rebuff he had received when he had offered to repay his father for the sacrifices he had made, in the only currency he knew and recognised – money. Only at this moment did he realise the depth of the insult, the cruelty of the rich. But now the insult could be redeemed, there was still a way to reconciliation.

"You want to crawl," she said, and for the first time, her anger flared.

"Yes," he said, slowly, with dignity, "I want to crawl." She still hadn't comprehended how many years last night had aged him, not calendar years but experience years, suffering years. For once crawling would be an act of adulthood.

"Forgive me, Father, for I knew not what I did." He ignored her contempt. He ignored her presence. He dialled the Commons and listened to the tone.

He waited for the half-forgotten voice, words of atonement still scrambled incoherently in his mind: Thank you, Father, for the education paid for by your muscle and sweat; for the protection from your own youthful fate, the black galleries, fire-damp, broken bones, filthy sweat, disfigurement and perhaps the violence of death – the dignity of labour. Here, now, perhaps too late, is my love and abasement.

The line clicked.

"Mr Tom Westwood, please."

He waited, nerves stretched like piano wire. The line signalled again. It was not his father's voice.

"Donovan speaking."

"I'm trying to get in touch with my father. This is Richard Westwood." He knew from his City contacts, his social drinking, when he met an old Etonian voice.

"I feel I know you already." A nudge-nudge laugh. "A lot of people are trying to get in touch with your father. Can I help? I'm his campaign manager."

"You?" He couldn't contain his surprise. In his own way, Donovan was just as much a phoney Socialist as Richard Westwood: having invested his father with nobility, had he discovered human weakness, a trickery, a Tammany Hall thinking, the product of which was intended to give Westwood the votes of the Parliamentary Party's misfits – the rich, conscience-stricken refugees from the Tory Party – which would otherwise go to Pam Bruce?

"You sound surprised."

"I oughtn't to have been?"

But the reminder of the sordid did not affect his determination to seek a reconciliation: his old man would play the game under existing rules. He was in a dirty game but he was unstained, stout as an oak. And he wasn't fighting a weak woman, he was fighting Joe Hepworth and his bag of assorted dirty tricks.

"You're thinking I'm not his type? I know I'm a freak. But then, as a Socialist, so are you."

"I pay my dues, I vote Labour, but I don't knock on doors and I don't preach any of the various gospels. How's it going?"

"The campaign?" There was a chuckle of mirth, followed by a collision of mutual dislike. "Well, it *was* going well. If you do succeed in catching up with your father, I shouldn't ask *him* how it's going."

"I've seen the *Daily Excess* myself."

"I couldn't really blame you, old boy. Liz Bruce is certainly a smashing piece of fretwork to get your saw into. It was just a pity to get caught, today of all days."

He wondered how his father could have been deceived by Donovan's excessive bonhomie. He supposed a politician met fewer con men than he did in the City. But he was an experienced man and Richard Westwood had only just grown up, except in his specialised field – skating just inside the constrictions of the Companies' Acts.

"Perhaps I shouldn't tell you, but he's at Transport House. He's had to give me a free hand with his campaign because he's busy working on the general election. I believe it's chaos."

"The dear old Labour Party. It always was chaos. That's why it's so endearing. Thanks, anyway."

He hung up and faced the bed. Liz hadn't accepted her rejection. She was now waxing her shaven legs. They were brown from exposure to the summer sun as she pointed them, one by one, at the ceiling. She bent forward provocatively so that he couldn't avoid the sight of her perfect breastwork. She was the only girl he knew with freckles on her tits. He turned his back and dialled again.

"Who are you ringing now?"

"Transport House."

"I never had any time for chivalrous bastards."

Transport House was busy, the call went on ringing and ringing.

"What have I got to do to get you going?"

He did not answer.

She gave him the gamine smile with which she was accustomed to appeal to his sexuality. She did not know that for the first time, as he was contemplating her body, he was simultaneously deploring the shallows of her mind.

He still waited for Transport House to clear the queue of callers. He realised now that yesterday they had been fools to think that the ballot wouldn't affect their relationship: it was Westwood versus Bruce here in the scented atmosphere of a brothel, just as much as it would be in the Grand Committee Room at the Commons. At last the line was clear.

"Mr Westwood's office."

"It's urgent that I speak to Mr Westwood."

"He's very busy. He isn't taking personal calls."

"This is his son, Richard."

A short, antagonistic pause.

"One moment, Mr Westwood."

In the long, long silence which followed, he was aware of her listening below him on the bed, turned on her side so that a bared breast was visible. He was aware more of the dryness in his throat, the guilt behind the quickened drawing of his breaths.

The voice said, conclusively: "Mr Westwood says he hasn't got a son."

The line went dead. He stood there, stricken, looking at the silent instrument. Gently, he replaced the receiver and it was then she began to laugh, peal after peal of musical laughter, mouth wide open, head thrown back. He stared down at her recumbent body.

"You tart," he said, tonelessly; "you Girton-gilded tart."

7

Apart from being an efficient Parliamentary Party functionary, Nick Hayling was a very cautious man. Having been booby-trapped by Jerry, liberally showered in the nether limbs with fragments of best Krupp's steel, he had left the Army with a mean disability pension, a Military Medal, a plum-coloured demob suit, and a built-in mental survival kit. He foresaw booby traps everywhere. He knew that after the tasty sex morsels in the morning papers, involving the Bruces and Westwoods, the Party couldn't survive a ballot-rigging scandal.

So, he had taken precautions. It wasn't simply that he didn't trust Joe Hepworth – although he didn't. It was an automatic reflex of his self-defensive apparatus. The fact was that only Nick Hayling, the two duplicating machinists, and the three scrutineers, knew that every hastily prepared ballot-paper bore a small symbol, no more than the size of a full-stop, strategically placed, which would establish its authenticity. In addition, every person entitled to vote had to sign personally on receipt of his ballot-paper.

He knocked his perfunctory knock on Joe Hepworth's door and walked in. He limped towards his customary haven, the green leather upholstered chair facing Joe Hepworth, who merely looked up from the division list on his desk. There was thunder in the air: Hayling knew that, for hours, Joe had been poring remorselessly over his figuring in the margins, his assessment of certain or probable voting intentions. The question in Joe's mind was certainly: how many of Pam Bruce's supporters would defect after the unfavourable publicity?

"Five minutes to go," said Nick Hayling, feeling mechanically for his pipe, his comforter. Seeing Joe's frosty reaction, he made no attempt to light up but merely played with the cold bowl, turning it over and over in his fingers. "What size of a poll do you make it?"

He leaned over the desk, not really curious about Joe's calculations. It was not a serious question, just words to form a barrier against the topic which filled both their minds. How would the Party take it? Joe answered in the same vein.

"Surprisingly well." He meant in view of the circumstances. "At least 80 per cent." Then he said, brusquely: "Don't let's play silly buggers, Nick. Tell me, how much harm is it going to do Pam?"

"You mean Bassett's refusal to serve under her, or –"

"You're being whimsical again, Nick," said Joe, warningly.

"Well, I'm paid to be neutral and I couldn't even hazard a guess." There was method in his evasion. Nick Hayling wasn't going to involve himself in personalities. He carefully committed himself to his limit: "I suppose it depends how strong the old puritanism remains in the twentieth century Labour Party, how many bible-bashers are left. I believe they still blast out Handel's Messiah every Sunday in the Welsh valleys and in the Noncomformist north. But I don't think many wear out their knees praying nowadays."

"Six?". Curtly. Joe wasn't in a fun mood. Hayling realised why he was so grim. That was the figure of defectors.

"It could have been much worse in the old days," said Nick, soothingly, deciding that a word of consolation would not infringe neutrality. "As you know there was a time in the Parliamentary Labour Party when the conscience clause covered only the fors – for pacifism and temperance; and the againsts – against adultery and all promiscuous sex."

"It's those self-righteous buggers I'm afraid of. I keep thinking of poor Jack Profumo. His career was ruined because he had lied to the House. But how many other Ministers have lied to the House? And all that shit about the possible danger to the security of the State. His real crime was that he fucked Christine Keeler and she wasn't a fully-paid up member of the Tory

Party. This nation is a shower of bloody hypocrites. It almost makes me proud of my reputation of being a bastard."

All the time, Hayling had been watching the second-hand circle the circumference of the clock-face.

"Time to go, Joe."

"Give it a few more minutes."

Immediately, Nick Hayling knew how much Joe Hepworth was worried. His list showed that some of his troops had gone AWOL and he still hoped they would report. He persisted stubbornly. He couldn't afford a scandal.

"It's on the dot. The ballot's closed, Joe."

Avoiding Joe's glare, he rose painfully and made for the door to the outer office to collect the ballot-box. Joe Hepworth joined him silently: he didn't confide in Nick his belief that, in spite of all the set-backs, he still thought Pam would lead the first ballot by a margin of seven votes over Westwood. But the evidence was all circumstantial – his own impressions, reports from his agents in the Whips' office, and secret intelligence from the enemy camp by Donovan. No one knew better than Joe Hepworth there were those who would promise his vote, shake hands on it, look you in the eye and then secretly vote for your opponent. But even if he was right, the lead wasn't enough to promise victory in the second ballot.

"You have the key?"

"Check," said Hayling, patting his pocket. He had done duty at many leadership ballots but this was a real cliff-hanger. Someone might be destroyed in the process. His safety apparatus was ticking away like a time-bomb. "Adam will be getting impatient."

"Bugger Brother Bolt." In the outer office, Hayling took charge of the ballot-box. "You know he tried to get the television cameras into the count?"

"Well, it's positively his last appearance as a politician." Bolt, the Prestcote man, was the chief scrutineer. That was another reason why everything had to be proper, precise, and seen to be so.

All the way along the Ways and Means corridor to the lift, Hepworth tried to quench his sudden fears of detection. But worry continued to gnaw at him: every mistake he might have made in his computations would mean a difference of two. Yet, he reflected, he had erred, *if* he had erred, on the side of caution. He couldn't conceive that Westwood could win an overall majority on the first ballot. There would have to be a run-off after Bassett had been eliminated, and he had already received McBrane's coded signal, Eureka.

And Donovan claimed to have accurate information about Westwood's support which could be crucial. Despite his creed of distrust, he felt he could rely on Donovan because he knew how to deal with old Etonians. He could do business with them because they understood mental thuggery. It was the old Wykehamists with whom he had never been able to establish a rapport – the Gaitskells and the Crossmans, the Dons and country-house Socialists.

He suddenly felt insecure as they left the lift and collided with the Lobby corps, crowding the committee corridor. Soon, after the count in Room 15, he would have to face the Parliamentary Party in the Grand Committee Room next door, when the result was declared. His face flushed with humiliation at the thought of smutty jokes already circulating about Joe and Pam.

He pushed angrily through the ring, reserving his special detestation for Edwin Battle, of the *Daily News*, the yellow rag which had administered the poison draught. The florid face smiled back a wicked message: *I'm not afraid of sanctions*.

"We were beginning to wonder what had happened to you," said Adam Bolt, portentous with self-importance, his Welsh wizard act.

"Adam, you're a pain in the arse," Joe Hepworth said, harshly. "We waited until the stroke of time. Give him the box, Nick."

Bolt took it with reverence.

"Key, please."

Hayling passed the key over and Bolt unlocked the box ceremoniously. Joe thought: The bugger could be laying a foundation-stone, launching a liner, or opening a new motorway.

"Adam," he said, "why must you make everything into a

Warner brothers spectacular?" It didn't help his peace of mind to know that his needling was a sign of nerves. What the hell was the matter with him? Hadn't he fixed everything so that Pam couldn't lose? But the strain was beginning to tell: he was on a tight-rope – on one side of the chasm the shady deal with McBrane; on the other his double-agent Donovan. Adam Bolt was still fussing.

"I am going to empty the box here – " he pointed to the expanse of desk. "You – " he indicated the second scrutineer on his immediate right – "will go through the voting papers and allocate them in separate piles for each candidate. You – " he indicated the third scrutineer further right – "will count each candidate's votes into bundles of 20, putting these elastic bands round each packet. When we have finished, I will personally check each bundle and certify the result for the Chairman to announce next door."

"Adam, you're certainly determined to go out in a blaze of glory."

Bolt dismissed Joe Hepworth with a look of withering scorn, his Lloyd George number two act. Then he tipped the ballot-box up and the count began. At once two piles began to gather in front of the third scrutineer. Five minutes passed before Bassett got his first vote. Joe Hepworth cheered ironically. It was another sign of nerves.

As the piles for Pam and Westwood began to mount in equal size, Joe Hepworth's mouth went dry with tension. He knew he wasn't often wrong, but he might have misjudged Pam's popularity badly.

But it cheered him that Pam was first to the 20-mark. The natural optimism of his nature asserted itself, a warm glow of confidence settling his stomach. But Westwood's first 20 followed at once. Bassett was never in contention.

The agile fingers went on with their monotonous task. It was difficult to persuade oneself that what was taking place was an election which might decide who was to lead Britain for the next five years. But Joe Hepworth knew, and with the knowledge grew the guilt. History was being made and he, Joe Hepworth, was a secret part of it, a double-dealing, immoral part of it. Now that the packets of 20 had begun to multiply, he felt a genuine fear. The count seemed to be going slowly: only Joe Hepworth didn't know each slip was being checked against forgery.

Westwood's votes were growing alarmingly. Pam Bruce was already trailing with the figures Westwood 80, Bruce 60. Bassett's first 20 was still to be signalled. Joe Hepworth was no longer in a jeering mood. Could it be that Westwood was stealing votes from both Pam and Bassett? If so, it could be curtains for Pam here and now.

The third scrutineer slipped an elastic-band round another bundle of 20, and said, emotionlessly: "That's Westwood's century."

Because of the dissolution there was no central heating in the Palace of Westminster and committee room 15 was chilly.

Despite the cold, Joe Hepworth felt the sweat bursting out of his pores. He watched the counting fingers with growing apprehension.

One of his major failings as a politician, Arnold Prestcote thought with self-candour, was that he had never had a suspicious mind. It was probably not his biggest defect but, now that it was too late, suspicion had begun to solidify within him.

He was sitting in an otherwise deserted Cabinet Room, recriminating about his past. It showed the state of his mind that every play-back, flickering on memory's screen, was a portrait of a loser.

He rose, thinking now of the present, the battle going on at Westminster in his self-inflicted absence. There was something he had to know, a suspicion which had to be confirmed, either for the worst, or at best, laid to rest. He remained motionless at the double doors a moment, looking back at the pillared room, particularly with sudden anguish at the vacant Prime Ministerial chair. It could never be. History would write him off as a failure.

Firmly he closed the door on the past and walked up the red-carpeted staircase to the flat Janet Hargreaves would be quitting tonight, before the new occupant moved in.

He knocked before he entered. He searched her face for guilt, but found none, only the innocence he had always believed in. He sat down beside her and they were silent a few moments while he contemplated the backs of his hands, resting on his knees. He cleared his throat.

"The battle is on," he said, tentatively.

"But I should think it's really all over – bar the shouting. Isn't Tom Westwood sure to win?"

"So it would seem. But –"

"But what?"

"Oh, the figures, the odds, the permutations, all point the one way. It's just that Joe Hepworth is personally involved in this one. In the last ten years he hasn't lost a vote which mattered, and this one matters an awful lot to him."

"Even Joe Hepworth can't walk on water." She quickly shrugged off any possibility of doubt. He began to fear the worst. She asked: "What influence do you think this morning's revelations about the parentage of Liz Bruce will have?"

"It could be decisive." He was quick to comprehend the significance of the question. "Janet," he said, sadly, "you saw Edwin Battle yesterday? He was here."

"Yes," she said, defiantly, "I saw Battle."

"Then *you* did it," he said. "You gave the story to Edwin Battle." It should have been a question, but he knew the answer.

"Yes," she said, but it wasn't a confession, it was a boast. "Yes, I did it."

With four words, she destroyed the peace of mind he had built up over the past twenty-four hours, the cleansing which had followed his honest admission of defects and failings, the voluntary abandonment of ambition and responsibility. In whatever evil she had done, he was implicated because she had done it in *his* defence, an act of malice and revenge. Now his sense of peace – the acceptance that he had always been a maybe man, a perhaps man, but never a clear Yes or No man – was destroyed.

"I have shocked you?" But she had no regrets, no compunctions.

"Yes, you've shocked me."

"You just gave up," she said, accusingly. "Someone had to hit back at your enemies."

"In politics, Janet, it's a Machiavellian belief that some man must be ruined for the good of others."

"I know all about *The Prince*, Arnold. I lived with one of his students for a lifetime. And Joe Hepworth was his hangman. He was your enemy, Arnold. You should be cheering. Your trouble was that you were too scrupulous."

"I wouldn't be too ashamed of that as a political epitaph." He had prided himself that, up to now, he had gone out with dignity. But to her, dignity equated with timidity or cowardice. Up to now, he had been prepared to admit that ever since he went to the Treasury, his political career had been downward. But only those fit for power were humble enough to fear their unsuitability. Sometimes greatness had to be thrust upon them.

"Well, I'm not made like that. I couldn't let you abdicate without striking back."

After all, he confessed, he *had* fled the field. Wilson had stood against Gaitskell at his first attempt knowing that he would be defeated; Herbert Morrison had stood despite the pleas of his friends who didn't want his Cockney heart to be broken; even blabbermouth Brown had fought Wilson at the expense of his colossal ego. After all, *they* had possessed the courage to stare defeat in the face. They had met triumph and disaster and treated them as imposters just the same.

"I expect you despise me," he said. "After all, I did run away."

"I love you," she said. "That's why I sent for Edwin Battle."

Love? How could he, an experienced politician, a supposed expert in the judgment of human conduct, love a woman for years and yet not penetrate her depths, the subtleties of the hidden mind? He was completely shaken by her sadism, directed against Joe Hepworth and Pam Bruce; and the determination with which she pursued Hargreaves to the very grave.

Once again his damnable honesty intervened. He still had to

face the fact that she had conspired with Edwin Battle, not to appease her own injuries, but to avenge the affronts to Arnold Prestçote's dignity, to repay Joe Hepworth for snuffing out his hopes.

"You were always too generous to your enemies, Arnold."

"If that means I was weak, I won't deny it." He felt the shame as he donned his hair-shirt. "I should have quit after the Treasury fiasço but I didn't want to go out like that. I should have realised Hargreaves was giving me a title without power. He saw that I never took any part in the decision-making. My only job was to stand at the Despatch-Box every Thursday and announce the business for next week"

"But before you abdicate, Arnold, you have one last duty." The hard, inflexible note was back in her voice. She hadn't yet completed her revenge, he thought sadly.

"I've finished," he said, and only after he had spoken the words, he felt instinctively his last note of resolution would have a comic ending. "Tonight, I tell the winner I don't want to be considered for any office."

"But first, you have a national duty to perform."

"National duty?" He waited, with caution for her to disclose more of her disfiguring hatred for Joe Hepworth and Pam Bruce.

"You know any administration led by Pam Bruce would merely be a perpetuation of Joe Hepworth's power. You are the one man of substance who opted out freely. That puts you above the battle. Your colleagues would respect your counsel."

"You mean. . . ?" He paused interrogatively, but he feared he knew the answer.

"You must come out publicly in favour of Westwood."

"Janet," he protested, "that could be a kiss of death. They would tell me to mind my own business. You know the Party – one man, one vote."

"You under-estimate your influence, Arnold. The Party knows you've been victimised and treated shabbily. You've always put country before Party and Party before self. You've been a sportsman."

He laughed, bitterly. He knew what effective politicians thought of sportsmanship: it was simply the lack of the killer instinct and the will to win; an absence of the essential immoral fibre.

"All you have to do is to ring the Press Association. That's what I ask." There was a note of command, an authority behind the "I" which suggested she was not asking, but insisting. There was a threat, withheld, but in reserve. "It would be on the news, in time to influence the ballot."

He was already struggling with his conscience. He realised for the first time that it was not public life to which she had objected, it was political life tied to a man who shamed her by his sexual philandering. She had a personal avidity for power. She went on insisting: "It's your patriotic duty."

This time the threat was naked. At risk was the understanding that they would spend the rest of their days together, days shared between his flat within the sound of division bells, and his home in the country. But she was demanding her price: first he must yield his entrenched neutrality and join in her conspiracy of vengeance. He knew – they both knew – that his need of her was greater than her need of him. He ought to resist, his sense of decency and fair play insisted on that. He ought to convince her that, merely by his death, Hargreaves had atoned, wiped his slate clean, paid his debt to society in general, and Janet and Arnold Prestcote in particular. The silence – lengthening between them, had become an ultimatum – intervene or get out of my life.

"Well?" She made it clear she had given him sufficient time. He must decide now.

"I could announce I don't intend to stand for office again and let it be known I am personally voting for Westwood. It would be folly to go further than that."

It was, he knew with self-disgust, one of his infernal compromises; the same kind of compromise which had haunted his political career. But it sufficed.

"That's all I ask," she said, exhaling a long breath of triumph. "That should be enough to make absolutely sure."

He did not answer. He could justify his concession without

staining himself with her motive. Joe Hepworth had fought a dirty campaign. But then, he remembered with crippling impartiality, so had Janet Hargreaves in association with Edwin Battle. In justifying his action to his conscience, he vowed it would be the last defeat of his honour. After his call to the Press Association his political career would be over. He would become a singularly unimportant man.

"Do it now," she said, and he realised that if he had become Party leader and, by some miracle, Prime Minister, he would have had to accept a power-sharing role. She would have been the dominant partner, a second Lady Falkender. She would have manipulated him. He devised his statement.

He made the call as she listened. The News Editor gave him a sympathetic ear. In a few moments, the news would be teleprinted into newspaper offices in Fleet Street and throughout the provinces. Through Reuter, it would travel round the world via satellite. For a while at least, Arnold Prestcote was still an international figure.

He hung up. He had a sense of finality. He had severed the umbilical cord which had joined him to the political womb.

Six of the buggers ratted, Joe Hepworth thought, seething with suppressed rage. The figures of the ballot were burnt deep in his brain:

Tom Westwood, 126;

Pam Bruce, 121;

Eric Bassett, 30; Spoilt papers, 3.

He stared down at the division list on his desk, trying to probe the anonymity of the six presumed Bruce supporters who, according to his calculations, must have turned their coats and voted Westwood.

By now he was over the first stunning shock and his thoughts were on revenge. Pam, sitting in the visitor's chair in his office, had taken it well. Here, deeply entrenched from the outside world, in the bunker-like security, they could be honest. She hadn't expected to win in her heart. She was already resigned.

"So much for fanciful dreams of power. I warned you, Joe. I

should have obeyed my woman's instinct and stood down. The Labour Party isn't ready for a woman leader."

"Don't talk to me about a woman's instinct," he said, bitterly. "It was Janet Hargreaves' instinct which caused this upset."

It was, he thought, more than just an upset. It was a body blow. But the secret knowledge of his own plans kept hope still alive, if not buoyant.

"Come, Joe, you've got to face it now. I've already lost. I want to throw my hand in. The only dignified thing to do now is to give Westwood a walk-over. It would be in the interests of unity."

At first her words did not penetrate his enraged mind. He was deeply preoccupied analysing the list, head low over the ticks and crosses in the margins, almost as if he was smelling out treachery. Then the words sank in.

"You're mad," he exploded. "You mean you would let yourself be deflected because of one dirty trick, and a slice of bad luck. We've only lost the first round."

"Joe," she asked, quietly, "are you thinking of me? The Party? The nation? Or of Joe Hepworth and his glory?"

"Damn it," he said, "I'm thinking of all those things. But most of all, I'm thinking of you, Pam. I never work on false hopes. We had more than reasonable expectations and something's gone sadly wrong. But I'll find out what it is. I'll go through the list with a small-tooth comb and recover the votes we were promised. It's going to be closer than I thought, but we'll win."

"And how will we do that, Joe? Or, would it be best if I didn't ask? Is it that the Chief Whip moves in a mysterious way his wonders to perform?"

The worry was still in her mind. She was obviously thinking back on all the times she had given him her absolute trust, accepting the benefits which had accrued, without another thought. He realised she was questioning for the first time, the wisdom of having allowed him so much control over her political career.

"To me," she said, "It seems a matter of simple arithmetic. Westwood will scoop up the majority of Bassett's votes and I shall be left trailing."

"Pam," he implored, "trust me a little longer. No one has the feel of the Parliamentary Party at his finger-tips more than I do, not even Nick Hayling. And anyone who relates simple arithmetic to this Party is a fool."

"That wasn't exactly a gallant compliment to my intelligence, Joe."

"I'm sorry, Pam. But you're a woman, and all women have illusions. So let's hear no further nonsense of quitting."

Now he wanted her to go because he needed complete freedom to think. He had suddenly become uneasy before her clear gaze. He needed solitude. He needed to let off steam. He needed, most of all, to identify and crucify the defectors and waverers.

"Pam, there hasn't been much time for making up minds firmly. Believe me when I say a lot of people might change their votes next time round. Would I risk making a fool out of you?"

"I know you wouldn't risk making a fool of yourself," she said, with a penetration which surprised him. "But *I'm* not a quitter either."

He began to breathe more freely. He hadn't expected a total revolt from Pam. She was an experienced politician true, not an innocent; but he was accustomed to her immediate acceptance of his advice and coercion. In a way, she was under an obligation to him because of his love. Because of her rigid honesty it was essential she should know nothing of his real plans. She must still have absolute confidence that he would do nothing to smear her good name.

She got up and he walked her to the door. But for once, neither made the movement towards the ritual parting kiss.

"Remember," he said, "behave normally. Chat with your friends when you meet. But don't solicit votes. Leave the prostitution to me. I'm more experienced."

"If I'm going through with it Joe, it's mainly for you. I know you've taken this ballot as a personal challenge." He couldn't cite the evidence for hope because she would never condone. It would be the end of their association, or any feeling she had for him. She turned at the door.

"Do you realise," she said, "win or lose, I shall have to shake Tom Westwood's hand."

"It will be for the sake of the party. You'll have to sink your personal feelings."

The Party. It came first, Joe Hepworth thought. Behind the unremitting bickering and struggle for power; personal animosities, hatreds, cynicisms, intrigues and character assassinations; all bore the same unnatural love for the ugly, monstrous, inefficient confusion they called the Movement, that coalition of inimical persons and bodies with the death wish. They all shared it: Hepworth, Bassett, Bruce, Westwood, Donovan, Prestcote, Bolt. Ramsay MacDonald had once shared it, with Snowden and Jimmy Thomas.

When she had gone, he sat at his desk, nervously drumming his fingers on his desk-top, waiting for Donovan to report. He was still wondering whether there had been a switch of votes because of the scandal, or whether his original estimate, based in part on Donovan's secret reports, had been wrong? The possibility poisoned his suspicious mind. Had Donovan done the dirty on him? Had he proved to be a double-double agent?

In choosing Donovan he had gone for pedigree. But pedigree wasn't reliable. Now, in his doubt, he remembered another blue-blooded aristocrat. "We are the masters now," he had declaimed, after the holocaust of 1945. But the red in the corpuscles hadn't lasted, and he was soon back with his spiritual masters. Sir Shortly-Floorcross.

The telephone rang. It was Donovan, dead on time. At least he was prepared to answer for his performance. He asked harshly; "What the devil went wrong? Our figures forecast a majority of 7 for Pam. How could it have possibly turned out like this?"

"That's exactly what I'm asking myself. I had 6 down as waverers. There must have been a dozen."

"And they wavered the wrong way. Donovan – " There was a dangerous cutting-edge to his voice – "you haven't been double-crossing me? If I thought – "

"Joe – " There was a genuine wound in the sound of the voice, identifiable even through the mechanical earpiece. "I've done exactly what you asked – 100 per cent."

He was reassured, he could be contrite. "Sorry, old man. The figures had me rattled. Can you identify the rats who deserted?"

"It must come down to the ones I had down as waverers. I told you I couldn't regard them as certainties."

"Give me the names again." He picked up pad and pencil and wrote down the names at Donovan's dictation. He knew them all well as he put a black mark against them in the margin of the division list. Each mark had the same significance as the cross put on suspect trees by the lumberjack, the death sentence by felling. Unless they toed the line in the final ballot, they would have no political future in the event of a Bruce victory. They were all trying to pick the winner, they were all in need of persuasion. All right, he would persuade them Pam was going to win, and they would make it so.

"Go to work on them," said Hepworth. "Leave the others and concentrate on these 12. Things aren't so black as they look. Believe me – " He had a more optimistic feeling when he thought of McBrane and the inter-cities speeding with their lost votes towards the Border. "Believe me, I've taken other precautions."

"Thumb-screws?"

"So far I've been decent. You have no problems? You still understand the terms?"

"Absolutely. If Westwood suspects, or questions me, I'm on my own. You can depend on me."

"I'm not a fretter by nature. And I know you're tough." His mind was already at work, digging into the mental files of the placemen, recalling the black marks against them, preparing to confront them with their delinquencies. They could have it either way: drowned in Bollinger or screwed by the balls. He split up the names on separate pieces of paper and went into the outer office. He handed out the names and gave detailed instructions, in each case based on personal knowledge, how to apply the pressure. Finally, he instructed the Whips' runners that when any one of the 12 signed for his second ballot paper, he was to be sent into Joe's inner office.

He knew he could expect efficiency and obedience. And *he* would have the last word. He went back to his office, satisfied that everything possible had been done to repair the damage.

He sat back in his chair, brooding, head resting back in the palms of his hands, looking at the wall. For him, the crucial moments would come when the delinquents, if delinquents they admitted to be, faced him across the desk and he told them privately, one by one, just why they would be well advised to put their cross against the name of Bruce.

Richard Westwood became a national figure at 5.40pm.

It was then that Angela Rippon announced, as the first item in the early-evening news bulletin, that he had donated the whole of his personal fortune to the Labour Party's general election fund.

In her cool, modulated voice, she sketched his career: he was the thirty-years-old son of Tom Westwood, the distinguished Cabinet Minister, who was favourite to win tonight's final ballot for the Party leadership, victory in which would lead, temporarily at least, to 10 Downing Street.

Although a professed Socialist, the son had made his fortune and a reputation in the City as a tough, ruthless tycoon. He had skilfully survived the collapse in the property boom and, until today's divestment of his wealth, had lived an elegant life-style which had led to his estrangement from his father.

It was at this critical stage in the political career of his father that he had made his dramatic gift to Party funds, and declared his intention of devoting the rest of his life to the welfare of the Labour movement.

"Over now to Transport House, where Mr Tom Westwood is about to open a Press conference. . . ."

Late arrivals were forcing their way into the crowded room, the cameras were still being moved about. Tom Westwood spoke: calm, confident, resonant.

"First question, please."

"How do you feel towards your son, Mr Westwood?"

"Naturally, I am delighted. And proud."

"Of course, one can assume the estrangement has ended?"

"What would you think?" Tom Westwood paused. For a moment emotion showed. No one could say whether it was professionalism or genuine, but the voice *did* quaver: "I had always regarded myself as a hard-headed realist but I must confess I am deeply moved."

"Have you seen your son today?"

"Not yet. We have spoken on the telephone."

"Was Liz Bruce with him at the time?"

Stony eyes. Frozen face.

"No comment."

"It has been stated that the reason for the estrangement was that you disapproved of his activities in the City?"

"My convictions about the unacceptable face of capitalism are well known. I could not accept double standards in judging my son."

"Mr Westwood, if I can repeat the question in another way: Do you approve of this widely publicised affair between your son and Liz Bruce?"

"No comment again."

"But you are public figures. The public is surely entitled to a comment."

"My son is not a public figure. Nor is Miss Bruce. They are each well over the age of consent and neither Mrs Bruce nor I would attempt to interfere in their private lives."

An arm was raised. Tom Westwood pointed. The cameras zoomed in on the rotund figure – unflattering head, golden hairs sparsely sprouting from its crown, squashed strawberry nose. The eyes were almost lost in rolls of fat. Edwin Battle spoke, a whisky-laden voice:

"If I can do it without offence, I would like to ask the question I am sure is in everybody's mind: Was your son's dramatic generosity the result of an appeal, pressure, or collusion, for which you or your agents were responsible?"

"I am grateful to you. It gives me the opportunity of saying categorically that the answer is No. The promissary note simply arrived on my desk, totally unsolicited."

The question was inserted into the proceedings so adroitly, the answer seemed so natural, that none of the non-participants suspected they were the victims of a well-known Parliamentary trick – the planted question. Tom Westwood wanted the collusion possibility firmly denied before the final ballot was too far gone, and television was the widest and most effective of the media.

Edwin Battle had been only too happy to oblige. Most of his success came from a wide range of contacts. And what better contact could a man want than a future Prime Minister who could be reminded of an obligation, a favour granted? Tom Westwood's gain would be that it spiked Joe Hepworth's obvious and desperate retaliation: that Richard Westwood's conversion was too timely to be true.

On the screen, Angela Rippon was back in the studio. "And now for further news of the fighting in the Middle East. . . ."

8

Thomas Arkwright surveyed the scene of his assignment with the apprehension natural to an outside commentator just before going into action under the all-intrusive eye of the cameras. It was natural because of the known and unknown hazards, the presentiment that something was bound to go wrong.

Standing in the dusk of evening at the open gates leading into New Palace Yard, he watched the unit putting the finishing touches to their preparations. Before him, like a reflection of the moon on water – he had already filed the phrase in his mind for use to cover up a silent moment in his commentary – was the illuminated clock-face of Big Ben's tower. The time glowed: in five minutes the final ballot would have closed and Thomas Arkwright would be on the air.

Tucked away at the entrance to Westminster Hall was the mobile unit, stuffed with electronics and monitor sets. Seeing it, fearing his commitment to the next hour, Arkwright felt the preliminary flutter in the stomach, then the mouth going dry with the familiar symptoms of tension, the fear of the freeze-up. It was his recurrent nightmare: Thomas Arkwright with anguished face, mouth opening and closing but wordlessly, like the fish faces behind the glass of the tanks in the aquarium. It was time to run his tests.

He pulled up the aerial of his radio link: "Calling committee corridor, calling Tim Mondale. Do you read?"

Instant relief. Mondale answered clearly. There was no static. The voice was only slightly distorted.

"Committee corridor here. You're loud and clear."

"Good-oh. What's happening?"

"The cloth-capped brigade is still gathering in the Grand Committee Room. There's going to be a fair old turn-out. The place is already full of tension and atmosphere."

"I'm sure. The trouble is how to convey that to the couldn't-care-less British public. Could you give me something early? Like, for instance, the tramp-tramp of the heavy hob-nailed boots of the proletariat?"

"Don't mock this historic moment. Later on I'll fill in with interviews from some of the more important personalities. Stand by for sound."

Arkwright waited with professional patience. He would need some drama, not chit-chat from some has-been politician. He had to make it exciting, yet he was cut off from the action, the scene, the colours, and the two principal characters. From him it would be nothing but a second-hand narrative. And he would have to cling on verbally a long time for the declaration, the moment of truth.

Suddenly Mondale sent him the first background noise from the committee floor. A little distorted but clearly recognisable as excitement, the swell and ebb, the lap-lap of waves of talk, the chatter of perhaps one-hundred-and-fifty men and women, falling like waves on a distant seashore.

"Well, did you receive?"

"Great. The noises off are okay."

"The door of Room 14 was still ajar. I inserted the magic mike through the slit and hey presto! There'll be such a jam later I can't promise to do the same with the declaration. If I could – "

"Kudos for you?" What for Thomas Arkwright? Nothing, but he was glad for Tim Mondale. Congratulations couldn't go to a finer operator and friend. If he could pull it off it would dramatise the commentary's end which, he felt pessimistically, would otherwise lack the essential reality. "When do you expect the result?"

"Well, there are three scrutineers. It shouldn't take them more than an hour, probably less."

"Let's hope so. It will be a drag up to then. Have you any

problems, Tim?"

"None here. I'm looking for Mikardo to find out what odds he's giving on his book. You've got the shitty end, friend."

"Yes," he said, grimly. "I wonder why? At least you're under cover. It looks like rain. That's all I need."

"With your ability, old man, what can go wrong?"

"Ability arseholes."

"What's it like down there?"

"Nothing more than the usual. The crowd of open-mouthed yobbos which gathers every time a camera appears, a portly constable on duty at the gates grooming himself for the salute when the car goes to the Palace, and cars arriving for the declaration. When I get desperate I'll come back to you to help me spread the shit. Signing off."

He shut down the pocket transmitter and saw from the moonlike face that he had only a few minutes to wait. Long enough to fret about the high casualty rate in outside broadcasts, the regular arrival of new faces, and equally regular disappearance of his contemporaries. It didn't take long for faces to wear out on an abrasive public. He just had time to brood about the wear and tear on nerves, and the unpredictable accidents which could ruin a broadcast. The gremlins.

Out there, all over the world, linked by satellite, were the waiting unseen faces, including those who so much disliked him, either his face or his voice, that they had taken the trouble to write to the mighty Corporation to say so. The Thomas Arkwright hate club. Fuck them for a start.

He got the signal. He warned Tim Mondale. He cleared his throat. He was ready. He drew a shuddering breath and faced the camera. He felt the flutter in his stomach steady and, miraculously, his nervous tension vanished. At once he felt secure in his television personality, fluently launched on his mentally prepared introduction, words and sentences lining up well drilled, like the guardsmen on parade along the road in Bird-Cage-Walk. His mind was working smoothly on its double-dimensional circuit: now he was skilfully setting the scene and he could do that with half a mind. He was confident, like a coxswain who had safely taken the lifeboat through the offshore breakers, so that the danger of capsizing could be forgotten.

"Inside the Commons building, together on the committee corridor, with other Lobby correspondents, is my colleague, Tim Mondale. We are in direct radio contact and I now propose to go over to him and find out exactly what the position is." Up with the aerial. "Are you there, Tim?"

"Yes, Thomas. I'm here."

The viewers couldn't see him; cut off from the monitors and the Commons closed circuit television in the mobile unit, Thomas Arkwright couldn't see him either. But he could visualise what the viewers could see: Thomas Arkwright live, Big Ben tower with the illuminated clock-face, New Palace Yard and the still picture of Tim Mondale, up in the left-hand corner of the screen.

"Can you tell us what is going on at the moment, Tim?"

"You could not have come over at a better moment, Thomas. Mr Adam Bolt, the chief scrutineer, has just emerged from the lift on the corridor. He is followed by his two assistant scrutineers, and a small retinue.

"One of them is Mr Nick Hayling, the Parliamentary Party's secretary. It is he who has been advising the Party in the unprecedented situation which followed the first death of a Labour Prime Minister in office. He has organised this emergency ballot with an efficiency which is generously acknowledged even by those original opponents of the decision.

"Also in the group is Mr Joe Hepworth, Chief Whip of the Party during the past ten years. He is undoubtedly one of Westminster's strongest personalities, the human dynamo who has for years been thrusting Pam Bruce into the limelight. Tonight, his ambitions for her might be realised. But on closer investigation, Mr Hepworth looks tired. And, more important, anxious. Is that an indication how close the result will be?

"The group has now disappeared through the door to committee room 15, Mr Hayling carrying the ballot-box. Behind that closed door, the count will take place. Meanwhile, the excitement is building up in the Grand Committee Room. By now there must be two hundred people in the room and the chatter is loud and continuous. It is already standing room only in the room in which so many historic decisions have been taken by all three Parliamentary parties. . . ."

Relaxed, now completely composed, Thomas Arkwright let Tim Mondale have his head. It reduced the pressure on him and the fewer words he spoke, the less the danger that he would blow it.

"Dear old Adam Bolt," said Arnold Prestcote, affectionately. "He'll make the most of his job but he's really past it."

"Knowing that, you chose him to be your champion at the Party meeting," she said, accusingly. They were sharing an after-dinner drink in the lounge of Prestcote's Gayfere Street flat, watching Thomas Arkwright on the screen, and listening to Tim Mondale's simultaneous report. "Couldn't you have found a younger and more influential backer?"

"It wouldn't have made a scrap of difference to the result," he said, loyally. Once a friend of Arnold Prestcote's, a friend for life. "I could have found someone younger, a more forceful advocate. But no one who appealed to all factions of the Party. After all, mine was really a claim for sympathy, a call to sentiment. We were beaten from the start."

"I shall never be reconciled," she said, bitterly, and he realised once more, how little he had really understood her nature during all the years of Hargreaves' rule and their own unconsummated love. "You've always been too modest. Your colleagues took you at your own value."

"Looking back," he agreed, "I've no doubt you're right." He had never had the self-confidence of strength. Joe Hepworth's contempt for his soft core was the biggest indictment of failure: he had not even merited the respect of his enemy. He had survived in politics, but he had never possessed the brutality to do better than survive. He had never possessed the guts to butcher colleagues in a struggle for mastery. Had any man with the same original handicaps of conscience and scruple ever reached the top? Had there ever been an *honest* ruler?

"What I hate about Joe Hepworth," she said, "is how much

he hurt you. He and Hargreaves were always plotting to thwart you. Basically, they feared your honesty."

"Believe me," he said, truly, "I am no longer hurt. All that is in the past." If this was hurt, sitting in his own home, in a twilight glowing from the television tube, close to a talented and beautiful woman he was now free to love, hurt was peace and pleasure. He warmed himself at her glow.

"I will make you a forecast, Arnold. Whoever wins will send Joe Hepworth for you. Or his successor."

He laughed. He felt indulgent towards her. For all her intuition, which had proved uncanny, for all the surprise of her political judgment, she still lacked the essential experience, the professional prescience.

"For me?" Hadn't they gone to extreme lengths to remove him first, to make a mockery of his feeble attempt to take power by right of title deeds? "I can't imagine anything less likely. In any case I have already announced my retirement."

"Despite that, don't you realise why, Arnold? Because you are still of use to them. They are both shrewd enough to know they will need the extra respectability you would bring to any Administration, the decency and respectable façade."

"You mean *my* honesty?" He laughed, cynically. They called honesty weakness in their language. "Joe Hepworth has never found any difficulty in faking honesty up to now."

But once again he felt warned not to disregard her intuition. Wasn't it she who really possessed the political prescience? It was suddenly too easy to see her being right. It was another confirmation that, if he had outflanked his enemies and seized power, she would have shared it avidly. No, damn it, she would have dominated it because she was the stronger character. All, he thought, had happened for the best. She was watching the screen with growing impatience.

"Is it possible they're having to have a recount?"

"It's certainly possible. Perhaps it's just Adam stringing the tension out. It gives him the feeling of authority."

He reached out and took her hand. He felt the warmth from the current of her blood. Once more he was glad he had given notice to quit. But what would he do if she was right, and Joe

Hepworth or his successor appeared with an offer of an elder statesman's post? Would he still owe allegiance to a country which never honoured politicians? Could he sulk in his tent? Suddenly, it was all very simple: he didn't know – the story of his life. But now it really didn't matter because he knew it would be Janet who made the decision.

He saw that, on the screen, Thomas Arkwright was still talking. There was, as yet, no sign of a declaration. And, as far as Arnold Prestcote was concerned, he wouldn't mind if there was no decision for a thousand years.

While the outside camera team relaxed, Thomas Arkwright had been listening to Tim Mondale. By now he must be praying for relief. He gave him the badly needed feed:

"I suppose the candidates are at the meeting, Tim?"

"I know Pam Bruce is because I saw her arrive."

"How did she appear? Confident?"

"She declined to discuss her prospects. One can hardly blame her, so close to the result. Like all experienced politicians, she is pretty good at hiding her real feelings. It must be quite an ordeal for her."

They kept up the friendly rally with experienced skill, filling in the time, feeding on each other's thoughts and ideas, seizing them like life-lines. They had always worked well together.

"Are you still there, Tim?"

"Yes, indeed Thomas. And in the last few moments the sense of expectation has risen. The count has been going on a long time and the result cannot be long delayed. The Grand Committee Room is jam-packed. Indeed, the overflow extends into the committee corridor. It really is one of those smoke-filled rooms about which one reads in novels on political intrigue.

"But the counting is still going on, almost certainly an indication that the result is close. One can imagine the scene in room 15, the two piles of votes accumulating, perhaps at the rate of one for each for minutes at a time. First one candidate slightly ahead, then the other. In the end, everyone knows, there cannot be more than a handful of votes separating the two candidates."

"Wasn't it Sir Winston Churchill who once said one is enough, Tim?"

"Yes, it was Winston." Hoarseness suddenly afflicted Tim Mondale's voice. It rose an octave. "Thomas . . . Thomas . . . I think. . . . Yes, the count is indeed over. The door has opened. We shall have the result in a few minutes now."

There was a brief, pregnant silence, then the sounds of excitement relayed by Tim Mondale from the committee corridor.

"As I speak, Mr Adam Bolt is leading out the little group of officials. It is moving towards the chairman's entrance to the Grand Committee Room, no more than a dozen paces. The step is solemn and the faces are inscrutable. This suggests to me that all have been lectured by Mr Bolt against communicating the result to us prematurely. He is a stickler for convention. It is his duty to convey the figures to the Parliamentary Party's chairman, and Mr Golding's duty to announce them to the meeting. The figures Mr Bolt carries himself, on a single sheet of paper, the certificate of the scrutineers . . .

"However, there is one clue which might be significant. Although the face of Joe Hepworth, Pam Bruce's champion, is expressionless, it is covered in sweat. That could be just an indication of stress or strain, or it could mean a Westwood victory. But there is no other clue . . .

"The chairman's door has now closed on the group. I am moving as close as I can get through the crowd to the door of the Members' entrance. Although there is no hope of getting my microphone into the room to record Mr Golding's actual announcement, I shall be so positioned that I can relay it the moment I hear from those nearest the door.

"The procedure, incidentally, is the same as at the declaration of the poll at a Parliamentary election. Names and votes are called out in alphabetical order. Therefore, the important point to bear in mind is that all experts who have studied the result of the first ballot, and judged the likely distribution of Mr Bassett's vote, are agreed that Mrs Bruce cannot expect to win with fewer than 140 votes. . . . Now the room is absolutely hushed – a sign that the chairman has risen and the result is imminent. Out here, in the corridor, forgive the cliché, the proverbial pin could be heard to drop. . . ."

Suddenly, there was a great roar over the radio link. Then the voice of Tim Mondale broke through – high, hoarse and cracked:

Mrs Pam Bruce, 131 votes. . . .

The rest of the announcement was interrupted, drowned by an even bigger roar, a spontaneous acclamation for the victor, whoever it was – the open throats, the banging of fists on desk tops, the drumming of heels on the floor. . . .

It had started to rain and, outside, without shelter, Thomas Arkwright was a bitter man. He was performing the menial task he most despised, thrusting the microphone into grinning, idiotic faces and asking the asinine questions: "Do you think the better candidate won?" "Would the victor make a good Prime Minister if Labour won the election?" "What do you think of the result?"

He went on doing his job mechanically, trying to forget that he was getting drenched and trying to hide his misery. Not for him the cosy, warm studio, and the privilege of hectoring and bullying the politicians without mercy. Thomas Arkwright would never be a Dimbleby, a Robin Day or a David Frost. His job was a mere current affairs interviewer on a daily roster, sometimes standing for hours out in the pissing rain. His role was to ask stupid questions and receive moronic answers, and accept them without answering back. So he went on with his job, inwardly rejecting the politicians' deceit when they pretended to have faith in the vision and wisdom of the British electorate. They knew it was all cock: ask the country to choose between a genius and a charlatan, and it would infallibly fall for the charlatan.

At last. With relief he detected signs of activity beyond the arch leading to Speaker's Court. He was able to ignore the stupid faces and turn again to the microphone.

"I see that the Prime Ministerial car is being prepared. In a few minutes the victor will be *en route* to the Palace.

Everything is happening according to ritual. The driver is opening the car door . . . no time is lost, the Queen has no doubt been telephoned with the result and knows whom to expect. She mustn't be kept waiting."

The camera was pointing at the exit from Speaker's Court as the car emerged, black and glistening in the rain. It panned with the car, converging with it towards the open gates, and the crowds on the pavement sheltered beneath umbrellas. The car slowed at the gates for the driver to investigate the traffic; the caped policeman walked sturdily into the road and held up an officious hand to hold back the vehicles heading for Parliament Square. The crowd surged forward as the car momentarily stopped and the Press cameras flashed.

In the back seat, Pam Bruce raised a hand and smiled a tired smile. At her side, Joe Hepworth, the real victor, was not so restrained. His grin was a positive gloating. The car surged forward.

Flooding with relief and exhaustion, a wet, disillusioned Thomas Arkwright began his finale: "Well, there it is, Pam Bruce rides in triumph to her appointment with destiny. In three weeks time it will be your responsibility to decide whether her tenure of office is to go down in history as the shortest ever of a British Prime Minister. This is Thomas Arkwright, outside the Palace of Westminster, returning you to the studio."

"Well," said Joe Hepworth, ecstatically, "We did it."

"You mean *you* did it, Joe. The question is – How?"

"I had it safely sewn up all the time, Pam," he boasted. How had better remain his secret. He suddenly realised that, despite the closeness of their bodies in the car, she was mentally distancing herself from him. There was a brief, penetrating silence except for the hiss-hiss of tyres on the wet, glittering road as they approached the Cenotaph. He knew he would have to beware of the residue of innocence and scruple still left to her, despite all the years at Westminster under his tutelage. He took her hand. It did not resist but it was cold, and did not respond. They passed the end of Downing Street, to which they would soon be returning in triumph.

"I'm sorry if I appear ungrateful, Joe, but I tell you now I never expected to win. I would rather have lost with dignity and honour, than find out later I won by shabby or dubious means." Like many others, she had begun to ponder on the meaning of the missing votes.

"There is no honour or dignity in defeat, Pam," he said, harshly, going back to the political primer, the first lesson of his political doctrine. "Honour, integrity, principle, loyalty –" He rolled the words off his tongue contemptuously. "Fine-sounding sentiments, like patriotism – and all counterfeit coins of a debased currency."

"Oddly enough, at this moment, I feel desperately sorry for Tom Westwood."

Then she was clearly appalled by her own admission. She would soon get over her attack of scruples, he thought, easy in his conscience. The car had stopped for the red lights at the end of Whitehall. The neon of Trafalgar Square was on and she was recognised despite the rivulets of rain on the car windows. Congratulatory hands were waved and she waved back. She had got the habit of power already, she thought. As Joe would find.

"Your reputation is absolutely safe," he said. But he wondered suddenly whether he could be so sure. If the truth of the McBrane deal ever leaked, could he protect her good name. Would the Party be satisfied with one disgrace? In the world's judgment wouldn't she be blamed for giving Joe Hepworth, the professional fixer, the known master of deceit, the unsupervised responsibility for her campaign? The lights changed, the car turned left and passed under Admiralty Arch.

"Joe," she said, tentatively, "you know what they all say about us at Westminster?"

"Pam, you know I know what everyone says about everyone at Westminster."

"They say that, without you, I would be nothing. That I'm your captive."

"That's only envy."

She went on, as if she hadn't heard his airy dismissal.

"That's why it can't be allowed to go on, Joe. It's better that I tell you now, Joe, so there can be no possibility of any misunderstanding in the future. It can no longer be a free hand, everything on your terms, your fist on the pen."

He watched the trees lining The Mall passing across the rain-pocked glasswork. He looked at her and saw a stranger. She had never challenged his authority, guidance or judgment. "If we win the election, I intend to work through a caucus within the Cabinet. It will consist of me, you, Tom Westwood and the Lord Chancellor." He was still staring at his former pupil with wonder. The pupil had suddenly changed into the mistress. She added casually: "Oh, and I shall include Prestcote, if he can be persuaded to join us."

"Pam – " He felt the foul taste of degradation. "Prestcote? The man's been totally unnerved by his rejection."

"He'll recover once he's got over his natural disappointment. He has sagacity and experience to contribute."

"But he's already announced he has no wish to serve."

"You can be very persuasive, Joe."

He couldn't believe it: she was sending him as a special emissary to humiliate him before Prestcote.

"I *can* be persuasive when the occasion merits it." She was forcing him to swallow his own vomit. He couldn't believe that she still wasn't pliable, that he had worked so close to her for a lifetime without realising the full potential of her steeliness. He had guided, coaxed and compelled, and she had always proved compliant. But, she was ready and equipped for power; she no longer needed him as prop. She meant to be in the classic position, able to play one off against the other; she would be the final arbiter, keeping the veto firmly in her own hands.

There was no mistaking the message. She was cutting Joe Hepworth down to size. It made him bitter when he thought of the risks he had run on her behalf. Thank God McBrane couldn't talk without ruining his own cherished reputation for being flintily honest. But the worst of all was to have to be the instrument of Prestcote's restoration.

"Prestcote's only contribution," he said, bitterly, "will be a gut-full of hatred from Janet Hargreaves."

"I hope they will find happiness together. They deserve it."

"I'm afraid I can't be as forgiving as you." He was still shocked at her revolt, the strength of her political will. He still could not accept her clear indication that he would never be more than *one* of her advisers; *one* counsellor, *one* equal amongst other equals. But she had made it clear she would not be a figure-head while Joe Hepworth manipulated the levers of power.

There was silence in the car again but for the click-clack of the windscreen-wipers sheering the streams of rain off the driver's vision. Each time they clicked he saw the flood-lighted Palace growing larger every second. Now he was aware of the distant threat – the day he presented his ultimatum to the campaign committee, the promise to flood Scotland with oil revenues, given without authority.

Well, he thought, nothing was going to spoil this peak of his career. Face the crisis when it came. As for her caucus, it would break up within a week, he would see to that. Joe would fix it.

They approached the gates of the Palace which opened to receive them. He felt her coldness again, she was freezing him out already: he thought of the long line of Chief Whips who had been squeezed dry and then cruelly discarded by Prime Ministers. He knew all about the baseness of ingratitude in politics, none better. His vanity, which had sustained him through his ten years of office, had been suddenly shaken. After all, he was the man who, for Wilson and Hargreaves, had ridden out storm and turmoil in the Chamber; quelled revolts within the Parliamentary Labour Party; arranged crowds to attend open-air meetings; just as he had survived the earlier evil days – Mosley's Olympia, Cable Street, and the other blood-lettings in the East End.

He could boast that he had never lost his nerve and he wasn't going to lose it now because of the coldness of an ungrateful woman. Responsibility would never cripple Joe Hepworth. He would do whatever it was necessary to do, whoever got in his path, friend or foe, whatever the consequences. He was no longer daunted by the risk he bore.

The car pulled up smoothly. A servant emerged, protective

umbrella already hoisted. He opened the door with calm servility. Pam descended, turned her head back at him with a nervous smile. It showed, he thought, complacently; she needed him already.

Joe Hepworth smiled back, his copyright mamba smile, the smile which was suitable for all seasons and all occasions.

On the screen, the Prime Ministerial car was just passing through the open gates into Parliament Square. Pam Bruce was acknowledging the cheers. Liz rose from the settee and switched off. She looked with compassion at his stony face, his fortitude.

"Well, my poor benefactor. Regrets?"

He shook his head violently. "Only for the old man."

She stretched her hands wide. "I'm no hypocrite. But how can I honestly say that I'm sorry." So much for the pact made in the car along Millbank – oh, how many years ago? It would be the height of dishonesty to deny self-interest, to pretend an impossible loyalty to an opponent's cause. In a few minutes she would be the daughter of a Prime Minister. "You still intend to go through with a life's commitment to the Party? It really was a blinding light on the road to Westminster?"

"Don't you feel pride in your mother's achievement?"

"Of course, but it's *her* own thing. I never gave a fig for the Party, the myths, the slogans, the shadow-boxing, the poseurs. As for economics, did you realise that if your fortune was spread over the dole queue it wouldn't amount to more than half-a-quid a head. As for Pam, you mean Joe, don't you?" Thoughtfully, she tapped her white teeth with a red lacquered nail. Two votes. Only two votes. How had the cunning bugger contrived it? "Well, my mourned ex-lover, what the hell are you going to do now?"

She still found it hard to believe in the permanence of his transformation, that he would continue to despise the playboy he had been, that he wouldn't miss the glitter of the world of finance, the self-indulgences money could buy, such as the Jag, and the pleasures of the flesh. How long before the effects of the aversion drug and the nausea worked off, and he thought of Number One again?

"I know I'm out," she said. "You've made that very clear. But you can't fuck Clause Four or the Party manifesto." She clicked her teeth in mock sorrow and he knew how hard she was working to restore his morale. "After all the bed hours I've put into your sex education. You were becoming quite masterful, very inventive."

He smiled bleakly. "Then perhaps you'd better give me a passing-out diploma." She had succeeded in assuaging the pain which had followed the shock announcement. She had admitted the defeat of her body against his father's influence, the family's honoured name in the Party's mythology, continuity of its service in the cause of the have-nots. He was no longer under threat from her sensuality. One pact had been annulled but it had been succeeded by another, a platonic comradeship. Neither of them knew but this, at least, was to last until the end of their lives.

"All I can do," he said, "is to start at the bottom. Dedicate myself. Work at the grass roots. Aim at a seat in the House."

"It might be amusing to start at the top," she said, sardonically. "May I suggest Labour candidate for the Cities of London and Westminster? All your old buddies in the City could rally round and vote you in. Don't think you flushed away your guilt when you pulled the chain on your swag. It's as brutal at Westminster as it is in the City, a pantomime world in which demon kings like Joe cut throats just as he cut your father's. By all means talk morality, integrity, and fighting the good fight. But, for God's sake, don't practise them. No one should know better tonight that there's only one winner. In politics there's no percentage for the loser." She paused reflectively. "You know, that has a familiar ring. I think I picked it up from Joe."

"Liz," he said, abruptly, "I hope you wouldn't be offended if I made you a gift – the Jag?"

Her eyes widened in surprise. Then she said, mockingly: "For services rendered? Redundancy pay? And what will you do? Ride out into the sunrise of your new career on the Tube?"

"Damn it," he said, explosively. "Can't you be serious? You

slip away from everything."

"Not everything. Everything but a hard cock. I'm grateful for one thing at least – you're not leaving me for another woman."

"If bedding was all I wanted, I wouldn't be such a fool as to say No to you. The moment I'm out of the way there'll be a queue. After Chichester's nude is hung, you'll be the most famous beauty in London."

"Why not the whole world," she said, airily. "And you have a glorious future too. Perhaps running the squalid slum of a local party headquarters, grinding the broken-down duplicating machine, falsifying membership figures, selling raffle tickets, and running the weekly bingo for Party funds. And if you ever want a woman there will be big bosomed women welders from the Boilermakers' Union with smelly arm-pits. That's when you'll sigh for your sweet-scented, red-headed, and nubile nympho. Cheer up, it might be worse. You might even have had Joe for a father."

"Why do you keep bringing in Joe? Are you suggesting the ballot was rigged?"

"Of course not. Joe's too clever for anything so unsubtle." Once again she mocked him with her insider's smile. "A fine politician you're going to make. Tell me, what do you think happened to the missing voters?"

"At least give him the benefit of the doubt."

"Oh, I can see you're going to make a great recruit." She tapped his knee with the point of her index finger. "Here cometh the first lesson in politics – never, never give anyone the benefit of the doubt. When in doubt, spray the bullets in the widest possible arc so no possibility of doubt remains. Try again. What happened to the missing voters?"

"They abstained."

"Of course they abstained. But why? The answer's simple. Pressure. And Joe is a walking encyclopaedia about his men's weaknesses and vulnerabilities. He knows who is in danger of being found with a guardsman in the Hyde Park bushes, or importuning in the Gents at Piccadilly underground station. We know from Tom Driberg that it happens, poor sods. One thing is certain: Bassett wouldn't do a deal with Joe. He's too pi."

"If it was one of Joe's dirty tricks, I'm sure your mother wasn't involved."

"That's kind of you. You have one consolation. Pam only holds No 10 on a short lease."

"I know."

If Labour was badly beaten, it would be hard to have returned to the fold in time to share the nadir of a great Movement. But he still had the faith of the novitiate – untested, unshaken, complete.

"Well," she said, firmly, "so this is the end. This is where we part."

He rose, felt in his pocket, took out a bunch of keys, selected two and extracted them from the ring. He handed them to her.

"Ignition and doors. She's yours from now on. I'll send you the log-book."

"If you're sure –"

"I'm sure."

"Then I'll take her, but only on the understanding it's a loan. You might want her back in a few months."

"There's no danger of that."

"It's a proviso that makes me less of a whore."

"Go easy with her. She can be lethal. And I know how you love driving with your foot on the boards. You can do me one last favour."

"All you have to do is ask."

"Drop me off at Transport House first."

"Of course. Give him my genuine condolences. No, damn it, give him my love."

"Love? A Bruce for a Westwood? Tonight of all nights?"

"I've got an intuition. We failed when we tried to bring them together. I have a feeling tonight will prove a reconciliation."

"I only hope you're right."

There was a silence in which both recognised there was nothing further to say, except platitudes. The quicker the parting the better. There was this measure of communication left from the debris of their voluptuous affair, even though it had involved only their bodies.

Outside the flat, he stood on the landing while she locked up, and then they went side by side down the stairs to the street. They were unmolested, abandoned temporarily by the camera and news hounds, who had lifted the siege. With the declaration they were stale news. He also noticed the green Cortina was no longer parked.

She unlocked the car door and slid into the driving-seat. No legal transfer of ownership had ever been so quickly or so informally transacted. She leaned over and unlocked the door on the passenger's side, and he slid in beside her. She paused with her hands on the wheel.

They were still drained of words and emotion. He looked at her and thought he would always remember her like this: radiant with youth and loveliness. He could not visualise her as, with the inevitability of the passage of years, she would become – old and withered, with shrunken, pendulous paps.

There was so much he wanted to say out of gratitude for the gift of her body so freely given. But all he managed was a gruff: "Now remember, you're not on the Brands Hatch circuit."

It was at this precise moment that the true and horrific meaning of the missing green Cortina entered his mind with the speed of light. . . .

His reaction was only human and could not compete. The message sped from his brain, through his blood, down to his arm, through his hand to the fingers. They clutched at her hand, but too late. She turned the ignition key. . . .

There was no introduction to death. It came instantaneously with the thunder of violence, an explosion which shook the whole of Battersea; it came with a flash of light and fire as their dismembered and shredded bodies hurtled upwards and sideways, mingled with the shattered chunks of the Jaguar's bodywork, separated from the twisted wreckage of the chassis.

Together with the echo of the explosion came the tinkling of the showers of glass blasted from the whole street's windows. The echoes died, but the flames burnt on furiously. In the awed silence before the screams of witnesses, the dismembered parts of two once-perfect bodies hung from the bared branches of the trees above, as the leaves fell in showers to cover the blood and flesh and broken glass in a carpet on the street. . . .

A few minutes later, the Night Editor of the *Daily News* received a telephone call. The voice was husky from years on the Guinness as it claimed the credit for the I.R.A. provisionals for the "execution" of Liz Bruce and Richard Westwood. The Night Editor rang Scotland Yard. Then he told Edwin Battle, and gave him a quarter-of-an-hour to rewrite the whole of his story of the triumph of Pam Bruce into the story of the tragedy of Pam Bruce and Tom Westwood.

9

The ringing tone went on and on. Liz did not answer.

Joe Hepworth said: "There's no one at the flat. Liz must be on her way over."

Pam, newly composed after the ritual acceptance of the public's cheers as she stood on the threshold of No 10 on her return from the Palace, said: "That's a pity. After this morning's publicity I particularly wanted to face everybody together – the three of us. From now on she needs a father's authority. I knew she was wilful and capricious. Now I'm afraid she's wanton."

He laughed indulgently. After Pam's triumph, he could face the world unafraid of reputation. "I'll have a talk with her. I'll make sure that if she can't behave, she won't get caught." That, he thought, was the only philosophy which guided him. "They are all waiting for you in the State Room. The bubbly is circulating."

He offered her his arm. It was, he thought, his hour just as much as hers. He had taken care of everything. Not quite everything. There was still Nick Hayling, the only other man to whom the evidence was available, or had been. And every man had his price. He thought he knew Hayling's. And Margaret Hayling's.

Pam clung fiercely to his arm. Her independence had been brief, he thought complacently. She was still his creation, his captive. They went through the communicating doors to the State Room where he saw at once the familiar faces, the Cabinet, ex-Cabinet Ministers, senior back-benchers, hangers-on, office seekers all; parasites and panderers; fawners and, worst of all, those creatures who, despite the secrecy of the ballot, he *knew* had voted for Westwood. All had one thing in common: they drooled for office.

So they all cheered and applauded and Pam acknowledged with a wave of the hand. She had insisted: no speeches. It mustn't appear a funeral celebration for Hargreaves. She began to move amongst them with a new grace which seemed to have come with the title; a word here, a word there, scattered amongst the circle of hopefuls, all pecking like pigeons at crumbs. Joe Hepworth watched the familiar phenomenon, thinking cynically of the ones it wouldn't do any good. *He* would pick her team, sychophancy and flattery were not characteristics he greatly admired.

He searched the crowd, looking with deceptive casualness for Nick Hayling; saw him standing beside one of the pillars, glass of champagne in his hand, regarding the scene through worldly eyes. He was leaning his elbow on the top of a tall table. Their eyes met speculatively. Joe Hepworth forced his way through the throng in his direction.

Hayling said: "It's a bit like dancing on his coffin." But he remembered the dead Prime Minister with scant respect. If there was a Hereafter, he thought, Hargreaves would laugh cynically at the revelation of how little he had been loved.

"Well, *you* drew up the time-table." Implicate him at all costs, that was Joe's objective. "And you know what they say?"

"The King is dead, long live the Queen?" The approach was too friendly, too bloody friendly for comfort. Nick Hayling remembered in a technicolour memory, the shell-racked ruin of the cottage left behind by fleeing Jerry, hotly pursued by the Armoured Division. It had seemed a very friendly haven until Hayling had gone through the shattered porch. . . .

"Well," he said, "you did it."

Joe Hepworth smiled, as if it had all been easy, hadn't involved a political assassination.

"Against all the odds and forecasts." He peered closely at Hayling. But Hayling knew he wasn't short-sighted. He wasn't merely looking, he was investigating. "I won't tell you how I did it."

"Christ, no. That's the last thing I want you to tell me." He knew exactly how to find out himself. All he had to do was to compare the list of signatures for ballot papers in the first ballot with those for the second ballot, and the pattern of abstention would emerge. So that, when he looked back into Hepworth's face, it too was an investigation. Joe lifted his glass.

"I'm usually very careful with this kind of tipple," he said, confidingly. His confidences were beginning to alarm Nick Hayling with the threat of implication. "I know through my job how many politicians it's ruined." He winked conspiratorially, all the time preparing the ground: How to suborn a potential enemy in three easy stages. "People talk too much when they're pissed, especially on this stuff. You know the joke of course, that Government Hospitality champers is exported from Japan." He laughed aloud and Hayling suddenly registered the fact that this was a rare event. "It first depresses the central nervous system and destroys the power of sustained reasoning. It loosens restraints, especially on the tongue."

"Then I'll have to be especially careful," said Hayling. But it was not necessary to be warned. Care was his calculated policy for survival. He was the Party's adviser on procedure and precedents, the chronicler of minutes, and its general dogsbody. But tonight, despite the caution, he was feeling a little complacent, a little truculent, because he had been very smart.

In a way, Joe Hepworth was his superior but, unlike Hayling, he could be toppled any moment by political upheaval. And too much connivance with Joe Hepworth would leave Hayling a sitting duck for a successor determined to throw out everything associated with the old regime. Why, he could finish up working at Transport House, and who would like that? Accidents often happened to those in political posts, so, when the barrages opened up from both wings of the Party Nick Hayling was Switzerland.

"I've been thinking, Nick." The champagne had already brought Joe Hepworth's cheeks up in a flush. "The Party's treatment of you is lousy."

Hayling shrugged non-committally. "The wife works. We manage. I could have got a better living standard but, as you know, there are other motivations." What he meant was there had been devotion before it had been tarnished by contact with political reality. He and Joe Hepworth still had one thing in common, however: they hated those weevilling away at the Party's foundations, creating its deformities.

"I wasn't thinking of money." Hepworth rapidly switched a full glass for an empty one as the tray circulated. Hayling declined. This time *he* would keep the clearer head. "I know someone ought to do something about money too. It's a disgrace that the Party supposed to be fighting injustice is the worst employer of all."

Hayling waited; puzzled, impatient

"No," said Hepworth, carefully. "I was thinking of a K."

Hayling was completely surprised.

"A knighthood?"

"Why not?"

So that was it. A bribe. A K. in exchange for a conspiracy of silence on whatever Joe had to hide. The deduction was obvious: Joe had a lot to hide. On the one hand, the idea of a knighthood tantalised. Sir Nicholas Hayling, M.M. and Lady Hayling. It would look imposing on Margaret's notepaper.

On the other hand there was the memory of all the jibes and jeers about Hargreaves' Honours Lists, the blatant patronage and nepotism, favours repaid, the shabby *quid pro quos*. And to accept a knighthood, the first ever given to a secretary of the Parliamentary Party, would not only breach his safety-first rule, his determined non-involvement in personality and policy affairs: if he took a knighthood from Pam he would be associated with the means by which her victory was secured. And Hayling knew instinctively from the way Joe Hepworth was watching him over the rim of the glass, there could be a God-awful row about that. Oh, yes, a K. would be very nice, but it could also prove very embarrassing. It could be more than embarrassing: it could mean, career-wise, total extinction.

Joe Hepworth was obviously disappointed at Nick Hayling's negative reaction. "You're not exactly bursting out all over with enthusiasm."

Hayling said, defensively: "You've taken my breath away. There's no question of any personal obligation." He saw a loophole and went through it at the speed of thought. "Perhaps when I retire –" It would be safe then, he couldn't be knifed by any faction.

"Retire? God, Nick, you know how long a week is in politics, never mind fifteen years. In this game, credit for services rendered doesn't last very long."

"I don't want any credit. I just did my usual job." Credit could turn into incrimination.

"That's just my point. You are doing the same work as the civil servant who sits opposite you across the Lobby. Yet he always gets a K. You're fully entitled to it. I'll arrange for it to be gazetted in the Dissolution Honours."

"No thanks, Joe. Believe me, I'm grateful. But –"

"Take it while you can. The chance might never be repeated. If we're beaten – and you never know – " A pause. Somehow Hayling felt it was loaded with significance. "Because of that possibility, I've just been cleaning out my confidential papers I wouldn't like a successor to see. Beating Tom Westwood wasn't easy."

"He could have made a great Prime Minister," said Hayling, most injudiciously. He hadn't realised so little champagne could do so much damage to his caution: he had volunteered a character assessment of one Party leader to another. In one moment he could be characterised as a Westwood man, a Transport House stooge, a machine man. He knew how the Labour Party worked, the deep emotional strata of internal strife. Underneath Joe Hepworth's scrutiny he decided, if he couldn't with dignity retreat, he could, at least, balance the scales. "Of course, the Party's chosen wisely. You and Pam will make a formidable combination." He was too wise to communicate what he really thought: that the Party was crying out for another Ernie Bevin figure, but this time a man of the Left, a man with the brutality and courage to whip the Party into a fighting mood, to restore morale. Under Joe and Pam, he foresaw the same old civil war.

He noted with interest the way Joe Hepworth was downing the champagne, like the best man at a wedding. Well, he had every reason to celebrate, or beg forgiveness for having fucked the bride.

"Our own little special toast, Nick. Here's to Pam."

It was almost as if he was determined to commit the professionally uncommitted. Reluctantly, Hayling raised his glass.

"To Pam." Then, with a quick mental flash of self-protection, he found an escape route: "To Pam, the Party and the next Labour Government."

His neutrality had become an issue. Joe Hepworth said, with alcoholic truculence: "Tell me honestly, Nick; if you'd had a vote, who would you have voted for?"

"In the Labour Party?" Nick Hayling was thinking quickly. He said, with careful profundity: "To tell you the truth, Joe, I shouldn't know whether to vote for the doctor or the undertaker."

Joe Hepworth threw back his head and laughed, all umbrage lost. "That's very good, Nick. I like that very much. I must tell Pam."

"I shouldn't do that."

"You think she might wonder whether she's the doctor or the undertaker?"

"I wouldn't like her to think I was being offensive." But he didn't really mind. In the face of Joe's challenge, his neutrality had at last turned malignant.

Joe Hepworth signalled the attendant with the tray. Hayling once again refrained. When Joe next spoke it was with a beguiling nonchalance.

"By the way, Nick. I've done a very stupid thing."

"That isn't like you, Joe."

"It was a pure accident. I told you about my disposal of my confidential papers. Well, I had taken away the two lists of signatures for voting papers in the two ballots. I wanted to find out what had happened"

"And what had happened?"

Joe spread wide his arms in mute apology: although the face was tipsy, the eyes were piercing, watching for Hayling's reaction.

"That's just it. We shall never know. The papers got mixed up with the other stuff."

"And went into the shredder? Official Party documents which should be a permanent record in my care? In the shredder?"

"I'm afraid so," said Joe, regretfully. But he was too sure of his importance in the Party to sound really sorry.

"Well, don't let it worry you," said Nick Hayling, cheerfully. His moment had come, the moment to repay all the forelock-touching which some of his arrogant political masters demanded. He said, happily: "I'm always particularly careful to safeguard the custody of official records. As soon as the ballot was over, I took photostat copies. They're in my briefcase."

He watched Joe Hepworth suffer at the realisation that all Nick Hayling had to do was to compare the two lists to detect the pattern. In his moment of shock the telephone on the table between them began to ring. Hayling lifted the receiver.

He recognised the voice. With Edwin Battle, Hayling had an odd relationship. They liked each other, they drank and socialised together, they had a mutual interest in politics. On that level they were friends. But their purposes in life were incompatible: Edwin Battle would kill his grandmother if it would give him a story injuring the Labour Party because he worked for a Tory paper; Nick Hayling would kill his grandmother to protect the Movement to which he had devoted his life.

"And what lying bullshit have you filed tonight?"

"Nothing to cheer the readers up, I fancy. Is Pam Bruce or Joe Hepworth within hailing distance?"

"Will either do?"

"For my purpose, yes."

"Here's Joe." He handed the instrument over to Hepworth. "Your very old friend, Edwin Battle," and enjoyed the look of intense distaste cross the red and shattered face. He wondered what Joe Hepworth's special enemy had dug up this time? He knew how much Joe feared Battle's forays deep into the secret files of Whitehall, his sudden revelations of inconvenient truths, the continued failure of Civil Service investigations to plug the leaks and punish the offenders. Somewhere, somehow, Edwin Battle had someone planted. Whatever his friendship with Edwin Battle, it was his duty to trap him if he could.

He had been watching Joe Hepworth while Edwin Battle spoke. This time, Battle must have the veritable whale of a scoop: he saw the champagne flush dilute swiftly into a parchment pallor, the eyes turn from glazed shock to disbelief and then unrelieved horror, the mouth fall open slackly to emit a groan of pain. From the suddenly inert fingers the glass of champagne slipped to the floor. Because of the thickness of the pile, the glass did not break, but the champagne slowly spread into a little pool.

"God Almighty." The telephone receiver fell from the limp grasp. Hayling retrieved it from the dangling line and replaced it in its cradle. "Liz and Richard Westwood," Joe Hepworth gasped. "They've just been blown to bits by the provos. The bastards, the dirty, crazy bastards. . . ."

The eyes fixed themselves on Hayling's face imploringly, pleading for succour. It was the first time Hayling had known the self-sufficient Hepworth dependent on love or sympathy. It was the first favour he had ever begged of him. And Hayling knew he was going to turn him down.

"How am I going to break the news to Pam?"

Hayling's eyes flickered away. He had shown on plenty of occasions between Dunkirk and the dash through Normandy to the Rhine, that he didn't lack courage. But this was a job he couldn't do. One of the lessons he had learned with the deadly shower of metal, was never, never to volunteer. Joe Hepworth was the father. Joe would have to do the father's job. When their eyes met, he knew that Joe had got the message, and now he had the guts. The colour was coming back to the cheeks, but this time it wasn't a champagne flush.

"Listen, Nick – " Joe Hepworth looked across the crowded, happy room. Pam was in the middle of a group of idolators. He had to detach her quickly and get her into a private room where she could break down unseen. "I'll get her out of here quietly. When you see us leave, give us a few minutes. Then announce the news and ask everyone to disperse. Pam won't want to see anyone."

"Leave it to me, Joe. And – " He paused helplessly – "if there is anything I can do. Or the office?" Joe Hepworth shook his head dumbly. Shoulders bowed, he headed in a hazy walk towards Pam. In the time it had taken to speak a few words from Victoria Street to No 10, triumph had turned to grief and anguish. He saw the detachment accomplished, felt compassion for the face of Pam Bruce, raised unsuspectingly and trustingly on the way to the exit, saw them pass out of view. In a few moments he signalled an attendant and asked him to call for silence.

In a shocked State Room, littered with scores of half-empty glasses, Nick Hayling made his simple announcement of the most recent achievement of civilisation. Everyone went home, stunned and silent. Some to weep. Some, no doubt, to fornicate and create, perhaps another generation's contribution to the human sacrifices to the unending demands of the ravenous Bog.

Joe Hepworth sat in his No 12 sanctuary, the room in which he had faced many crises in his political career. Normally, the room comforted him; it was a refuge from the office off the Lobby where he did his conspiring. His elbows were resting on his desk, his face was lost in his hands. He had discovered, as millions had discovered before him, there is no easy way to break calamitous news. As he had expected, Pam had been gritty. But, in a way, her outward bravery was an indication of the distance which had grown up between mother and daughter.

He knew Pam had been afraid of her daughter's exotic personality, her blatant appeal to the sensational in life, her venturesomeness and, it had to be admitted, her growing reputation for sexual adventures. Now his worst ordeal faced him, to fulfil Pam's delicate task. He could no longer delay. It was getting late.

He picked up the receiver and asked the switchboard to get him Tom Westwood at Transport House. He waited, weighed down with misery while the call matured. Suddenly, Tom Westwood was on the line.

"Tom?" He knew his voice was hoarse, tentative, apprehensive. There was a long pause.

Then, at last, Tom Westwood spoke: "It *is* Joe Hepworth?"

"Yes, it's Joe." This was the man he had dreadfully wronged, defeated with a twisted deceit. This was a man whose honesty he had despoiled. He wondered, while he made up his mind what to say next, whether Tom Westwood had been told of the outrage or whether he would have to break the news to the victim that he had lost a son as well as the Party leadership? Another guilt. He prayed: "Do you know?"

"My son and Liz? Yes, Edwin Battle told me." The voice was stony, a voice which was experienced in answering stoically the news of death: death in many shapes and forms, particularly the mutilations in the dark galleries underground. It was these particular deaths which were the obstacles between Pam Bruce and Tom Westwood. Now he had to try to negotiate that obstacle for the good of both of them, for the sake of the Party and country. He thought, as always, in the context of Party first.

"It's a grief we share," he said, remembering Liz, thinking shrinkingly of the beauty shredded in the street. "And I'd only just been able to acknowledge my parenthood."

"I never thought I would hear a maudlin Joe Hepworth." It was like a slap in the face. It made him remember how hard Tom Westwood could be. "Sudden death is a shock to the survivors. But there are worse things. Pains that go on a long time. Desertion and betrayal. But, for what they are worth, Joe, you have my condolences."

Joe Hepworth couldn't help himself although he knew he was being ingratiating: "At least, Tom, you'll be glad for what the boy did before – "

"Yes, I'm grateful. And the Party is no doubt obliged." Tom Westwood was a proud man but he wouldn't advertise his pride in his own son. He kept it to himself, like the depth of his pride and devotion to the Party. At the other end of the cable, Joe Hepworth writhed, knowing himself as a fraud, whose political chicanery would have been criminal in any other sphere.

Tom Westwood said: "I'm sorry I didn't congratulate you personally after the count, Joe. Especially about Donovan."

Joe Hepworth's hand tightened round the receiver.

"Donovan?"

"Yes, Donovan. I know you've pulled off some coups in your career, Joe, but to have the gall to plant your saboteur on me as campaign manager – that was really superb, Joe."

"I don't know what you mean," he blustered. He could only lie with his customary brass face, knowing that he wouldn't be believed. That had never bothered him. It was the record which counted. The record said that Pam Bruce was Prime Minister, at least for three weeks.

"It's no use, Joe. Edwin Battle told me."

"Oh, Edwin Battle," he said, contemptuously. *That bastard again, always in his hair*. "He hates my guts. He'd say anything to hit at Pam and me. Tell him I'll sue if he dares write a word about Donovan."

"Joe, Joe, Edwin got it from Bassett. And we all know Bassett is another Georgie Washington – never tells a lie. Don't worry, Joe. I couldn't expose you without harming the Party. And I won't tell Pam, although how she keeps her precious illusions about you defeats me. Battle isn't going to write anything because he thinks we've suffered enough. Have you suffered enough, Joe?"

"I'm sweating with it, Tom."

"That's not suffering, Joe. That's fear of exposure. How you swung the abstentions will probably never be disclosed and I certainly shall not follow it up. What matters now is to keep the country out of the greedy hands of the Tories."

"There's one thing," Joe Hepworth said, anxious to shed his guilt. "Labour should get a big sympathy vote."

"Joe, you're a bloody vulture. You'd poison your own mother for a hundred votes."

"That's always been my job," he said, defensively, "to deliver the vote."

"I know," said, Tom Westwood, "and bugger the cost."

"Tom – " He could not delay the approach any longer. Their relations were deteriorating moment by moment, not improving. He said again, interrogatively: "Tom . . . ?" If only they could meet half way.

"There's something important on your mind, Joe. What is it? I hope it isn't a favour?"

It came out in a gush, a gush of fear.

"Will you speak to Pam?"

There was a long, long silence. Then Tom Westwood said, evenly: "She's asked to speak to me? It isn't another of your false initiatives, Joe, a laying-on of hands to demonstrate your healing power? Not strictly for the head-lines?"

It was obvious from the voice that the issue between the Westwoods and the Bruces was still a gaping void. Two more violent deaths involving both families could not, in themselves, bring reconciliation.

"Honest to God, Tom, Pam asked me to ring you. I appeal to you, Tom, not only for her sake, but for the sake of the Party. Tom, don't snub her now."

He knew from the quality of the silence that Tom Westwood was contemplating a savage revenge – the rejection of an appeal for peace, the demonstration of the superior endurance. In his tension, he gripped the receiver more tightly: even then, he thought surreptitiously in terms of votes, this time, votes showering into box after box in the ballot-booths all over the country. Relief came in a gigantic gush.

"I'll speak. Put her on the line, Joe."

Neither of them had to speak. Each was conscious of the other's living, breathing presence in a silence as tangible as that which had lasted a quarter of a century. She had the sensation of being linked to a fuse, spluttering with flame, creeping nearer and nearer to the explosive charge. By total accident, they both spoke at once:

"Pam . . .?"

"Tom . . . ?"

The dark vaults opened. Their minds were suddenly ventilated by a golden gush of sanity.

Tom Westwood said: "It seems we can't escape the simultaneous spilling of family blood."

"If only the tears would come." But, she remembered, the tears had never come that other day. If they had, grief might have taken a less vengeful form.

"That day," he said. "It couldn't have been changed by wisdom, hindsight, compensation or a miracle. There is only one thing to do – wipe it from our memories."

"Yes." But, she thought, a person is only the sum of his or her memories. Lose those, and although the body lives on, the person does not exist. Wasn't it a laudable thing that the Pam Bruce of the last twenty-five years should no longer exist? She tried to imagine life without the memory: Pam Bruce as part of the pithead pathos, waiting with the beshawled relatives; tearless, counting and identifying, fearfully turning back the blankets covering the stretchers as they came from the cage out into the open pit-yard. The memory still seared a moment, and was gone. She was left with grief, but a new grief for which a Westwood bore no blame, a crime more bestial than manslaughter.

"Pam," he said, "let me say this, then I will never mention the subject again. You were right. There should have been prosecutions."

"It doesn't matter now, Tom. I used my grief as a justification for revenge. I set myself up as prosecutor, judge and jury."

"My father was negligent. But the extent was never disclosed. The real criminals were the owners, who would never spend money on the safety measures required. He'd pleaded for them. But the company pulled all the strings. You know how influence was applied in those days. The authorities couldn't prosecute him without implicating the owners."

"They couldn't have suffered." She was thinking of Liz and Richard, not the events of twenty-five years before. The past was dead, mountains of bitterness and hate demolished in less than a minute. "I can't forget," she said, "that almost the last thing they did was to try to reconcile us."

"And we walked out on them. I never saw him after that. I disowned him. Thank God we had made our peace before – " The strong, courageous voice failed.

"But you can be proud of him. The Party will always honour the name. But me – I failed as a parent. All my attention was paid to the Party, never to Liz. I deceived myself that neglect, shrugging off my responsibility on to schools and university, was a favour, a non-interference, an enlightened attitude."

"And all I cared was that his activities should not ruin my reputation as a Socialist who had kept his grass roots. I failed as much as you, Pam."

"You ought to know his last words when I walked out on them at Church House. They were: 'It's tribalism, pure, bloody, medieval tribalism.'"

"We both now know he was right."

Grief had once separated and distorted them; grief had now brought them together. She still saw life through a colliery image but it was a different picture: this time it was Pam Bruce at the coal-face in the underground gallery beneath the falling roof and splintering props, crawling on hands and knees, lungs filling with the inhaled dust; slowly, she was edging towards the distant glimmer of light at the end of the gallery. There, at the mouth of the tunnel, Tom Westwood was holding out a hand to drag her to salvation.

"Pam," he said, "whatever the grief, I have one great consolation. Richard came back out of loyalty to the Party. More than ever now, I want a Party victory to commemorate that. I will move heaven and earth under your leadership to bring it about."

"God knows, I need you, Tom."

At last the cleansing tears were running freely now, washing away the years of vengeful bitterness, a quarter of a century of futility. "They were so young and so innocent to die in a quarrel that never concerned them, a struggle going back to medieval days."

"Cry it out, Pam. It's better like that. Remember, there are no more of our families left, no more martyrs to the coal or the shamrock. We are the survivors."

She staunched the tears. This was no time for the weakness of a woman. God alone knew what trials and tribulations awaited her from dawn. "There's no more time for grief, Tom. We have a job to do."

"It's going to be a bloody fight. More than anything you'll have to win it on television. You must be absolutely honest. You'll be fighting under grave organisational difficulties. The machine is creaking badly. We haven't yet won back the activists. We haven't appeased the middle-class. The North Sea oil and the Scot Nats together mean that, if we lose, we're in the wilderness for a decade."

"I know I have no right to ask. But I need you as much as Transport House needs you." He had the muscular physical strength and unshakeable moral foundations which she lacked. It came from their common roots, nurtured below the ground, an all-exclusive need which omitted even Joe Hepworth, architect of her victory in the ballot; her sponsor, tutor and, hitherto, general-in-command. "Whatever the personal ordeal, I open the campaign with Hargreaves' programme at Manchester tomorrow. I want you beside me on the platform. I want the country to recognise you as my number two. I want the public to know our reconciliation is not a gimmick for cheap votes."

"Win or lose," he promised, "it will be hand-in-hand. I know the schedule. I'll see you on the 'plane. Now get some sleep . . ."

At his desk in No 12, long after the connection had been broken, Joe Hepworth sat on, receiver still clutched in a sweaty hand. Then he released his convulsive grip and hurled the instrument into its cradle. Eavesdroppers seldom heard good things about themselves, he thought. But he had not even merited a mention. She had totally ignored his position, his importance, his contribution, his victory campaign. She had promoted Tom Westwood, her old enemy, over his head.

It was to have been Joe Hepworth, the indispensable, who was to have planned and led a victorious cavalcade. He was to have been the mastermind. And he was to have inherited the reality of power if Labour won.

Now, in the course of a few minutes of sentiment, Tom Westwood had supplanted him. He should have been warned by Pam's unexpected touch of authority earlier in the day, the sudden disclosure of her plan for an inner caucus. That, he had too readily dismissed as a minor complication, which he would soon bring to an untimely end. It was an insult that he, among the four, would have been no more than equal. But this was the added insult; that, of the four, Tom Westwood was to be more equal than the others.

For a moment he had the senseless urge to storm into Pam's privacy and rage at her ingratitude and fight the issue out, present her with the ultimatum: Tom Westwood or Joe Hepworth? Then the craft and guile mastered the heat of emotion and comparative calm returned. The fact remained – he could not concede that he would win the ballot for Pam and then be satisfied with third place in the power ladder. He could never, never accept that what he had done, execrable as it would be recognised to be if it ever became fully known, had been for Tom Westwood's benefit.

He sat down and faced the situation. He would participate, as planned, in Pam's election tours. He would never leave her for an instant. Every picture would portray them side by side. Undignified though it would be, he would fight Tom Westwood every inch for the power and influence she might one day wield.

Even Joe Hepworth's iron constitution had to yield to the strain of the days of emotional grind and struggle. His head drooped towards his chest. His last waking thought was that Joe Hepworth had never expected gratitude in public life. Why should he be surprised?

10

For Edwin Battle it had been a long, exhausting, but totally satisfying day. There had been the drama of Pam Bruce's shock two-vote victory, the double assassination and now, thanks to Stella, the exclusive story of the reconciliation of the Prime Minister and Tom Westwood. He lay full length on his old leather couch, savouring the moment before he poured himself another drink. If ever a man had deserved it, he had.

He grimaced because he had heard the sounds of Stella undressing in his bedroom. Unhappily, he visualised her, down to the ugly buff, wrapping herself in his dressing-gown, preparing herself for the pay-off. Thinking of the required sexual reciprocity, Edwin Battle suffered a miniature physical collapse, a tiny reminder of the ultimate dissolution to come. He sat up and defiantly poured himself another Haig. As the glass touched his lips there was a knock on the outer door of his flat.

There was something peremptory about the knock that warned him at once that what he had long feared was happening here and now. With astonishing agility for a man of his bulk and unfitness, he reached the bedroom door in three paces.

"Stella," he hissed, "there's someone at the door. Keep absolutely quiet and don't come out unless I give the signal."

The knock was repeated, this time more imperatively.

"Coming," he called, and went slowly towards the door. Now that the inevitable had happened he found himself totally unprepared, no carefully rehearsed story ready. He would have to play it by ear. Then, he thought, half the cells in

Wormwood Scrubs were no doubt occupied by men who had played it by ear. He composed himself and opened the door. One look was sufficient to confirm his worst fears.

"Mr Edwin Battle?"

There were two of them, two flat-feet in civilian clothing. The one who spoke was obviously the Detective-Inspector; a hard-faced, lean man in a low-brimmed hat. He had the drably-dressed exterior ordinariness which was as conclusive an identification as any uniform – the Special Branch.

"I'm Edwin Battle. Occupation political journalist. Employer, *Daily News*." The aggression surfaced involuntarily: the citizen's undeniable right to respond to harassment, bureaucracy, red tape, curtailment of human rights, the mere existence of the fuzz.

"I am Detective-Inspector Barrett."

"Of the Special Branch. I've heard of you, Inspector."

"This is Sergeant Baxter, also of the Special Branch."

"Your side-kick. Now, *he* is a new one on me."

"No doubt you will soon be better acquainted."

The sergeant was a gum-chewer, otherwise a duplicate of the Inspector. Battle didn't invite them in. He kept the door inhospitably half-closed. There was no fire escape for Stella and he was only using the delay to think up a plan to save her by superior verbal cunning. He could bear his own martyrdom with almost pleasurable fortitude, but he wasn't going to make it easy for the bastards to get Stella.

"I must have proof of your identity. Sometimes people are not what they pretend to be. And it is pretty late."

"That is the very point I wish to discuss with you, Mr Battle." The inspector was true to type, all right. He could have fitted snugly into the lower echelons of the Diplomatic Service, M.I. 6, or merged himself, safely camouflaged in mediocrity and his seventy-guinea suit, into almost any middle-class background.

He remained in the doorway, blocking their entrance. The most he could do was prolong the delay and give his brain the chance to work.

"Well, gentlemen, what can I do for you?" He could see

himself as a heroic figure in the dock, facing the judge, refusing once, twice, thrice, to disclose the name of his informant and being sorrowfully sentenced for contempt. But could he save Stella?

"It may take a little time. Perhaps – "

The inspector courteously indicated the interior of the flat with an economic gesture of his hand, suggesting they might be admitted without commitment. But there was no doubt the friendliness of the approach was the usual form, the precursor of more distasteful tactics in reserve. Edwin Battle was not deceived. Barrett had a reputation in the Street. He was fair, but he was hard. And he went by the book.

"By all means. There is no need for a search warrant, I hope." By his counter-attack, he made it clear that there would be no search of the flat, and discovery of Stella without the formality of a search warrant. Anxiously, he watched their faces. "Can I offer you a drink, gentlemen?"

"Not on duty, sir."

"Then you don't mind if I have one?"

The inspector inclined his head in a gesture of consent. He still kept up the courtesy act, but Edwin Battle, pouring himself a confidence-booster, wondered how long it would be before he was on his way to Cannon Row, and whether Stella would be riding with him? How much did the bastards know?

In a moment it would be wit against wit. He looked down at the amber liquid in his hand and, for the first time, he regretted the niagara he had poured down his throat for fully thirty years. He needed to be razor-sharp to brazen himself out of this one. For himself he felt no fear: he was probably on his way to professional fame and glory, the recognition in the Street that he was a bulwark of liberty against the secrecy, the conspiracy of silence of the Establishment. In the bars in the Street and Westminster, Edwin Battle would be toasted as the man who had fucked the Official Secrets Act and had honoured a Scrubs cell.

The detective-inspector was producing a large Press cutting. With hopefully leaping heart, Edwin Battle identified the front page of the *Daily News*, recording the death of the Prime

Minister. Perhaps they only wanted him – on an impersonation charge.

"No doubt you have seen this before, Mr Battle."

"It has a place of honour in my cuttings book. Besides, my name is on it."

"It wasn't the text to which I wished to draw your attention." The inspector even paid pedantic attention to his grammar. "It was this person." The finger stabbed, spearing the portly Battle. "You identify yourself?"

"Of course."

"And the other man, Mr Battle?"

"I don't have to identify him. The caption does that."

"Well, it's my duty to tell you, sir, that Sir William Lawson has made a signed statement in which he says you told him you were an officer of the Special Branch and that you represented yourself to be the late Prime Minister's security guard. What is your reply to that allegation, Mr Battle?"

"I would not like to conjecture what I did say. I'm very hazy about that moment. You see, I was affected by all that excitement in Downing Street at that time of the morning."

"Then perhaps you would care to tell us how you found yourself to be in Downing Street at that significant moment, Mr Battle?"

"Oh, I often go for late walks. I suffer from insomnia. After all, Inspector, Downing Street is on my – what do you officers call it? – my patch"

"So I believe from television. In the absence of any more satisfactory explanation or denial, I am afraid it might be necessary later to charge you with falsely representing yourself to be an officer of the Special Branch. If so, you will first be formally cautioned. Meantime, are you acquainted with Miss Stella Martin?"

The question came at the very end of the sentence, shot out like a bullet, the name which left the guilt strewn all over his face. His mind blanked. It was from a distance he heard his own voice saying:

"Miss Martin is my fiancée."

For a moment he doubted whether it was he who had

spoken – a stupid, useless lie out of some unrehearsed gallantry in defence of Stella's reputation. The instant he admitted it was his act, he knew it was folly. He had used Stella, he had abused her stupidity, led her into criminality and conspiracy for the sake of his vanity, his by-line. It was too late now to save her by sacrificing his freedom and independence.

"Indeed?"

He had at least surprised the bullet-headed bastard as much as he had surprised himself. The sergeant went on chewing gum stolidly with a peculiar rotating motion of his upper and lower jaws. Battle disliked him more than the inspector. It was the kind of irrational dislike one had for the doll in a particularly bad ventriloquist's act.

"We haven't broadcast the fact," said Battle, pursuing his hopeless trail of falsity; no one knew better than he did how lie built on lie until the whole edifice became unsafe. "It's a bit delicate because of our relative jobs. You see, she's on the No 10 switchboard. But you would know that, of course?"

"Of course," said the inspector, dryly.

"Of course," echoed the sergeant, faithfully.

"So *it* speaks," said Battle, facetiously. The inspector was not amused.

"She would have access to secret information?"

"Oh no," said Battle, backing away with hand raised. "She's been scrupulous in observing her obligations. She sticks rigidly to the rules of the Official Secrets Act."

"Naturally. When did you last see her?"

It was the end-of-sentence-bullet technique all over again. The hard face, veteran of hundreds of skilled interrogations, trapper of spies, cracker of codes, was totally uninterested. It suggested boredom, having to deal with a trivial section 2 case. Battle studied the expression in vain for a clue as to how much Barrett knew.

"Let me see," he began hesitantly, and paused, once again examining the face.

"Gentlemen in your profession usually have reliable memories, Mr Battle." There was a heavy accent on the first word of the sentence.

"I've had a very busy forty-eight hours on the Labour Party ballot. But it wasn't today. Yesterday, perhaps?"

"Perhaps," interceded the gently, insinuating voice, "You have spoken to Miss Martin on the telephone lately?"

So that was it. The bastards had done a phone-tap on him: his mind raced back, tracking down incriminating conversations. It remembered particularly the one o'clock call that morning of the P.M.'s death. Now, he thought, he couldn't keep her out of it; they were both in the shit.

"I don't recall," he said, sullenly. In the absence of innocence, loss of memory was the only feasible defence. But silence, carried to its logical conclusion, became mute of malice.

"So you haven't seen Miss Stella Martin today, and you don't recall any telephone-calls recently? Are you quite sure you wouldn't want to reflect a little longer, Mr Battle?"

"I'm sure," he said, lying because it seemed the only hope of not committing himself unnecessarily. But he was only helping Stella to her inevitable doom.

Inspector Barrett said, still in his dry, uninquisitive voice: "Then how do you account for the fact that she was observed by Sergeant Baxter – " at the flick of the hand to identify him, the ventriloquist's doll nodded its head faithfully – "entering this block of flats by the service lift, and was seen to admit herself to your flat by means of a key she took from her hand-bag? Time: half-an-hour ago."

For a moment Edwin Battle said nothing as his little castle of evasions and downright lies collapsed, leaving him exposed. He was only capable of a flash of reckless humour.

"I suppose the expected thing now is to admit it's a fair cop." Then, with resignation, he went to the bedroom, opened the door a few inches, and said: "Stella, you'd better come out. Our friends of the Special Branch have had you tailed."

First, he saw that she had dressed. Second, that her face was aglow, suffused with happiness. She wrapped both her arms round his neck and kissed him. He smelled her antiseptic Lifebuoy smell, but he flinched as if caught in a disreputable act in public. He was trying to disengage when he understood: Stella had heard his commitment, made before witnesses.

Against her unaccountable love for Edwin Battle, the prospect of prison, public disgrace, loss of pension rights, faded into matters of unconcern. The realisation buttressed his ego, gave him a novel self-respect. The thought that he was needed so badly; that he, one of the nation's biggest shits, could bring such unalloyed happiness, totally surprised him. He felt the prick of tears rising in his ducts, something he hadn't known even when he'd thought of the slaughter of Liz Bruce and Richard Westwood. Pride? Vanity? Self-pity?

Whatever it was, it proved something he hadn't believed for years: he wasn't beyond redemption despite the contagions of the Street and Westminster, and the contamination of Haig. He kissed her, for the first time without embarrassment; for the first time affection wasn't a forced reciprocity. He could genuinely compensate her for the damage he had done to her life, the professional ruin. For the first time for years, he thought he might yet have the courage to forsake the easy road to self-destruction and take the tougher, steeper road to salvation. He wondered whether she had faced the possibility that, unless she got a suspended sentence because she was a deluded pawn, he might be dead before the gates of Holloway opened for her. Gently, he freed his arms. In the circumstances he could only strike a cheery, devil-may-care attitude.

"Well, Inspector, where do we go from here? Cannon Row, I presume. If so, I'd like to telephone my office first."

"I think I can grant you that facility in a moment," said Barrett, still with impeccable courtesy. At least, he treated Stella with respect, recognising her as the victim of weakness to the deceit of a praying mantis. But although he looked at the stupidly radiant face with compassion, his voice was stiff and formal:

"Stella Martin, I have reason to believe that you, having in your possession certain information obtained in contravention of section 2 of the Official Secrets Act, or entrusted to you as a person holding office under the Crown, did communicate the said information to Edwin Battle, a person other than those to whom you were authorised to communicate it.

"It is my intention to charge you with this offence formally later and to conduct further inquiries. In the meantime I have to advise you that you are not obliged to say anything, but anything you do say, will be taken down in writing and may be given in evidence against you."

Edwin Battle stood between Barrett and Stella, a broken-down shield. "She has nothing to say. In the meantime, I deny ever receiving any classified information from Miss Martin."

"I will have a note taken to that effect, Mr Battle." It was the sergeant, the ventriloquist's doll, who was writing laboriously in his official notebook, tip of tongue hanging out as a sign of concentration. Oaf, thought Battle, disgustedly. The inspector patiently gave his underling time, then addressed Battle.

"Edwin Battle, I have reason to believe that you, being a person not entitled to receive information in contravention of section 2 of the Official Secrets Act, did receive such information on diverse dates from Miss Stella Martin, a person holding office under the Crown. I hereby administer the same caution to you. Have you anything to say, Mr Battle?"

"Yes, I have. Write this in your little notebook, Boswell: 'I have reason to believe that the Special Branch did install telephone-tapping apparatus on my instrument. I demand a citizen's right to know if this is so?' "

The inspector did not reply. He merely smiled.

"Now write this, Boswell: 'Inspector Barrett declined to reply.' Now write: 'Mr Battle demanded the right of every private citizen to know whether the fiat of the Home Secretary, necessary to legalise such telephone taps, was so obtained in this case. I give notice that, at the proper time, I shall demand production of the fiat in writing.' "

Now the sergeant was writing at speed. He was proving himself an accomplished shorthand-writer. "Write also," Battle commanded, " 'Once again Inspector Barrett declined to comment.' Then add: "I have nothing further to say at the moment."

Inspector Barrett said, equably: "You can have a few minutes for that phone-call."

"Which I have no doubt you will have recorded." Once

again the inspector smiled. Oddly enough it didn't make him look happier. "You know, of course, that the Home Secretary has more or less promised the Press an amnesty from prosecutions under section 2 until the promised reforms are put into legislation. In this case, there is no question of endangering the security of the State."

"That is not a matter for me, Mr Battle. The question of prosecution is a matter for the Director of Public Prosecutions."

"You know that Fleet Street will crucify you for this, Inspector?"

"Perhaps you had better make a note of that too, Sergeant."

"Two cheers for democracy," sneered Battle, reaching for the telephone, his life-line. He saw that the glow of happiness on Stella's face had not diminished; it remained the glorious sunrise moment of her life. He dialled mechanically, thinking of the invisible recorder which would convict him. He asked for a copy-taker, performing his professional duty as if nothing out of the ordinary had happened to him. Then he realised he was not a trained observer now, he was a principal, a maker of news. He felt important, certainly not guilty.

"This is Battle," he said. "Yes, your Lobby correspondent. Can you take a piece? Yes, it quite short, but very important. Story begins:

'*Edwin Battle, political correspondent of the Daily News, was taken into custody at Cannon Row police station late last night. It is understood he will be charged with offences under section 2 of the Official Secrets Act, the section which the Government has promised to amend because of allegations it is mainly used to gag the Press.*'

"Para."

'*Mr Battle, a veteran Westminster journalist, secured this week's exclusive story of the Prime Minister's death and Whitehall's efforts to trace the sources of his information, which have been going on for months, had been intensified.*'

"End message. Give me the Night Editor, please . . ."

They all waited a few moments in silence. Stella watched Battle's every move adoringly.

"Jim? You've seen the piece I've just put over? Yes, I shall be at Cannon Row if you can arrange a mouth-piece to get police bail tonight. And there will be two of us, Jim. The High Priest knows. I have an undertaking about legal costs. Just in case the bail idea doesn't work send me a bottle of Haig. Don't worry, it's all good for circulation. See you soon." He laughed, a sound sharp and short. "I hope."

All the time he had been speaking, Battle had been watching the inspector's face. He was not, he decided, an imaginative man, but one couldn't expect that. He seemed fair. Like doctors, barristers, judges and even journalists, policemen couldn't allow personal feelings to affect their work or judgment. No? It was clear he felt sorry for Stella, sucked into dirt by a drink-sodden bastard who had used her affections to boost his by-line. The trouble was it made Battle feel a criminal, not a martyr. He held out his wrists, facetiously presenting them for handcuffs.

"Am I a desperate enough character to need the bracelets?" He intoned part of an old remembered line: "with gyves upon his wrists . . ."

The sergeant stopped chewing and spoke, only for the second time. "Thomas Hood," he said. "From 'The Dream of Eugene Aram'." He went on to quote, sonorously:

"Two stern-faced men set out from Lynn, through the cold and heavy mist;
"And Eugene Aram walked between, with gyves upon his wrists."

"Well, I'm buggered," said a surprised Edwin Battle. The sergeant wasn't an oaf.

"Oh, the sergeant is a man of erudition," said the inspector. This time his rare smile was one of pride. He pointed the way to the door and waited for Stella and Battle to lead the way. In the corridor, Battle put his arm round Stella's shapeless waist, still marvelling at the transformation of her features by the glow of possession. He thought compassionately: how the hell can she believe she's getting a bargain?

"You know I'm as worthless as the wreck of the Hesperus? I

can't stop drinking. I'm suffering from advanced brain and liver damage. I'm liable to go out like a light."

The inspector listened cynically. He knew what the bastard really wanted. He wasn't worried by the fear of going out like a light. Most suicides wanted that and, however much he might rationalise, Battle was a suicide. What he really wanted was insurance, a pair of loving arms into which he could creep at the last to hide from the fear of death. Barrett hoped, with a sudden explosion of silent fury, that Battle got his martyrdom – and eighteen months to go with it.

He pressed the button for the lift. There was still all the paper work at Cannon Row. It would be hours before he could creep into bed, which would be warm from his wife's sleeping body. And, he thought, it was no good feeling randy. She wouldn't thank him for wakening her. But, he thought, watching Battle's face, he'd still rather be a straight policeman than a bent journalist.